#1 MUSE

USA *Today* Bestselling Author

T. GEPHART

#1 Muse
Published by T Gephart
Copyright 2018 T Gephart

ISBN-13: 978–0-6480231–8-0
ISBN-10: 0–6480231–8-4

Cover by:
Hang Le

Editing by:
Nichole Strauss, Insight Editing Services

Interior Design & Formatting by:
Christine Borgford, Type A Formatting

#1 MUSE

DEDICATION

To Mini—Dear friend, awesome travel partner, with the most radiant heart.

Our trip was nothing sort of magical, it was exactly what I needed.

CHAPTER #1

THE END.

Those words sent a shiver down my spine every time I wrote them. Usually they were preceded by FADE OUT, but every once in a while, those last two little words were just for me.

Writing fan fic was never going to win me an Academy Award. It wasn't going to earn me the respect of my peers or give me the recognition I craved in the industry I loved. It didn't even pay the bills. But when I opened up that blank document—without the limitations of a script—it was like hitting a reset button.

It was my dirty little secret.

My guilty pleasure.

Just for me.

Don't get me wrong, I loved writing screenplays. I loved the feeling of molding an idea and playing God with all the characters. Controlling their destiny with the ultimate goal of seeing it play out on a screen, but that wasn't as easy as it sounded. The pressure sometimes made it worse. Which was why my "private" writing felt soooooo good. Zero pressure, and I *still* got to play God.

And if I thought there was *any* chance I could parlay my pages of nonsense into anything remotely resembling a book, I'd have hit the publish button months ago. Lord knows I could use the money. But a novelist, I was not.

My characters weren't mainstream enough, and my storylines often ridiculous—who cared, not like anyone else was going to read them. But more to the point, most, if not *all of them,* were literary daydreams that allowed me to fantasize about the hottest guy on earth.

Nick Larsson.

The man was so hot it was absurd. He was tall—six-foot-some-thing delicious—with a body better suited to an athlete than an actor. Even his hair was hot; a rebellious mess of just-fucked-tresses that looked like a perfect mix of I-don't-care and I'm-on-the-cover-of-GQ. And those eyes—luminous pools of warm wood brown that had the power to make you forget your first name.

I chuckled, feeling my skin heat at just the thought of him. He didn't even seem to know how hot he was, striding through life like he hadn't appropriated more than his share of sexiness from the rest of the male population.

I'd had the pleasure—and really, there was no better word—of meeting Nick when I was a writer's assistant five years ago. He'd played a bartender on an episode of the series I was working on and never had *"what can I get you to drink"* ever sounded as good as it did coming out of his mouth.

Of course, I introduced myself, smiling slightly inappropriately while trying to think of a good way to ask him out. Suggesting a drink seemed cheesy, and I was attempting to think of something witty and clever to say when he was whisked off by the director. I was gutted by the loss of opportunity, scouring the call sheets to see if he was going to make a reappearance. And thankfully, I was given a second chance, *Hot Barman* bringing sexy back, two episodes later.

I'd spent the morning following one of those ridiculous *YouTube* makeup tutorials that used fifty different types of beauty products just to make you look fresh faced and natural. *Quick, flawless routine—my ass.* Tamed my long hair into a cute messy bun that had taken me almost an hour to perfect and thrown on a dress and heels that were bound to get a raised eyebrow when I waltzed into work.

There wasn't a chance in hell I was walking away this time without at least a number, a date—the ultimate objective. Of course, that was before I found out the studio had cancelled the series overnight. So not only was I *not* going to see Nick reprise his sexy—despite not being integral to the script—role, I was also out of a job. Oh, and the phone number and date were probably not going to happen either.

Fast forward to the present day where I had moved from shitty writing gig to shitty writing gig—nothing noteworthy or monumental—treading water and needing to write copy ads to make ends meet while Nick Larsson's career had exploded.

Heading up an all-star cast in their second season in an Emmy award-winning series, he was the next hot thing. I had yet to go a full twenty-four hours where I didn't see his astoundingly handsome face staring at me—that billboard on West Hollywood made sure of that.

So even if our paths *were* to cross again—either through the intersection of mutual projects or at a social function around town—I was almost positive he wouldn't know who I was, have any recollection of meeting me, and have almost zero interest in "hanging out."

No, he was lost to the beautiful people, gripped by the clutches of fame and success, and nestled at the bosom of the "it" crowd. Conversely, I was the weirdo with my face pressed against the glass, staring at him and writing him into fictional scenarios like I was a medieval conquering queen requesting his talent at her majesty's pleasure. I wasn't much into historical, but putting the man in a sexy-ass coat of armor sounded hot as hell. My fantasies weren't genre specific; paranormal, historical—I was an equal opportunity creator.

But there weren't any vampires, kings, or warriors in tonight's installment. Instead I had kept it close to reality, blurring the lines enough, so it seemed believable he'd end up with a girlfriend that happened to be me.

Blaire, the female protagonist—* uh-hum * me—was a smart twenty-six-year-old with amazing brown hair and stunning hazel eyes that changed color with the light. There had been no need to embellish; I had a head of hair that could earn me a shampoo endorsement if I only applied myself and eyes that I counted as my best physical feature. I liked that they morphed like a chameleon, reflecting rich golds, greens and browns depending on mood or how the sun's rays were refracted by my iris.

Blaire * uh-hum me * had graduated from USC with an impressive GPA and a heart full of hopes and dreams. Unlike me, she was plucked from obscurity and hired to write meaty scripts for Hollywood heavyweights who gave her complete creative control and even asked her opinion on casting. What can I say? I was writing fiction after all.

Also, unlike me, Blaire was a stunning five-foot-nine, with legs that went on for an eternity and perfect breasts that pressed against her blouse like two ripe melons. Not the porno, inflated balloon kind that looked like beach balls had been stuck to her chest, but the nice kind that filled up a large man's hand and made his dick stand at attention when she wore a bathing suit.

Yes, it was shallow, that poor Blaire—or was it me?—wanted a man to admire her for more than just her intellect and creative talent, but wasn't feminism about wanting whatever the hell you wanted and not having to feel bad about it? In my version of events—which currently were the only ones that counted—it was, so Blaire could have perky tits, be breathtakingly beautiful *and* be smart.

I didn't mind being five-foot-six, my legs not as impressive as Blaire's. Although there wasn't a woman in her right mind that'd scoff and decline a few extra inches if offered. *Not just in height, I'll have you know.* And while my breasts only achieved melon-sized greatness when aided by a well-fitted bra, my curves were well portioned in an old-school bombshell kind of way. Sure, I could diet, work out six hours a day, and become a size zero, but I valued joy, happiness and cookie dough over a skinny ass.

Besides, my ass wasn't so bad, it cushioned the blow whenever I landed on it, which was more often than I would have liked. I was being ironic of course, the landing on my ass more metaphorical than literal, which was why I had eaten a pint of New York Super Fudge Chunk ice cream straight from the tub as I typed the final words on Nick and Blaire's adventures.

I didn't even bother changing his name, liking the way my fingers felt every time I typed it. N I C K, the letters on the screen enough to give me goosebumps.

"Hey, are you done? I need something to read." Scully walked in, her hand rubbing her swollen pregnant belly.

Scully—her parents were massive X-Files fans, enough said—was one of my best friends/roommates. A sassy twenty-five-year-old who worked in the wardrobe department with one of the major networks despite being seven months pregnant. *Baby Daddy* had bailed after the second month, citing the need to go find himself before he became a dad and told Scully she'd have to raise the baby on her own. He was not only an asshole, but incredibly misinformed if he thought one of my BFFs was going to be doing ANYTHING alone when she had Luke and I.

Luke—my other best friend/roommate—was Nick-Lars-son-level hot. He could throw on a pair of jeans or a suit and make you want to write letters of thanks to the designer. But being handsome wasn't the half of it. He could not only successfully pick the perfect fantasy football team every year based on stats, but also had a freakish ability to do all kinds of "stuff." Be it unclog a drain, build an impressive investment portfolio, or know what kind of motor oil I needed for my Toyota, it was *all* in his wheelhouse.

And when he wasn't playing Superman, impressing us all with his male prowess of smarts and looks, he was a talented Production Buyer, getting to spend studio money for films on things I could only dream of. He had an incredible eye and an acute sense of detail, and when mixed with his charming personality and a devastating smile, it made him irresistible. And if it weren't for the small detail that he preferred men to women, Scully and I probably would have battled to the death for him.

So rather than some crazy sister-wife arrangement, we instead were fierce friends who shared space and adoration. It meant we could afford a decent three-bedroom house in Los Angeles, and we'd take care of each other in the event one of us fell on the skids. Case in point, the screenwriter who was writing fan fiction instead of a script.

"I'm not sure if I'm honored or embarrassed you want to read the sordid tales of Nick and Blaire. I feel like it should be weird or something." I hit print on the document and white sheets of my nonsense started spitting out on the printer tray.

"Please, you have no shame. Don't pretend like you care now." She tapped her foot impatiently, like that would somehow make the pages print faster.

"It's unedited, and rough, and . . ." I bit my lip as my voice trailed off. Not really sure what else I wanted to say. "And different to the last one."

"Different how?" Scully raised an eyebrow, her hand circling her belly stopping mid-stroke.

My feet hit the floor as I stood and stretched, my body tight from sitting at my keyboard for so long. "Like there is an actual storyline, not just a vehicle for me to have sexy time with fictional Nick."

"You mean for *Blaire* to have sexy time." Scully grinned, pretending like there was still some mystery as to who Blaire really was.

"Yes, *Blaire.*" I shook my head, finding it slightly ridiculous to be talking about myself in the abstract. "I just needed to write something good this time—funny, clever, emotional—if for no reason other than to prove that I'm not a shitty storyteller."

My self-esteem had taken a battering. And while my "private" writing gave me a much-needed mental vacation from the reality that I had yet to sell a script, I wanted to prove to myself—because no one outside our apartment was going to read it—that I could still craft a decent tale.

Scully pulled me into a hug, her belly hindering the effort. "Stop being so hard on yourself. You know you're a great writer and an amazing storyteller. Why else would I be sitting beside your printer waiting for an unedited manuscript? And I'm not trying to inflate your ego, but lately, this has been some of your best stuff. Not sure if it's because of the subject matter or that he inspires you, but I swear I can't put it down."

"New Blaire and Nick?" Luke stopped in the open doorway, a towel slung around his waist. "Print me off a copy too."

"Do not use it as jerk off material." I narrowed my eyes as I added another copy to the printer's list of jobs, knowing the appreciation for Nick's fine form was one that was shared by Luke. Not that I blamed him, he wasn't the kind of man easily ignored.

Luke laughed, rubbing his hand down his muscular chest seductively. "I can't help it if I feel inspired. Scully is right though, this is some of your best stuff."

I probably should have been offended. That the best writing

I'd churned out recently was fantasy-induced scenarios that would probably never happen. But they were right. Nick inspired me, excited me, and lit a fire in me I hadn't experienced in a while.

He was . . .

My. Muse.

The human incarnation of my creativity, making my fingers fly across the keyboard with an ease I hadn't ever experienced. Words poured out of me effortlessly, filling page after page that had previously sat empty.

I wasn't sure if it was the way he looked, his on-screen persona, or the fake reality I'd built in my head, but he unlocked a part of my brain that allowed magic to happen.

And it wasn't only restricted to my "creative" writing, I felt myself improving professionally as well. My dialogues weren't as stale, my directions more precise, my scripts overall sharper than they had been before. So if nothing else, me "musing" him wasn't a bad thing, right?

No, of course not.

Some people went into the desert, chanting naked, while eating peyote. I, on the other hand, conjured up fantasies—without the aid of hallucinogens—about a guy I barely knew.

"Best stuff or not, I don't want to know." I waved my hand in Luke's direction. "Read, enjoy and then banish it to the box with the others." I patted a plastic storage tub that housed my previous Nick-themed-efforts. "Meanwhile, I'm going to watch the man on television for what is probably an inappropriate amount of time. And while doing that, I can decide which shitty writing job I can pick up for the next month so I can cover my share of the rent."

It had to count for something that I was still writing, right? And no matter how unimportant the job was, at least I hadn't given up. I hadn't tossed it in and become a waitress just yet. Trust me, it would have definitely been easier, especially in a city that was pretty much paved with broken dreams.

"You know, we can cover you." Luke turned serious, the smile dropping from his lips.

Scully shifted uncomfortably, and if the silence wasn't enough to tip me off they'd discussed this before, the awkward sideways glances they shared did.

I didn't like it.

Not one little bit.

"You guys, you know I love you, but I don't need your help. And I know you would cover me if things got desperate, but I'm an adult and I can pay my way like both of you."

I hadn't even told my parents I'd hit the skids, preferring to syphon what was left of my savings than admit I couldn't cut it in my chosen career. It helped they lived out of state, my dad, mom, brother and sister moving to Colorado years ago when my dad got transferred for work.

"We know that, but both of us have steady jobs right now, and if the situation was reversed, you would help either of us, wouldn't you?" Scully's hand reached out, gripping my arm. "Besides, I'm probably going to need the two of you to help me out when this baby is born." Her eyes dipped down to her belly.

"She's right, you know. And all we are offering to do is toss some cash at the situation to give you some breathing room. Scully here is brining a whole human into the mix. I figure floating you for a month or two is nowhere near as big an imposition."

Scully rubbed her belly, her smile returning as she—like Luke—tried to lighten the mood. "He's full of shit, he can't wait until this baby is born so he can finally have a legitimate excuse to watch kids movies and not look like a deviant."

"I like fucking animation, it's an art form," Luke fired back defiantly. "But yet a single guy walks in there and suddenly you're a pedophile. Everyone is so fucking judgmental."

"In any case, I'm good. I know my big break is just around the corner. One of my scripts is bound to sell." I summoned all the enthusiasm, trying hard to convince everyone in the room— including myself—that my low point was ending soon.

After all, it's not like I was a bad writer.

Unless.

Shit.

Maybe I was merely a bad writer and I was deluding myself.

"Do you think . . ." I felt my old nemesis, self-doubt, rear its ugly head. "Maybe I should do something else?"

Confidence was a funny thing. It could change minute by minute with the feeling of being brilliant only to be quashed in the next breath. I consequently loved-hated-loved almost everything I ever wrote. All except the fan fic stuff because that was for fun and remained free from scrutiny.

"Noooooooo. You're a brilliant writer." Scully slapped her hand down on my desk.

"I hate to read, and I love your stuff." Luke collected the latest installment of Blaire and Nick from the printer.

I sunk down in my chair and studied my work still on my screen. "As much as I love hearing that, I really need to do something to get me out of this rut. Maybe I need to go on a heist or something, give myself some inspiration to pull from."

"I'm driving the getaway car," Luke offered a little too quickly.

My eyes dipped down to his mostly naked body. "Just make sure you wear clothes, heisting is serious work."

Scully laughed, retrieving her copy from the printer. "I'll be on comms, tip you off to any incoming trouble. And if shit goes bad, I'll go into fake labor."

"Well now that we have all that worked out, we simply need to find this perfect crime." Or me a decent job, at this point I wasn't too fussy.

"I'll keep a lookout, let you know if I find anything," Scully mumbled, her head lowered ignoring both of us as her attention diverted to my words. "Nick's show is starting soon. Watch and be inspired for me. I'll think of some trouble we can get in later." She waved goodbye as she left the room.

"Thank God she can't get pregnant twice." Luke chuckled giving me his own farewell as he left me too.

I grabbed the remote and switched on the T.V., the opening sequence already on.

There he was.

The hottest man on the small screen, and currently the only subject I could write about and not suck.

Maybe I should write him a thank you note.

No.

That would be creepy.

CHAPTER #2

THE WEEK PROGRESSED predictably.

No bites on any of my submissions, no agents interested in representing me, and no openings at any studios. I did have a guy message me through *Upwork* looking for someone to help him script pornos. I considered it for about a second, but then hesitated when he suggested we meet to discuss the project at his "studio." Yeah, I wasn't that stupid, and not that desperate . . . yet.

I did, however, manage to get some temp work as a script reader. I was almost positive Luke had called in a favor, but I wasn't about to turn it down. Sure, it wasn't the best job in the world, but at least I didn't have to fetch anyone's coffee. And I could do a lot worse than sitting around reading other people's work all day—writing pornos for one. And if nothing else, it showed me what *not* to do, all while keeping me in the industry.

My luck was about to change; I could feel it in my bones.

"WOW." Luke stood at my open doorway, the look of disgust on his face unmistakable. "I'd have thought you would have been celebrating your new job, not sitting around in yesterday's sweat-pants eating ice cream straight from the tub."

"This *is* me celebrating." I shot him a grin, waving my spoon around.

He grimaced, folding his arms across his chest. "Looks more like a break-up. Go shower, get dressed and when Scully gets home, we'll go out to dinner."

I didn't need to check my phone to know it was late, somewhere closer to midnight than it was to dinnertime.

"Ummm . . . Luke, I think we'd have better luck with breakfast."

"Can you go shower already? I'll text Scully and find out if she's going to grace us with her presence."

Usually I was up for whatever. Dinner, a movie, drive-by to egg the house of the father of Scully's unborn child—I was game. Just tell me the time and place and I could be ready to mobilize in less than thirty minutes. But I had lost my motivation of late, probably fueled by my dwindling savings. Which meant more than once I had given Luke and/or Scully the sorry-I-can't-tonight-I-need-to-do-laundry. That was *before* though, my newfound job making things a little easier on my bottom line.

"Sounds good," I agreed, forgoing my night with ice cream and yoga pants in favor of dinner/breakfast with my best friends. Well, at least one of them. Scully was still out at a wrap party for something and had yet to come home.

So after a quick shower I was back in my room, still within my ready-to-mobilize thirty-minute window when Scully walked in. She looked pretty pleased with herself, popping her hand on her hip as she stood in my open doorway while I applied a thin layer of makeup.

"So, guess who I saw tonight?" Her eyebrow rose, goading me further.

With Scully, it could have been anyone. She once slammed on the brakes on the 405 because she swore she'd seen Henry Cavill in the piece of shit Buick two cars behind us.

Spoiler alert.

It wasn't him.

Just someone who looked remarkably like him.

But she did manage to get his number and date him for about three months before she faster-than-a-speeding-bullet told him to take a hike. Thank God *he* was not the baby daddy.

"Babe, I didn't even know where you were for sure tonight, how the hell am I supposed to guess who you saw?" I added another lashing of mascara as I kept my eyes on the mirror in front of me.

I could hear the smile in her voice as she enlightened me. "I was at a wrap party for *The Blue Line*."

My hand stopped mid-stroke, the mascara wand inches away from taking out an eye.

"YOU WERE AT NICK LARSSON'S WRAP PARTY?" The words barreled out of my mouth like they'd been shot from a gun. Just as loud too, any hope of controlling a silly thing like volume getting tossed out the window the minute she'd mentioned the show that Nick happened to be the star of.

She rested her hand on her chin, staring off into the distance as she started to recount her evening. "Well I didn't start there. I was supposed to be at our wrap party, you know that documentary on thirteen-year-olds I've been—"

"Scully focus, I don't care where you were *supposed* to be." I tossed the mascara wand, grabbed her with both my hands and gave her a little shake. "I need to know how you ended up being at Nick's party? Details, all of them. Start talking," I demanded as heavy footsteps came down the hall.

"Jesus Christ." Luke entered the room like he was SWAT, almost knocking Scully over as his eyes darted between us. "I had headphones on and still heard you. How did you get to Nick's wrap party?"

Scully rolled her eyes, the smile beaming on her lips. "I was trying to explain but apparently I'm not allowed to say what I was supposed to be doing."

"Just give us the condensed version." I shook her again impatiently, not any closer to the details. "Please, tell me everything."

She took a deep inhale, opening her bright pink lips as she blew out a breath. "Well the short version is one of the girls from wardrobe is dating Ben—one of the support actors—apparently it's new because she's never mentioned it before. So when we got to our party and saw it was only a bunch of old people standing around drinking wine and eating Brie, we had to bail. I mean, I'm pregnant and both of those things are on the "no" list from my OB/GYN. And if I'm going to spend my evening out torturing my feet in these heels, I don't want it to be with a bunch of old dudes in cardigans eating cheese and crackers. At least give me something decent to eat."

I nodded, hoping my head bobbing would encourage her to keep going and not elaborate further on the shitty menu.

"So anyway, Lisa—our wardrobe girl—said she knew of something better, we slipped out and went to Max's on Sunset. And there he was."

There was no need to clarify the *he*.

I knew who *he* was.

I had dreamt about him, weaving his dreamlicious smile and sexy body into pages upon pages of literary fantasy.

"What was he wearing?" asked Luke, like his choice of attire was important.

"Did you speak to him?" I added my question, wishing there was some way I could connect a cable to Scully's mind and download the experience like some weird science experiment and watch it back live.

"Jeans, T-shirt, and the sexiest smile I've ever seen." She answered Luke before turning back to me. "And yeah, I spoke to him almost all night. He's amazing, so nice."

"Tell me. What. Words. Said. You. Him." Language became

something I didn't know, reduced to out of sequence words in sentences that didn't make sense. I needed to know everything. *More* than everything.

What he said, how he said it, tone used, the visual cues and the fifty-seven ways it might have been interpreted. Not a freaking byline, but a leather-bound thesis with footnotes and citations.

She laughed, not surprised by my reaction, as her eyes lit up with a playful mischief I wasn't sure was a good thing.

"Okay, so he was hanging back and watching the rest of the crowd who were drinking and having a good time. It was sort of dark so I wasn't sure at first, but once I saw the smile, I was positive. There were also about thirty girls who were circling him, but he seemed more interested in merely chilling rather than which blond or brunette was in front of him. So I took a chance and walked over and started a conversation. He was so sweet, even asked me how far along I was."

"Skip how sweet he was and tell us how hot he was," Luke interjected, his impatience probably for different reasons than mine.

"So we got talking about the industry, and he mentioned he was taking the summer off because he hadn't read any decent scripts he wanted to work on. And because I was looking for a way to work you into the conversation—I totally have your back girlfriend—I gave him a copy of your latest work which I had tucked away in my handbag."

BOOM.

That was the sound of my mind exploding, my brains flying across the room while I clasped at my skull screaming "medic."

My mouth opened, releasing a soundless scream. The lack of volume wasn't intentional, the absence of air in my lungs responsible for the silence.

"What work?" I managed to rasp out, praying to God the *work* she was referring to was the script I'd written three weeks ago and not my Blaire and Nick stuff.

I mean, she wouldn't give him that, would she?

She wouldn't.

Please.

No.

One look at her face and I could tell it was, Luke as equally quiet as we stood in stunned silence.

"Why do you look so horrified?" she laughed nervously, her eyes flashing between me and Luke. "I thought you'd be ecstatic. He took it and said he'd be happy to read it, and we've all agreed it's some of your best writing."

"I'm going to die." My hands clutched at my throat as reality set in. I was having a panic attack or a heart attack, my pulse racing at a rate I was positive was more favorable toward mortality. And it was just as well too, the idea that he had his hands on words *I* had written about *him*—not something I could even reconcile right then.

"Breathe, Claire!" Luke's arm wrapped around my waist stopping my body from crumbling as my knees buckled. I wasn't really worried about hitting the floor, a broken bone or two were the least of my problems.

"No. He can't read that. It's not . . ." I spat out between gasps, "for him or anyone else to read. That stuff was for fun, private. Oh. My. God, Scully. How could you give it to him?"

If I'd been in better shape, I'd have plotted her murder. I mean she was a good and loyal friend who'd had my back more times than I could count, but clearly we'd come to the end of our run.

Satanic possession.

That, or she'd finally succumbed to the absence of mind that apparently accompanied growing a human in your body.

Those were the only explanations on why she would give my muse the fantasy he'd inspired.

"I was trying to help," she squeaked out, her smile dropping as concern set in. Either she'd come to the realization that it wasn't her best idea or my interpretive dance of a zombie was freaking her out. "I thought that if he read it and saw how good it was, then maybe he'd—"

"Want to meet the crazy person who wrote it?" I didn't let her finish. "Sure, that doesn't make me sound deranged or delusional or even worse . . . like a stalker."

It couldn't be real; it was a bad dream—a nightmare—I was going to wake up from.

Wake up, I chanted silently. *Wake up.*

Nothing.

It wasn't a dream.

"He probably isn't even going to read it. Didn't you say he was bored with all the scripts he'd read?" Luke nodded to Scully as he tried to smooth things over. "A hundred bucks says he threw it into the trash the minute she left."

Okay, so there was that. I nodded, agreeing it was completely ridiculous that he would bother keeping it *and* then read it.

Actors got unsolicited scripts all the time, and most of them never saw the light of day. Banished, their fate to either be recycled into something more useful, or used as kindling for firewood in the cooler months.

"Don't be mad, Claire. I'm pregnant, I wasn't thinking clearly." Her voice warbled, her chin shaking a little like she was about to cry.

Of course it was an act, something she'd throw out there whenever she wanted to escape trouble, pretending it was mood swings brought on by the pregnancy. Not that she couldn't or didn't get emotional, but crying on cue—even with the hormone surge—was not Scully.

Overlooking her bad acting routine, I pointed to her bump like it might yield the answer.

"Of course, that's why he took it in the first place. He probably was just trying to be nice because you were pregnant." I tried to convince myself more than anyone else. "There's *no way* he's going to read it."

Newsflash. Scully wasn't the only person in the room who was a bad actor.

Her lips pulled into a tight smile that didn't signal good things. "Actually, he sat down and started reading before I even left."

"Not helping," Luke cursed under his breath as a renewed wave of panic washed over me.

"Okay, Okay." I nodded, reassuring no one in particular because I didn't possess that kind of power. "So even if he read it. My name isn't on it; he has no idea who wrote it. It's not like there is anything tying it to me."

And chances were he wouldn't even like it, wondering why a pregnant woman he met at a party handed him a story that wasn't even a real script. He'd laugh, tell his friends about it and chalk it up to a glitch in the Matrix.

All of which I was totally fine with.

Because the truth was so much more horrifying.

The silence wasn't reassuring. Neither was the look of guilt that clouded Scully's eyes as she rolled her bottom lip against her teeth. She did that when she was nervous, almost chewing her lips to pieces when we were waiting to find out if she was indeed with child, and its reappearance could only mean one thing.

"My name wasn't on it, was it?" I asked again. I hadn't even bothered with a cover page, leaving no indication at all as to who could have authored it.

"I maaaaaay have scribbled your name on the back page."

"Oh dear God!" a strangled voice called out, and from the look on my friends' faces, it had been mine.

"Yeah, there's no coming back from that. Let's hope he has a short attention span and doesn't finish, though I have to tell you, it was compelling reading." Luke laughed, no longer able to hold on to the pretense there was any silver lining.

"We need to go get it back, we need to figure out a way and get back the pages and remove all traces of it."

There was a chance—albeit slim—that our paths would cross in the future. A project we'd both work on, a party we'd attend, or at the Academy Awards when he acted in the movie that I won best screenplay for. Okay, the last one was a long shot, but you get the idea. But he hadn't hit his older brother, Eric's, level of stardom yet, and I hadn't been banished to the colony of the pariahs. So, until either one of those happened, I was holding onto that middle ground like my life depended on it. And on the *chance* that one of the above transpired, I couldn't risk him thinking I was a hack with stalker tendencies.

Luke scoffed, loosening his hold on me as he shook his head. "Hold on there, *Mission Impossible*. How the hell are we supposed to do that? Break into his house and steal it back?"

Hmmm, I hadn't thought that far ahead but breaking in sounded like a good idea. It was a stack of A4 paper, not the crown jewels. He'd probably leave it on a coffee table or something like that, easy to find and recover.

"Sure, why not? It's L.A., people get broken into all the time." And technically I wouldn't be taking anything that wasn't rightfully mine anyway.

The fact I had no experience in crime and unlawful entry was swept aside, there was always room to expand your personal set of skills.

"I know where he lives," Scully volunteered, finally being proactive in helping us sort out the mess she'd created.

"Do not encourage her," Luke warned her with a raised brow before turning to me. "My suggestion is you take your chances he thinks you're a fruit loop and leave breaking and entering to people who want to go to jail."

"She only goes to jail if she gets caught," Scully interjected.

Luke blew out a frustrated breath. "Still not helping."

Maybe risking jail to save myself embarrassment seemed extreme, but it wasn't *just* my pride at stake. It was my career—which had yet to get off the ground—on the line as well.

Nick not only knew *hundreds* of people in the industry, but also by virtue of his brothers, had a reach I couldn't even begin to fathom. Did I really want to leave it all up to chance? The chance he'd take pity on me and my slightly creepy compulsion for writing *him* into my fan fic and not think I was a weirdo with no talent? This was the kind of thing that could ruin me, reduce me to cocktail party fodder and exile me to the graveyard of I-could-have-been-a-contender.

No.

If I was going to be a washed up nobody, then it would be on my terms alone. I didn't need anyone to help me with my fall from grace, and I wasn't going to allow writing that had been the bright spot in a fairly bleak creative landscape, be the source of my undoing.

"You know where he lives?" My body stiffened with a renewed sense of purpose as I focused on Scully.

Luke shook his head. "You can't be serious."

"Yes," she answered, choosing to ignore Luke and his warning.

My heartbeat thumped out of control under my skin as I looked to the open doorway of my bedroom. "Then let's go."

I was no closer to knowing how I was going to get my manuscript back than a few minutes ago. Who knew if he'd even be back? He could've potentially still been partying somewhere in Hollywood, celebrating being awesome while I was having my nervous breakdown. But encouraged by Scully's claim he'd been uninterested by women and the surrounding festivities, it was worth the risk he'd ditched the crowd and headed home. Or I could be delusional, always a possibility. Either way, I was damn well sure not going to sit in my room and watch my world burn.

Resolution settled in. I was willing to do whatever it took.

Let's hope "whatever" didn't see me end up with a conviction and shitty mug shot.

CHAPTER #3

LUKE DROVE.

He pretended like he didn't want any part of my madness, citing it would make him an accessory, but deep down there was no way he wasn't going to be involved. He was like a magnet to drama, pretending like he didn't buy into it but being unable to resist the allure. Of course he wanted to be involved, he didn't move from Peoria, Illinois to sit at home and play it safe. Plus, his shiny new Lexus was a better getaway car than either of us had, and he'd offered to be the wheelman when we'd planned our fictional heist. #NoTakeBacks

Scully was our lookout and if need be, the diversion. It was the least she could do considering she was the reason we were in the mess to begin with. Like me, she was a native to L.A. and she knew the right level of crazy to bring. If shit went down, she knew how to cause just enough of a distraction so no one would call the cops.

Our mission was simple, get in, get the story, and get out.

Of course, the closest thing I had to breaking into anything was the one time I jimmied open my mom's snack stash when I was sixteen. She had a drawer in the kitchen she'd put all the good stuff in—Peanut Butter Cups, M&Ms and enough candy to make our Halloween haul seem like amateur hour—and I had managed to force it open with a ladle and a wooden spoon. It wasn't epic level gangsta stuff by any stretch, but in the eyes of my younger brother Cody and sister Courtney I was a hero of unrivaled proportions.

"You know this is crazy, right?" Luke again tried to persuade me to forget our planned lawlessness as we rolled to a stop two houses away from Nick's duplex in West Hollywood.

"I'm already committed." I squinted my eyes, trying to see the front of the house.

Except for the streetlight, it was mostly dark. There was a big hedge to the side, which was currently obscuring my view but from what I could see, it looked to be empty. While I hadn't known his exact address, I didn't need Scully to tell me he lived alone. He'd previously shared a house with his brother Dave, but thankfully his older brother had recently moved in with his girlfriend. It was a useful piece of information too, because no roommates meant less chance we'd be discovered. Unless his neighbors had a strong sense of civic duty and were watching from their windows.

Or he had surveillance cameras.

Or an alarm.

Shit.

Maybe I hadn't thought this all the way through.

"Or you *should* be committed." Scully laughed, finding it amusing that she was soon going to be party to a crime.

"Just make sure you do your job," I warned, popping open the door of Luke's black sedan. "If I go down, I'm taking you down with me and no one wants the baby to be born while you're serving time in lock up."

"It's a first-time offense, we'll get off with community service." She waved me off, watching as I slipped out of the car and onto the street.

If I was trying to be inconspicuous, I failed miserably, tiptoe-ing like a moron on the sidewalk as I stalked closer to his house.

In my perfect world I would have been dressed in a sleek black full-length body suit, wearing sexy and yet practical boots. But there hadn't been time to procure a Catwoman costume, so I had to make do with skinny jeans, a black T-shirt and a pair of Converse that had seen better days. I was still wearing my makeup from when we were going to be going out for dinner/breakfast, so at least my mug shot would look good.

With the blood roaring in my ears, I slowly climbed the cou-ple of steps that led to Nick's front door. I'd watched a dude on YouTube pick a lock with two paperclips, but as I pulled mine out of my pocket, I didn't like my chances. I hoped by some miracle he'd forgotten to lock the door, or left a side window open wide enough for me to shimmy through.

"Fuck." I felt my feet go out from under me as my body crashed forward. My hands reached out, bracing myself and stopping me from falling as I looked down to see what the hell I'd tripped on.

Oh.

Fuck.

What I had suspected was some crazy or intricate security measure was actually a body. A very tall, very muscular, and very horizontal body that was strewn on the front stoop like a prop for a crime scene. And if not for the two beautiful eyes looking back at me, I'd have assumed that was exactly what I'd stumbled into.

"What are you doing here?" he slurred, his keys dropping to the ground as he tried to shuffle himself into a sitting position.

"Ummm." My brain scanned for any plausible explanation and came up blank. "I'm here to help you back up?"

It probably would have sounded more convincing if I hadn't phrased it as a question, or if I had offered to do anything that resembled helping him up.

But I hadn't.

Instead I was staring at what seemed to be a very drunk Nick Larsson, who looked so gorgeous it didn't seem fair. God he was hot, his messed up hair and glassy eyes somehow working for him. He clearly wasn't human because no mortal man looked *that* good when they were struggling with gravity and sobriety.

"My agent sent you, huh?" He used his hand as leverage as he slowly rose off the ground.

Did I lie? Pretend that his agent had sent me, help him into his house, steal back the manuscript—I mean, I still had an objective here—and then disappear into the night?

Who would even do that?

What kind of sick, reprehensible—"Yes, your agent sent me." It left my mouth before I had a chance to stop it.

I'd admit that when it came to being decent, I didn't always do the right thing. That didn't mean I was a bad person, it merely meant that sometimes I made bad choices. Case in point, me putting my arm around Nick Larsson and helping him with his keys while he believed I was there for altruistic reasons.

"I told him I was fine." His weight pressed against me like his feet weren't up to the challenge of holding him up. I didn't mind, the heady mix of cologne and beer wafting up my nose as I helped guide his hand to the lock.

"Yeah, you look fine too," I muttered under my breath.

I meant it sarcastically because he was far from "fine." But even though he was inebriated, Nick Larsson was still most definitely *fine*.

What I was doing—entering his house under false pretenses—was thirteen types of wrong, but I tucked away my conscience for later. It served me no purpose, especially as Nick unlocked his door and I was granted access to his house. I hadn't even needed the paperclips, managing by some insane strike of luck to score an invite—well the closest thing I was going to get—as I waltzed through the front door.

He moved forward, dragging me with him as he tossed the keys on the coffee table, my body tingling at the contact.

Nick Larsson had his arm around me.

And I was holding him.

It was totally *not* in the context I had ever imagined, and so far away from anything romantic it was almost pathetic it got me excited. But I wasn't going to argue semantics at that point. Or give up the opportunity. For whatever reason, the universe had thrown me a bone, and I was going to be grateful.

Please God, don't let him realize he let a strange woman into his house and call the police.

His head dipped down as his eyes tried to focus, looking at me properly for the first time. "You're not Audrey." He swayed unsteadily on his feet.

Busted.

"No, I'm not."

Part of me—the irrational, moronic part—wanted to ask who Audrey was and what was her business with him. Not because I was jealous—because that would be dumb—but because if I'd known maybe I could have done a better job at impersonating her.

There you had it, ladies and gentlemen, not only had I been ready to commit a crime—my first foray into breaking and enter-ing—but I was willing to carry on the charade of impersonating *Audrey* if I'd only been given enough information.

His hand moved across my face, his fingers grazing my chin like my bone structure would yield some hint as to who I was. And for someone who had let a strange woman into his house, he sure was calm. I mean, I could have been a psychopath or a crazed fan, he really should have been more concerned than he was.

"You going to tell me who you are? Or am I supposed to guess?" His mouth twisted into a smirk that could only mean trouble. Not just for him, he was clearly waaaaay too intoxicated for his own good, but also for me because I had trouble thinking straight when he looked at me like that.

The manuscript, I reminded myself. Asking him out on a date wasn't an option; that ship had well and truly sailed. Also "out" was staring at him adoringly and cataloguing every inch of his body for future reference. The research argument wouldn't fly in a courtroom.

"I should go." It had been almost a whisper because I wasn't convinced it was what I *should* be doing. It sure as shit wasn't what I *wanted* to be doing, because if I was doing *that* we'd have already been on the couch and making out by then. Because that was smart, making out with a man who was clearly not able to give proper consent. I swear if I didn't end up in a jail cell before the night was up I was going to hand myself in.

"Really?"

He didn't let go, his hands moving from my face down to my waist as I was frozen in place. I had no idea what he was doing. If his handsy approach was an attempt to try to steady himself—most likely—or it was some weird version of flirting. For all I knew he had a strange and dangerous kink and liked to make out with strangers.

Lord, please.

Please.

Please, please let it be the latter.

Stop it. I chastised myself as my eyes widened no closer to knowing. *There is no way he is trying to seduce you.*

Why the hell not, my hormones argued. *If the man wants to kiss you, drunk or not, we're going to reciprocate.*

"I think I—" Even if I had known what the rest of that sentence was going to be, I didn't have a chance to finish. My feet lost contact with the floor as he pulled me down with him, my body landing on his as he hit the couch.

I didn't dare move, holding my breath—lying on top of him—undecided if it was the best thing to ever happen to me or some cruel joke.

Oh.

Dear.

God.

He was hard.

And I was turned on.

His hand touched my ass as his lips made contact with my neck, and I felt every cell in my body simultaneously jerk awake.

Like I'd been electrocuted, I leapt off him, landing on the floor in an ungraceful and uncoordinated heap. Thankfully he hadn't seemed to notice the pile of arms and legs tangled on the floor beside him, closing his eyes like he hadn't witnessed the most awkward dismount of all time.

I was definitely going to jail.

Ignoring my impending future with a cellmate named *Brenda* and chunky shackle jewelry, I was positive was not going to look cool, I tucked and rolled on the floor trying to right myself with some dignity.

Not sure why I bothered. Dignity, self-respect and common sense hadn't been with me when I showed up and I highly doubted they were going to make an appearance any time in the future.

As I rose to my feet, still silent because I didn't trust my mouth and/or didn't know what to say, and I noticed that sexy hot Nick was also silent. Not totally like he-might-have-died quiet, but other than the heavy breath pushing past his lips, there was no other noise.

Holy shit.

Was he . . . unconscious?

Still unsure as to what I wanted the answer to be—it might be easier to ghost out of his apartment if he was out for the count—I tentatively moved closer, keeping a safe distance in case he was faking me out and going to tackle me the moment I got in striking distance. You could never be too sure, and the night had already taken a weird and unexpected turn, so I wasn't about to assume anything.

"Nick?" My hand curled around his shoulder and gave him a hesitant shake.

No response.

Nothing.

Satisfied that he wasn't using his superior acting skills, and he really was asleep, I moved closer to examine him. I mean, I had to make sure he was okay and not going to choke or something. Not that I had any first aid experience and/or knew what the hell I was doing, but I wasn't going to let something like logic get in the way. It was probably a little late in the game to start acting smart.

My eyes were drawn to his face, his beautiful dark lashes resting peacefully on the top of his cheeks hiding those stunning chocolate eyes. His plump lips—almost too perfect to belong to a man—were slightly parted allowing the soft rush of air to pass them. I swallowed hard, my gaze following the curve of his muscular neck down to his impressive chest. The T-shirt did nothing to hide the masterpiece underneath, his strewn arms and legs giving me a front-row seat to the magic that was Nick Larsson's body. He was a work of art, perfection in the purest form, and even casually draped across furniture, he looked beautiful.

Seeing him on television was one thing, appreciating him and marveling at how hot he was. But up close like this—close enough to touch him—and my skin broke out in goosebumps so badly I wasn't sure they weren't hives. The lingering memory of him five years ago was nothing compared the reality of how perfect he was, the view almost overwhelming. The butterflies in my belly were also disconcerting, throwing my game off further as I wondered what the hell I was supposed to do.

Caught in a tug of should-I-stay-or-should-I-go, I moved closer, my hands tentatively reaching for the strong, sexy curve of his neck. His steady pulse thumped against my fingertips as I hovered above him like a creeper.

"What the fuck?" Luke's voice hissed from behind me. "You killed him?"

I guess I shouldn't have been surprised. I mean, I was supposed to get in, find the manuscript and get out, and who knows how long I had been gone. I'd say if Luke, Mr. I-don't-want-to-be-involved, had left the safety of his car and come to investigate, it had to have been a substantial amount of time. Not that it mattered anymore, the problem of what to do next not made easier with an extra participant.

My head whipped around, trying to keep my voice low as I hissed back. "I didn't kill him. What kind of person do you think I am?"

"Well, considering you broke into Nick Larsson's apartment, not really sure how to answer that."

At least he was honest. I wasn't sure what kind of person I was either considering I should have already left but there I was, still in the unconscious man's apartment, touching him. Oh, and side note, I had yet to feel regret or remorse.

"I didn't break in, I helped him unlock the door," I whispered, ignoring the fact it didn't make the situation in any way better than the mess it currently was.

Luke moved closer, inspecting Nick carefully before turning back to me. "So what, you knocked him out?"

Funnily enough he didn't sound surprised or shocked. Not sure what that said about me that he thought A. I was capable and B. I had the physical strength to accomplish it. I sat on my ass for eight hours a day and got winded doing Pilates, rendering a grown-ass man who had close to eighty pounds on me incapacitated was something I'd put in my resume if it was anywhere close to true.

"No, Jesus, Luke. He was drunk." I huffed out an exasperated sigh as I quickly explained. "I found him on the floor at his front door, struggling with the keys, and he thought I was some girl his agent had sent to check on him. I didn't correct him."

I didn't bother with the extra stuff—Nick's hands on my body, me considering kissing him and then finally falling on top of him— because it sounded sleazy. Let's be honest, it was *sleazy*, and even still—no regrets.

Luke screwed up his face in horror, recoiling from me like he'd discovered I was carrying some hideous horrible disease. "You pretended to be someone else? *Deceived* him?"

"Wait a minute." I waved my hands in the air, trying to get a handle on his shock. "I came here to break in, and then you assumed I'd either killed him or knocked him out, but me pretending to be someone else has your panties in a twist? And here I was thinking I was the craziest person in the room."

Luke opened his mouth ready to respond when he was stopped by the soft groan coming from the couch.

Oh, I hadn't forgotten that our little disagreement was happening in the living room of a man who didn't know either of us. Or that at any minute Nick could wake up, see two strangers in his house and call the cops. Realistically, calling the police was the best-case scenario. Him thinking we were thieves and trying to take us out was also a very real possibility, and we'd already established I got winded during Pilates. I wasn't at all confident I was going to be able to defend myself against a not-so-sober man-giant who probably fought like a ninja, even three sheets to the wind.

"Scully is still waiting in the car, we should go before this gets any worse." Luke's head jerked to the door.

I bit my lip, glancing around the room before my eyes fell back on a still-sleeping Nick. "But I didn't get my pages back."

"Honey, I think the manuscript is the least of your problems. Cut your losses and let's get out of here before the woman who you were impersonating turns up and we have some serious explaining to do." Luke circled his hands around my arm and yanked us away from the couch.

Of course he was right; we needed to get out.

And I had every intention of leaving.

Except . . .

"Can you help me move him to the bedroom?"

The look of horror had returned to Luke's face, dropping his hands from my arm like my body had caught fire. "Are you fucking crazy? What part of we're not supposed to be here and we need to get out do you not understand?"

"Oh please, don't pretend like you expected me to be logical about this. We're both here aren't we? It's too late for that." The time for exploring my sanity, and whether or not any of it was a good idea, had probably expired the minute we'd all climbed into the car like vigilantes and driven to his house. I'm not saying it was my proudest moment as an intelligent human, but there was no point splitting hairs that late in the game. "Stop being so dramatic and help me get him to his bedroom."

There was no reason for me to do anything other than leave. Sure, I hadn't recovered the manuscript—the prime reason for me being there—but I highly doubted that was going to happen at this point. Leaving made sense, but as I looked at him, his body tossed on the couch, I felt compelled to make sure he was okay. Or at the very least save him from falling off the couch and hurting himself. Maybe it was my way of finding redemption, my good deed to try to negate all the shady shit I'd recently done. Or maybe I'd woken up from a rough night of drinking and felt like absolute hell and wanted to make it easier for him.

In any case, whether it was apathy or for restitution, it felt important that I do it. And then lock the door behind us in case some other nutter had similar ideas. He'd been too trusting, too unguarded, and even though he lived in a nice part of town—it had been too risky.

Luke huffed in exasperation but thankfully didn't continue to argue. Instead he followed me to the couch, where I gently grabbed Nick's legs while Luke took the lion's share of the heft, wrapping his hands under Nick's arms and lifted.

In what could only be described as an awkward dance, the two of us managed to shuffle him off the couch and haul him down the hall to where we assumed his bedroom was. At least I hoped that's where it was, because I wasn't sure what else we were going to do if his bedroom was in some secret hidden room. Not going to lie, he weighed a ton, the sigh of relief both literal and metaphorical as we passed an open door that revealed a room with a bed. I didn't even care if it was his room, my arms starting to shake as we lowered him down onto the mattress.

By some miracle—or from the copious amount of alcohol that no doubt had been consumed—he didn't wake up, allowing us to manhandle him without so much as cracking an eyelid. He moaned softly as I positioned him, curling to his side the minute I'd taken my hands away.

He looked so innocent, so vulnerable that I almost felt bad for seeing him like that.

Almost.

Because as I'd mentioned before I had questionable boundaries and wasn't the best person in the world.

"Claire, we need to go." Luke's hand curled around my elbow and jerked me away from the bed.

I nodded, or at least that was what I thought I did. But as my feet stayed on the floor at the edge of his mattress, I couldn't get over how beautiful he was.

Lying in front of me.

Vulnerable.

"Oh my God, you killed him?"

Luke and I whipped our heads around, finding Scully in the doorway, her hand covering her mouth in horror.

"Seriously?" I hissed back. "You both have been watching waaaaaay too much television."

Knowing we were well past the point of pushing our luck, I grabbed Luke's arms pulling him outside Nick's doorway as we gently pushed Scully out of the way. Thankfully the room was mostly dark, the only light streaming from the hall which I put the kibosh on the minute I shut the door.

At least if he woke up, he wouldn't be able to identify us in a lineup. Not physically anyway. I hadn't *completely* lost my mind.

"Hey, I didn't even get to see him properly," Scully giggled, retreating back to the living room as we moved further away from his room.

"You saw him plenty tonight when you gave him my story, which I might add, still hasn't been recovered."

Ironic that my sole objective had become an afterthought. Still, no point dwelling on it now.

Scully tapped her lip, looking at the closed door. "Do you think he gave it to Audrey?"

It was the second time I'd heard that woman's name, and in both instances I didn't like it.

So maybe I was a tiny—microscopic—albeit irrationally bit jealous. Clearly I needed to reevaluate my earlier statement that I *hadn't* lost my mind.

Dumbass.

"Who cares?" Luke tapped his foot impatiently. "Maybe he gave it to Santa Claus, it doesn't change the fact we need to get the hell out."

Yes.

Leave.

We needed to.

"Who's Audrey?" I asked as Luke pulled us to the front door. It was more like a huddle at the line of scrimmage being moved down the field, my feet barely touching the ground as we made it to the threshold.

Scully pushed back, arching her back defiantly as she stood her ground. "The writer's assistant, they are supposed to be looking for a project together. *And* stop pushing me around, one of you needs to tell me why the hell he was unconscious on the bed." With her hands anchored on her hips, she dared either one of us to move her.

As quickly as I could, I gave her the rundown.

He was extremely drunk.

Tripped on him.

Helped him into his house.

See, your Honor, there was no foul play and/or trespassing when I entered Mr. Larsson's premises.

"Wow, he must have hit it hard after I left then because he was totally sober when I saw him." Scully looked perplexed and in no hurry to leave.

Great, maybe it had been my writing that had driven him to drink.

Shit.

Because I didn't have enough self-esteem issues, I had to add hypotheticals to it as well.

Luke looked between us, tipping his head to the street. "Again, this is a conversation we should have in the car. Preferably as we drive home."

"We *can't* just leave him here," Scully protested, her body stopping us from getting to said car.

"Of course we can, he *lives* here. This is exactly where we *should* leave him. We on the other hand, should—" Luke didn't get to finish his sentence when he heard a faint—but definite—moan coming from the bedroom.

Scully looked at me, my urge to go check at odds with my self-preservation as I twitched where I stood.

"If he was so drunk he was unconscious, he needs someone to look after him." Not sure if it was her maternal instinct showing up a couple of months early or she was genuinely concerned, but either way, it gave me a reason to stay.

A reason I hadn't even realized I was looking for until then.

Well look at that.

I really *was* crazy.

Abandoning any pretense that I had my mind right, or that I wanted to leave—one and the same really—I threw my own argument into the ring. "She's right. What if he hurts himself? Or worse? He ends up a headline tomorrow, drowned in his own vomit, I'll never forgive myself."

"Not to mention our DNA is all over the place, and I don't want to have this baby in jail." She rubbed her belly to reinforce the point.

Luke shook his head, the I-can't-believe-you-guys written all over his face. "You said back in the car it was a first offence, they're not going to lock anyone up."

"Murder is a felony, Luke. I have to stay for all our sakes." I stood with Scully in solidarity. "You two go, and I'll hang out until almost morning, make sure he's fine, and then catch a cab home." I pushed lightly on Luke's chest.

Another head shake and with few "fucks" muttered under his breath, he took Scully's arm and pegged me with a final look. "If this goes bad, call me immediately. And for the record, I think this is crazy."

I nodded, agreeing that as far as sensible decisions, this wasn't one of them, but made my peace with it.

"I'm fine, go."

God I hoped I was right.

Because, as I watched my two best friends disappear from view, I had no idea if any of it was going to be anywhere close to fine.

It was the opposite of fine.

It was definitely *not* fine.

CHAPTER #4

I LOCKED THE door after my friends had left. I didn't want Audrey or anyone else paying us—listen to me, *us*, like we're a fucking couple and I belonged there—walking in unannounced, and tossed the keys on the coffee table.

Then I patted myself on the back for my good deed—which would hopefully balance out my not-so-good intentions—before I returned to the bedroom, crossing my fingers to find a still-sleeping movie star.

It would be helpful if he was still breathing as well, considering that was the reason I was supposed to have stayed.

My body tensed as my fingers wrapped around the knob. Slowly—and praying to the DIY Gods someone had had the good sense to WD-40 the hinges—I opened the door.

Breath.

Held.

The exhale only came when the light from the hallway illuminated a stunning, alive, but still sleeping Nick, thankfully where I'd left him.

Thank you, God.

With his welfare confirmed, I seriously considered snooping

around and turning up the manuscript I'd come to find in the first place. Even though he hadn't seemed to have had it when he walked in, there was a chance he'd dropped it in the bushes or tossed it in his mailbox before I'd found him at his front door. Or maybe my manuscript was shoved into his pants, just waiting for me to extract it. All I had to do was reach down there and . . .

Ugh.

Not even I could sink that low. Besides, as I watched him, the guilt ate at me.

Because as dumb—and irrational—as it sounded, it felt wrong to take advantage of him.

He looked awkward, still clothed and wearing heavy black boots. I was almost positive it couldn't be comfortable, my own shoes getting toed off as I stalked closer to the bed.

Don't do it. My subconscious warned, the idea not even fully formed in my mind as it was discounted.

Maybe only the boots, I rationalized.

It's not like touching his feet was a violation. He'd be wearing socks, there'd be no skin-to-skin contact at all.

No.

No touching.

Ok, fine . . . just the boots.

I got closer, my fingers quickly undoing his laces as I loosened both boots. My hands wrapped around the heel, attempting to be both agile and delicate as I shimmed the boot off his foot. He stirred but didn't wake, letting me get the other one off before setting them both down at the base of the bed. His socked feet wriggled as I came back up to inspect him.

He purred a sigh of satisfaction, like my small act of kindness pleased him, tempting me to take more off. Socks maybe?

No.

I had already pushed my luck too far.

My hands were shoved into my pockets—my attempt at restraining myself—as my head shook, returning to the safety of the doorway.

As tempting as it would be to lay on that bed with him, I would be spending the night on the couch. There, I could "observe" him, make sure he was okay without infringing too much on his personal space. Hopefully I could leave in the early hours of the morning before he woke, and no one would be any wiser.

Or he could potentially emerge from his drunken slumber, find me in his house, mistake me for a burglar and bludgeon me to death with one of his award trophies. It really could go either way.

And with that little nugget ping-ponging in my brain, I retreated to the living room, laid on his couch and stared at the ceiling.

Remember when my biggest problem was writer's block and not having a steady job? Funny how I thought it couldn't get worse.

Thank God my parents weren't around to see.

Even though I'd been a grown-ass woman in college when they left, they'd still worried I'd end up in some kind of mess. Not anything illegal per se, more likely low-key mayhem. Cody and Courtney were born a year a part with Cody—the elder of the two—five years younger than me. We'd get up to stupid pranks as kids, making my parents gray before their time. And yeah, as I sat in the living room of a famous man who probably didn't remember me, I questioned if perhaps my parents were right.

Although, my evening escapade would make a great idea for a script. Who didn't like an intriguing spy-esque tale about a girl who only had her wits to keep her out of trouble? Maybe she had to infiltrate a hostile foreign embassy, her *mark* a devastatingly handsome diplomat from an eastern European country. I imagined Nick in a suit, traveling covertly with a polypropylene ballistic black suitcase as he rendezvoused with contacts in different countries trying to find the mole. He'd fall in love with the beautiful spy of course, torn between betraying her and serving his country or defecting. Maybe she'd be playing him, using his feelings for her as a weakness to destroy him.

Man, he was good.

Or more to the point, *I* was in the presence of him.

Perhaps there was some science behind it that could explain it. As to why he helped me tap into creativity I couldn't seem to reach by myself. I'd always preferred sex to masturbation, liking the assist rather than being there alone with my own hand. So maybe it was sort of like that.

Like my brain had been rewired and recalibrated, ideas and thoughts percolated. It was fresh, unforced and made me excited to write again. I hadn't had the compulsion to put pen to paper like that in a long time and sitting around and fighting the urge wasn't an option even if the setting wasn't ideal.

Except, the setting—and the person it belonged to—was exactly what prompted the urge in the first place.

I needed to make good life choices, and as I looked around wondering if this was my bottom or the beginning of my magnum opus, I wasn't going to squander the opportunity I'd been given. Not today, Satan. Not today.

So while I camped out on Nick's couch like a squatter, I pulled out my phone and opened my notes section. I'd have preferred my laptop but I would have to make do. The sexy spy wouldn't moan about her lack of materials. No—she would get shit done, which was exactly what I was doing as my fingers plotted out ideas and tapped out notes.

Damn, it felt good.

"Thank you, Nick Larsson," I whispered, turning my attention to my phone.

Maybe the night wouldn't be so bad after all.

I just had to make sure I didn't fall asleep.

CHAPTER #5

I DIDN'T SLEEP.

Instead, I wrote like a madwoman, backing up my notes every twenty minutes to my cloud so I didn't lose anything. It wasn't fan fic either, but an actual script—something I could potentially shop.

And best of all.

It *didn't* suck.

Well, at least I didn't think it did.

Delirium had probably set in, madness consuming me as I purged out words, which unfortunately had happened while I was trespassing. Still, you couldn't control when the creativity struck, and maybe all that bullshit about Nick being my muse hadn't been bullshit after all.

There was something about Nick that affected me like other men didn't. Not that I hadn't dated other guys or found them good-looking, but not to the level I was attracted to Nick. Maybe it was because he was insanely hot and talented, but I wasn't going to rule out magical powers either.

Hell, if being in his vicinity was enough to revive my productivity and bring back my mojo, I'd drink his freaking bathwater and not bat an eye. I'd probably drink his bathwater even without the additional incentive. And yes, I needed serious professional help.

Due to dedication, delirium, or possibly just stupidity, I hadn't realized that those nighttime hours had faded, and the morning was no longer a distant possibility. Unlike jail time, which was probably going to be in my future.

SHIT.

The door I'd left open a crack last night so I could hear him, meant I had no real warning, Nick groaning as he stepped out into the hall. His bare feet—the socks gone—moved slowly from his doorway, making his way to the kitchen.

My whole body froze, every muscle still, as I watched, wondering how hung over he was, and whether or not I could lay flat, camouflaging myself or try my luck at impersonating a lamp.

I didn't dare even blink, worried that just the fluttering of my eyelashes would be enough to attract attention. As for my heart, it was beating loud enough I was shocked he hadn't heard it.

If he'd noticed me, he sure as hell wasn't letting on, his slow dance with next-day regret happening in front of me while I looked on like a silent voyeur with a panic-induced fever.

And.

Oh.

My.

God.

At some point of the night/morning he'd obviously shucked his clothes, the boots I'd helped him with nothing compared to what else he took off. I guess even drunk he'd managed a certain amount of dexterity—something else to admire. But currently, that wasn't the *talent* I was most in awe of.

He was topless, a pair of sweats hanging off his hips seductively so he didn't flash anything indecent—not that I would have complained—and more of his bare, taut skin than I had ever seen up close before.

So smooth and delicious, my eyes feasted over every curve of his chest like it had been the first time they had seen a man. And I wasn't overly religious but covering all of that perfectly rippled and curled muscle had to be a sin. And those sweat pants? That drawstring must have been Wonder Woman's lasso because anything less would have surely succumbed to the power of all that awesome.

He had inadvertently given me enough material to feed my creativity for a month. Maybe even longer.

Oblivious to me, my impending nervous breakdown, and my staring, he raked a hand through his hair, squinting in the daylight that streamed through the kitchen window.

My throat constricted, making the shallow breaths being expelled by my lungs almost painful as my heartbeat accelerated. God, I hoped I wasn't having a heart attack, the thought of dying only mildly more mortifying than being discovered. Well, technically death wasn't going to save me either considering then he'd have to deal with a body.

Shit.

This was so bad.

My life flashed in front of my eyes as I internally argued whether this was the most amazing or most terrifying experience of my life. Probably both, which was why I wanted to simultaneously vomit and cheer at the same time.

Did I hope he didn't notice me or send up a flare and announce my presence?

Why hadn't I thought this through?

And did it still count as a first offense if I'd been there all night?

God, I hope he didn't call the cops.

"Hey." It slipped out of my mouth while I was trying to still work out what was to follow.

His eyes swung around, lazily landing on me while I attempted to think up my next move. I should have thrown myself behind the couch and waited it out.

"What are you doing inside my house?" he asked with zero recognition.

No *"get the fuck out, I'm calling the police,"* which was exactly what I was expecting. He was calm, unconcerned, like random women he didn't know loitered on his furniture all the time.

He eyed me up and down like a second look might jog his memory. Somehow, I didn't think it was going to help.

"Well?" he asked again, reminding me I had yet to answer him.

I froze, so mesmerized by him and that body that I completely forgot what I was doing and why I was there. Selling insurance? Looking for a lost pet? I could've been petitioning for a seat in the Senate for all I knew.

Say something.

My mouth opened, my lips moving, but no sound came out. He'd rendered me mute, unable to find words—any of them—as I sat, looking at him like a pervert.

"I'm sorry, what?" he asked, moving closer which unfortunately wasn't helping my situation. "I've got a killer headache, and I didn't hear you the first time."

He mistakenly thought my gold-fishing lips had said something audible when in fact they hadn't. I wasn't going to point that out though, glad he was still hung over enough not to notice how much of a weirdo I was being.

"Hi, I'm Claire." I jumped to my feet, throwing out my hand and trying to remember if I'd actually introduced myself last night.

His brow rose hinting that he might not be as hung over as I first thought. Or maybe my weird was too much that even an elevated blood alcohol level didn't help. It could have gone either way to be honest.

"I helped you inside last night." I tipped my head to the front door, hoping it might prompt the recollection.

I didn't like my chances.

"Claire?" His hand reached to stroke his chin, flexing the muscles in his chest and arm in the most glorious way.

If saying something intelligent was my objective, then I was going to have to stop looking at him. All that naked hot male skin on display, just being able to remember my name was a challenge.

"Yes," my one-word answer not giving him much to work with. "From last night. I got you inside your house," I repeated because obviously saying the same thing a few extra times would help clear up the confusion.

Dumbass.

"Oh, from *last* night." His lips twitched into a grin, a spark of recognition flashing through his eyes. "Shit, I'm sorry. My head's a little fuzzy. Where are my manners, want some coffee?" He raked his hand through his hair again, no less sexier than the first time.

"Umm?" *Did I want coffee? Did I want COFFEE? What the hell was happening?* "Don't you want to ask why I'm still here?" Because clearly he needed a reminder to toss me out on my ass.

I swear I'm not an idiot.

"So . . ." his sexy smile widened, *"last night."*

Great.

If the grin was anything to go by, we had wildly differing recollections of what actually transpired. I'm sure it was novel for him, have a woman put him to bed and not get in it. Something I probably would have done if he'd been conscious and coherent.

I mean, no I *wouldn't.* I absolutely didn't sleep with men I didn't know.

Except . . . I sort of did know him.

And he was super hot.

Plus, I was positive we all got at least one free pass on reckless sex.

Gah, that was so not helping.

And if that little conundrum wasn't enough, I wasn't sure if I should be flattered he believed we went there or offended he didn't remember we hadn't.

"No, not like that. We didn't have sex." I waved my hands in front of me. If I was going for smooth, I'd missed my mark.

Part of me would have been happy to play it out and see where his assumptions took us. Did he think I stuck around for a repeat performance? Was that what he was looking for? The coffee necessary to recharge before the next round. Ding, ding.

But the rational part of me—I swear, it did exist—didn't want to complicate things any more than they already were.

We were *not* going to sleep together.

Crying freaking shame too.

"Huh?" He looked confused, his brow furrowing and his smile dropping. "I know we didn't have sex. Did you think I was imply-ing—"

"No, no, no." I was quick to answer, mortified I had misread him completely. "I just wanted to set the record straight. Make sure you knew I didn't take advantage of you."

Somewhere in the Pacific was the Marianas Trench, a part of the ocean so far down that the pressure would literally crush you. But that bad boy wasn't even close to how deep of a hole I'd dug for myself.

His smile was back, hooking at the side because clearly he hadn't been charming enough for today. "I wasn't worried about you taking advantage of me." He rubbed his chin as if deep in thought. Or he was a cartoon villain and looking to calculate the next move. "But I will say I'm usually a better host. My agent put you up to this or my brother? Both have been a pain in my ass."

Nice ass it was too.

"Sorry, what?" Because the morning hadn't been confusing enough as it was, we had to add conversation I couldn't follow.

He tilted his head to the side, speaking slowly in case *that* was the reason I hadn't caught on. "Dave or Jeremy? I assumed the threat of a chaperone was an idle one, but I guess not. By the way, I would have been fine last night."

"Firstly, I'm not your chaperone, I haven't spoken to either your agent or your brother. And secondly, you weren't in the same neighborhood as fine," I shot back. As long as I maintained eye contact I was good.

New rule: don't let my eyes drop below his chin.

His eyes squinted in confusion. "But you look familiar, don't we know each other? And if they didn't hire you, then who are you?"

If I hadn't essentially been trespassing, I might have been excited that he had a vague recollection of me. Clearly, our brief encounter five years ago *hadn't* been permanently etched into his memory like it had been mine, but I would take what I could get. Okay, so maybe I *was* excited.

"Well . . . we sort of met a while ago." Lord help me did I sound lame. *We sort of met a while ago?* Who was I and why did my voice sound like I came from the valley?

"We worked together briefly, a long time ago." My effort to recover nowhere near as smooth as I'd hoped. "Anyway, that's not what's important. I was visiting a friend and noticed you having a hard time getting into your house and thought I could help."

My explanation was sketchy at best, but what choice did I have? The truth? Sure, might as well go flush my career down the toilet at the same time because the truth was so freaking ridiculous, I wouldn't even hire me.

His eyes narrowed, looking at me closer like he could sense the inaccuracies in my story. "So, you helped me inside and then . . . decided to stick around?"

If his mouth hadn't curved into a smile, I might have assumed he was angry or even annoyed, but if anything, he looked . . . intrigued?

Could I have been reading that right?

"You were really drunk, I didn't want you to drown to death in your own vomit or break a leg or something." *And possibly end up the suspect of your murder when the place was dusted for prints.* I'll admit, I didn't say the last part, some things were better left unsaid.

His smile got wider. "I'm not sure what's funnier? That you had me destined for an untimely demise, or that you were trying to be my hero. I think either way, I should definitely buy you breakfast as a thank you. Then you can tell me all about our *brief time working together.* I'm looking forward to you refreshing my memory."

What the . . .

Was he asking me out on a date?

No, surely he wasn't crazy enough to ask a woman he didn't know, who essentially muscled her way into his house under false pretenses—granted he didn't know that, but my motives had to be questionable at least—and ask me to breakfast.

My mouth refused to accept the invitation the rest of my body was begging to RSVP to. It *surely* was a test.

When I didn't respond, his eyes scanned my body with increased interest. I didn't know if he was looking at me in a sexual way or if he wanted to measure me up so he knew where he could stash my body. I mean, I didn't really know him, for all I know he might have had plans to make a skin suit, and a girl like me seemed to fit the bill.

No.

I wouldn't accept he was a psycho—questionable sanity perhaps—but not *Silence of the Lambs* level crazy.

He moved closer, bringing that body of his, which was still very much on display, inches away from mine as he leaned into me. "You have other plans? Other men that require your civic duty?"

Jesus.

Freaking.

Christ.

There was no chance I could say no to that.

I mean, who cared if he was certifiable, everyone had to eat and if I could do it with an amazing view, what was the harm.

Think of the material it would inspire.

And, it would possibly give me the opportunity to find out what had happened to the manuscript Scully had given him. I'd bring it up casually while I stared into his beautiful eyes and try not to choke on toast.

"Sure, I'd love breakfast." I tried not to sound too eager, which wasn't hard considering part of me was terrified. "Mind if I use your bathroom to freshen up?"

Not sure how much "fresher" I could get considering I didn't have a toothbrush, clean clothes or deodorant, but worrying about technicalities clearly wasn't my MO. Current situation—the evidence.

He folded his arms across his chest prompting my eyes to drop. Bad move. Not that he seemed to notice that my eyes were about to bug out of my skull or that I was holding my breath as he leaned in closer. "You spent the whole night at my house. I think we're a little past asking to use the bathroom, don't you think?"

Well played, Mr. Larsson.

Well.

Played.

"Right," I coughed nervously, trying to regain some composure while I formulated a plan. "I'll be right back." I grabbed my phone off the couch and the small handbag I'd come in with last night. The two paperclips I had tucked away in there when I'd planned to pick his lock weren't going to be any help. But hopefully I had a rogue breath mint or something else that would be useful. Next time I planned a break-in, I was bringing an overnight bag.

I felt his gaze on me as I shuffled past him and headed to the bathroom. The problem, I wasn't exactly sure *where* that was. My feet froze in place, my eyes scanning the door directly in front of me, which was where Luke and I put Nick last night. I probably should have snooped when I had the chance. Again, hindsight was 20/20.

"Down the hall, the door on the right," he called out with a chuckle.

Against my better judgment—there was an oxymoron—I turned around, treating myself to his delicious smile.

He looked *good* when he was amused.

Straightening my spine, I gave him a smile of my own. I might have zero idea what I was going to do in the next few minutes, but I refused to dissolve into a puddle on his floor. "Thanks." I turned back around and strode to the bathroom like I had always known where it was.

It was only once I was safely inside that I was able to take a huge deep breath. The exhale spilled from my lips as did the sigh of relief.

The situation was far from ideal, but it wasn't terrible either.

No cops had been called, no suspicion raised—and as far as he knew, I was just some do-gooder who helped him. At least, that was what I *hoped* he thought. He could have very well been on the phone while I was staring at my reflection in his bathroom mirror and organizing a free ride for me. And chances were it was going to be the 9–1–1 variety and not Uber.

Quickly—because I didn't trust him or myself to spend too much time alone—I cleaned myself up as best I could. Hijacking his toothpaste—he was a Crest man, while I preferred Colgate—I used my finger to brush. Then I finger combed my hair, patted my underarms with a damp tissue and wiped off any smeared makeup from my face. I also found a perfume sample card in my handbag that still had some scent to it and wiped that on my skin praying it would transfer. It was the best I could do and when I surveyed the result I was pretty impressed. It wasn't my best work, but I didn't look like I'd camped on the couch of a man I barely knew. There was a positive if ever there was one.

With my appearance refreshed, I needed to take care of a few other issues. My two roommates who could at any minute knock at the door and blow this whole ruse were my first priority. The repeated text messages telling them both I was fine the first few hours of last night had been enough to quell any rescue operations, but I wouldn't be able keep of either of them away if I suddenly went radio silent.

As quietly as I could I dialed Scully's number. I figured out of the two of them she would be the mostly likely to be awake considering the three million trips to the bathroom she seemed to take.

"Hey," her voice a little groggy from sleep, "what time is it? Where are you? Do you need me to get Luke?"

"I'm fine, I'm still here." The *here* not needing to be explained as I purposely kept my voice low. "I wanted to let you both know I was fine and there was no need to worry, I'll catch a cab home later."

"What do you mean you're still there?" she almost screeched into the phone. "You were supposed to make sure he didn't die from alcohol poisoning and get out. Stick with the plan and get out before he wakes up."

I winced, knowing she was not going to like what I said next. "He's already awake, I'm in his bathroom as we speak. Just trust me, okay. I promise I'll be back soon."

There was a pause, followed by an exasperated sigh. "Okay, okay but promise me you'll call if you need back-up."

"I promise. Now, I better go before he gets suspicious," I whispered into the phone, wondering if I'd already taken too long. And with a quick goodbye, I ended the call and shoved my phone back into the bag.

Pushing my shoulders back and trying to harness as much confidence as I could possess, I stepped out of his bathroom and strutted to the living room. Sadly, my little show seemed to be for nothing when I found myself alone. The hung over, partially clothed movie star was MIA, the room as empty as it had been the night before.

What I should have done was sit on the couch and waited because common sense dictated that he wouldn't be far.

But doing what I *should* was never my forte.

Instead I inched to his partial opened bedroom door and peered inside like the pervert I apparently was.

OH.

MY.

GOD.

Those insane sweatpants—the ones that seemed to have a hard time with gravity—were gone, and there was nothing in their place. *Nothing.*

Instead, I was staring at Nick Larsson's incredibly taut ass as he toweled off his hair, tiny beads of water clinging to his back like it was their life's mission. I understood the compulsion, though if it was me I'd have definitely aimed lower.

Two thoughts passed through my head.

One, I was a deviant and should be disgusted with myself.

And two, he had the most spectacular ass I'd ever seen.

Oh, and clearly he had a second bathroom because he'd not showered with me.

Not that all of that mattered if he turned around and caught me gawking at him. Which was why I peeled my eyes and the rest of my body away from the door and almost ran back to the living room. There I sat my butt down, folded my hands in my lap, wondering if my prayers for forgiveness would be answered even if I wasn't truly repentant. A decent person would be sorry for violating him like that. But I, ladies and gents, was having trouble with the sentiment.

"Get through breakfast, hope to God that between the party and his drunken slump on his doorstep he lost my story, and get out of this situation without a criminal charge," I muttered under my breath. That was as close to prayer as I could manage without choking on my words.

Somehow, I didn't think it qualified.

CHAPTER #6

"SO, WE WORKED together?" He took a sip from his juice, waiting for me to fill in the gaps.

While I had managed to stay out of his room, and avoid any further infringements of his privacy, avoiding the conversation wasn't going to be so easy.

He'd emerged from his room looking better than he should, considering he had barely been able to stand less than twelve hours ago. And other than the dark sunglasses, you'd have never known he was rocking a hang over.

By the grace of God, I'd managed to keep the conversation completely benign as we walked to a nearby diner. The weather, how his head was feeling, whether the Laker's were going to have a good season this year—which showed how desperate I was because I knew jack shit about sports—hoping I wouldn't accidently blurt out anything incriminating. You know, like I'd seen his ass and that I'd had ulterior motives for my Florence Nightingale routine.

Of course all of my efforts were redundant when he asked what was probably a very logical question. Something I had readily admitted when he said I looked familiar. I was going to have to learn to be a better liar in the future.

I forked my eggs, waving my other hand like it was no big deal. "Oh, it was years ago. You played a bartender on *Crash* and I was the writer's assistant. I think we had like one conversation, maybe two. It really wasn't anything you'd remember." *Unless you were me who clearly held onto the interaction waaaaay more than was probably appropriate.*

"Oh yeah, I was on that show for like a minute before it got canned," he laughed. "Thankfully, my acting has improved."

Yeah, and you got hotter.

He narrowed his eyes, lowering his juice as he studied me. "I'm trying to remember you because you don't look like someone I'd easily forget. What did you say your last name was again, Claire?"

The way he said my name was unnecessarily suggestive, like he wanted to roll it around in his mouth a little before spitting it out. And let me be clear I had no problem with that. I was more surprised he even remembered it, our introduction more focused on the fact I was a stranger in his house.

I cleared my throat, trying to ensure my voice sounded normal, so I didn't look too pathetic. "It's Becker. Claire Becker." *I wisely didn't point out I hadn't said previously.* "Anyway, it's not important." *At least not right now.* "Sooooooooo that party last night sounded great. You happen to remember chatting to a pregnant lady?"

As far as smooth segues, it was a train wreck. Seriously, it was like a conversational version of Sudoku, and let me be clear, I sucked at the number version of that game as well. But I couldn't be sure the attention he was paying me wasn't a fact-gathering exercise to tell the police, so I didn't want to give him too much. And besides, I still had to work out what the hell happened after Scully gave him my story. A stack of crisp white paper wasn't easily misplaced.

I wasn't sure if it was my awkward word stumble or something else that had him looking at me like I'd grown another head, losing interest in his breakfast and as he grinned. "What did you say?"

"You met my friend, Scully, last night at your wrap party," I offered, hoping it was starting to make more sense. "She was pregnant, wearing a red dress, likes to talk to people more than she should." I pushed around the eggs on my plate, trying to sound casual. "I think she might have given you a script?"

"A *pregnant woman* gave *me* a script?"

"Yes."

His smile turned into a laugh. "Is this some kind of riddle?"

"No, Scully said she ran into you and handed you . . ." I couldn't finish the sentence, a knot tightening at the base of my stomach.

He shook his head. "I know I was drinking heavily but I think I'd have remembered getting a script, especially if a pregnant woman gave it to me."

"Are you sure?" The blood in my veins ran cold with no way to be positive if it was disappointment or relief I was feeling.

He scrunched up his nose as he grinned. "I was doing shots at the bar most of the night with my buddy Rich. Barely spoke to any women. I don't like to date my co-stars, too much drama, if you know what I mean."

"I guess." Nick's good work ethic not even close to being important right now. "She must have been mistaken." My heart was beating so fast my ribs felt like they were going to explode. "Excuse me for a second."

Grabbing my handbag, I shuffled out of my chair, trying to keep the smile on my face as I powerwalked to the bathroom. If this was Scully's idea of a joke, pregnant or not pregnant, I was going to put her in a chokehold until she blacked out.

My fingers furiously dialed her number, managing to get the bathroom door shut before I heard her voice on the other end of the line. "Where are you? You need help?"

"Who the hell did you give my story to?" I choked out. "Because it wasn't Nick Larsson."

"Of course it was Nick Larsson, I'm not a dumbass," she spat back indignantly.

I tried to remain calm, reining in my panic as I paced the bathroom. "Scully, he doesn't remember you. He doesn't remember getting the story. And didn't you say he hadn't been drinking? Nick Larsson was hammered last night, is it conceivable that maybe you got him mixed up with someone else?"

"Claire, I know you're freaking out but who else could it have been? It's not like there is anyone who . . . Oh. Shit."

"Looks like him?" I finished for her. "Shit, Scully. Did you give it to Dave?"

Nick and Dave were born a year apart, with Dave being the older of the two. And unlike their more-famous older brother Eric—blond-haired and blue-eyed—they both shared darker hair and brown eyes. They were far from looking like twins, but the family resemblance was definitely strong. Add in shitty lighting attempting to create ambiance, and Scully wouldn't have been the first person to get them confused.

"Shit, shit, shit." I chewed on my bottom lip, my brain in free fall as my throat tightened.

Scully's voice warbled as she whispered into the phone. "Please don't be angry, Claire."

"It's fine, it will be fine," I said more for my own benefit than for hers. "I'll just go back to Nick, make up some bullshit excuse and leave. Then when I get home, you can help me formulate a new identity. New name, new phone number and I also need a new backstory. I'll be Jane from Palm Springs and my parents can be date farmers. It's been a while since I've been a blond. We should dye my hair as well."

Scully laughed, probably assuming I was kidding. "You don't even look like a *Jane*. But seriously, think of the positive, at least you got to see Nick Larsson again."

My head shook, there were so many random thoughts going through my mind and none of them positive. "Yeah, it turned into a real silver lining. I'm hiding out in a bathroom while I'm sure he is probably wondering how crazy I am."

It was tempting to leave the bathroom and give Nick the slip. Unless he was watching, he'd never see me slide past the tables and to the exit. Then once I was safely outside, I could call Luke to extract me like a soldier behind the enemy lines. The new plan could be formulated on the drive home, perfected once I was securely in my room.

"I better go, talk soon." I wasn't sure what I was going to do but phone calls in the bathroom weren't helping. "Tell Luke to be on standby." I hadn't ruled out a rescue mission just yet.

"Sure thing. Bye."

My feet rocked with uncertainty, the itch to go to the door and keep moving almost overwhelming, but I wasn't someone who cut and ran.

Ha! If that had been the case I would have given up my dreams of one day seeing my name in the credits and taken that job writing scripts for porn. No, I was a lot of things but quitter wasn't one of them. So with my shoulders pushed back I opened the bathroom door and walked back to the table.

ARE YOU SHITTING ME?

Like a gremlin, he'd multiplied, and right beside him was another tall, good-looking Larsson.

Damn it.

"Everything okay?" Nick asked, his smile widening as I took my seat.

I tried to hide my panic, my jaw locking as I looked at his brother. Too late to rethink my stance on not being a quitter because leaving sounded like a really good option.

"All good. Sorry, I needed to check in with a friend." I shuffled in my chair trying to make sure I didn't hyperventilate and pass the hell out. That would be bad. Worse than the situation I was already in.

Nick pointed to the guy who not only shared a similar smile, but also his last name. "Dave, this is my friend Claire. Claire, this is my brother, Dave. He felt the need to check up on me even though I told him you'd cornered the market." He shot me a quick wink.

Shit.

Shit.

Shit.

Because I didn't have enough challenges, I had to deal with his charm as well. A woman could only take so much, I was dangerously close to making couch jumping Tom Cruise look sedate.

"Hi, I'm Claire." I extended my hand, ignoring that I had already been introduced as I scrambled for something to say.

He called you his friend, the excited fifteen-year-old girl inside of me shimmed.

Well it wasn't like he could admit he was having breakfast with a crazy stalker and not make himself look bad, the realist countered.

Who needed angels and demons on your shoulders when I had all the voices in my head?

Dave accepted my handshake, wisely looking at me with skepticism. "I heard you took care of this loser last night. You have my thanks."

"It was nothing." I tried to laugh it off, "I was just doing what any decent person would have done."

I tried not to choke on the word *decent*, mentally bargaining with whichever higher power was running this sideshow that he or she would be merciful.

"Still, I'm thankful." Dave added, piling on some extra guilt in case I didn't have enough of my own.

"Honestly, don't mention it." *As in seriously, let's stop.* My fingers fumbled with my fork as I attempted to eat my breakfast. The bacon and eggs were cold, but I didn't care, more concerned about getting through the meal with my sanity intact.

"You checking on your friend, the pregnant lady from the party?" Nick asked causing my eyes to bulge. He'd been paying attention—awesome.

"Ummm. Yes. Her." I gave as little as possible, trying to force a smile.

"She tell you what she did with the script?"

No.

No.

I shook my head doing my best not to make direct eye contact as I tried in vain to laugh it off. "She didn't mention it. Probably made the whole thing up, you know pregnant ladies. Ooooh this breakfast is so good." I shoved a loaded fork into my mouth, attempting to chew and smile and not look deranged.

Dave's brow furrowed, rubbing his chin as he looked between Nick and I. "You mean the pregnant lady from last night? Wearing the red dress? It was hard to hear her over the noise, but I think she said her name was Sally? She pulled a script out of her handbag, interesting reading. Huh, small world."

I was going to die.

The last moments of my life were going to be in the chair of an L.A. diner, taken down by some mediocre scrambled eggs while the man who had played in almost every fantasy I'd had for the last five years looked on in horror.

So undignified, I really wished it could have been a more elegant death.

Before my sight faded, I was able to witness Nick leap from his chair and pull me out of mine, tapping my back with authority I was too dizzy to appreciate. "Shit, Claire, are you okay?"

"Fine," I wheezed out, sucking in breaths that felt more like razor blades. "Water."

While Nick held me, Dave lifted a glass of water to my lips, my eyes widening as I took a sip.

Nick Larsson was *touching* me.

And this time, he was sober.

I nodded, mumbling more *fines* as my esophagus stopped spasming. I'd even managed to swallow the water and not spray it in his face—fate finally throwing me a bone and showing some benevolence.

"You good?" Nick righted me on my feet, his smile warming my body like the sun on a summer's day.

I was so dead.

My head bobbed, my lips parting without the extra rush of air. "Yeah, all good."

Bullshit, there was nothing good. Not unless not expiring in front of an audience counted because that was about the only thing *good* about this whole scenario.

Both Larssons waited until I was safely seated in my chair before retaking theirs. They had manners as well as good looks, because that wasn't greedy at all.

"Did you want to order something else?" Nick asked, looking down at my mostly uneaten plate.

"No, no. It's fine." I think I'd probably broken the record for the most fines spoken in the last few minutes. "I'm not that hungry."

As tempting as it was to shove a forkful of breakfast into my mouth in order to shut it, I figured one brush with asphyxiation was enough for the day. Of course it did feel slightly better than the alternative, admitting that my *pregnant friend* had somehow mixed up the brothers and had given my personal fantasy fodder to either of them for consumption. I wasn't even sure I could blame hormones; this was classic Scully—acting first and thinking later.

Nick didn't suffer the same concerns, sipping his juice without the worry of drowning. Literally *or* figuratively. "So the pregnant lady who gave Dave the script was your friend?"

Why did God hate me so much?

Sure, I wasn't the best Christian. Hell, I couldn't even remember the last time I walked into a church. And yes, I cursed a lot, and had broken at least four of the Commandments last night, but I was a good person. Why must I continue to be punished?

"Yes, Scully. She works for one of the networks and was at your wrap party last night." I purposely avoided all mention of my pages, hoping it was like Beetlejuice—as long as I didn't say it out loud three times it wouldn't be able to haunt me. "We're roommates."

"I think the two of us were the only ones not drinking." Dave smirked at his brother.

Nick rolled his eyes. "It was a celebration. I was celebrating."

Dave lowered his voice, looking at me before adding. "Well maybe next time do a little less of that. And you need to call Audrey, she said she missed you."

And suddenly Scully, my writing and my almost dying wasn't the most interesting thing getting brain space.

Audrey.

My nemesis.

From the limited information I was able to gather last night from Scully, Audrey was the writing assistant on the show Nick starred in. She had a job I once had, and would kill for again. She also got to work with Nick, so she was two-for-two against me. There were no indications they were romantically involved—Nick's comment about not dating anyone he worked with being the strongest evidence—but that didn't mean she didn't want to.

Of course she did.

As irrational thoughts of disliking someone I didn't know and never met, I decided it was time I needed to go home and get some goddamn perspective.

"I should get going. I have work I need to get through." I stood up, committing to my exit before I had a chance to change my mind.

Nick joined me on my feet, reaching out and grabbing my hand as he smiled. "Are you sure, I feel like I haven't properly repaid my debt."

"No, no, you've done plenty. Like I said, it was no big deal." I smiled back, trying to ignore he was touching me again, and this time he was sober, *and* I wasn't choking. "And now that your brother is here I don't have to worry about you getting home okay. That top step of yours is a killer." I gave him a wink before sticking out my hand.

He glanced down at my outstretched hand, raising his eyebrow as he accepted it into his own. "We're handshaking now? Seems a bit formal considering we spent the night together." The smirk that followed just about undid me.

No.

It was insanity.

The longer I stayed, the greater the chance he'd find out the truth. That I had an unhealthy obsession with him, and I was using him for my creative musings. Crap, it was only a matter of time before Dave went home, picked up the "script" and discovered the awful sordid story.

I bit my lip, unable to help myself. "Yep, handshaking. Enjoy breakfast and stay out of trouble." I extracted my hand before turning to Dave and waving goodbye. "Nice to meet you. Take care."

With the promise of freedom ringing in my ears like William Wallace's warrior cry, I was about to take my first step toward the doorway when I felt a hand on my arm stopping me.

"Wait, you're not even going to give me your number?" Nick looked surprised, like he'd expected me to scrawl my digits in red lipstick on a napkin and seductively whisper, "call me" on my way out. Because *that* wasn't the most cliché thing ever.

His hand around my arm loosened as I looked down at it, bringing my eyes back to his. "I'm sure we'll see each other around," I lied, knowing the chances were virtually nonexistent.

It was for the best, turning and heading out the door while they still believed my actions and intentions last night had been altruistic. When in reality I had been trying to save myself the embarrassment. So with my head held high, I gave one final wave and walked out of the diner and into the warm Californian sun. If nothing else, I had gotten my mojo back. And that had to count for something.

CHAPTER #7

I'D BARELY MANAGED to get inside my house when Scully threw every single pound of her pregnant body at me. She was like one of those monkeys at the zoo, clawing at you like you held the last banana. "What happened? Did you kiss him? Tell me everything!"

"No, I didn't kiss him. Can I at least go have a shower first? I'm still wearing yesterday's clothes and haven't slept." I was more concerned about the shower to be honest, I had so much adrenaline running through my veins there wasn't a chance I'd be sleeping.

Luke was leaning up against the wall, casually standing back while I got the third degree from Scully. "You know this has bad news written all over it. You should have left last night with us. He's a big boy, sure he could have handled himself."

Thinking of how *big* he was and how well he could *handle* himself weren't helpful, which was why I chose to ignore it. Along with anything else I might like him to handle. Damn. My body wasn't the only thing that needed a shower; my mind could do with a good scrub too.

"Look, it's done. He thinks I was visiting a friend, saw him, and helped. Let him live the fantasy that I'm the citizen of the year for an afternoon. In the meantime, his brother will probably go home and read the story Scully gave *him* by accident, and one or both of them will file a restraining order. All good."

While my future sounded bleak, it was by far the most excitement I'd had in the last few weeks. Not only was my body humming like I'd jammed wires underneath my fingernails, but I had written more last night on a "workable" script than I'd had in months. One of those reasons was probably why I was smiling so wide, and I wasn't going to try to extrapolate which.

My roommates looked at each other, a silent dialogue passing between them as they stared at me. They probably wondered if somewhere between last night and the morning if I'd had a mental break, snapping into full-blown psychosis.

Luke moved closer, narrowing his eyes as he lifted his phone and shone the light from the flash into my face. "Pupils reactionary, she isn't high."

I shoved the light out of my face. "Of course I'm not high, you think in between helping Nick into his bedroom and being discovered in his living room I had time to score some weed?"

"Well, it was a long night, and you did say you didn't sleep," Scully offered like it would be reasonable.

Well, realistically, it might be reasonable. But in this instance, the high I'd received *wasn't* synthetic. "I did something better than get high. I *wrote* last night," I declared proudly.

"You wrote sexy times while he was asleep in the other room. Babe, I'm impressed." Scully beamed, her pride shining through.

Luke joined in, his own smile wide. "I like this deviant side of you. Good girls finish last you know."

I raised my hands in protest, wondering if it said more about me or them that they'd assume my writing would involve sexy time. "I was writing a screenplay, not fan fiction."

"Like something you'd actually shop?" Luke's smirk dropped, his face turning serious.

My head bobbed. "Yes, and I don't know if the sleep deprivation has made me delirious or I'm just delusional, but I think it's good."

It could have easily been a huge pile of shit, a bunch of words that made no sense or had no artistry, put on the page just to make a word count. Hell, it certainly wouldn't be the first time.

But last night felt different, like I had a renewed sense of . . . inspiration.

"Awwww, you got your groove back," Scully cooed. "I should have given him a copy of your story months ago."

I barked out a laugh. "You didn't give *Nick* anything. And I could have done without the embarrassment and pending banishment from Hollywood. I still have to work out how I'm going to spin that."

The feel-good mood didn't negate that I still had all that shit to deal with.

The Larssons were like showbiz royalty. The eldest brother Eric was a god, an A-lister who could pick up Academy Award winning roles like he was going down to the corner store for a gallon of milk. Dave and Nick, only a few steps below, but not by much.

The closest I could get to the kind of names and numbers they probably had on speed dial was stalking profiles on IMDb. Just a few whispers in the right ears and I would be a pariah. Dirty, laying in a gutter somewhere on Hollywood Boulevard in tattered clothes and a bad haircut like a poor man's version of Les Misérables. "*I dreamed a dream . . .*"

"Well, there's still the option of Jane from Palm Springs," Scully offered, not being helpful.

Luke shook his head. "She doesn't look like a Jane."

"Well, while you two try and find me a better pseudonym, I'm going to shower. We can have a crisis meeting later."

If I stuck around any longer, they would have tried to argue the need for more details, wanting to pump me for information so they could dissect it. Which was why I left them to ponder while I found sanctuary in the bathroom. And for a few moments, I was able to lose myself in the steam and spray.

I could pretend that the excitement in my belly was because of my work and not from seeing Nick. That the goosebumps on my skin weren't from imagining his touch. And that I wasn't hoping to see him again.

Instead I convinced myself that if I did see him it was only for the greater good of my art, purely for inspiration because that would make sense. Wasn't there a whole movement of Renaissance painters who coveted curvy women? Well, this was no different.

As I toweled myself dry, I replayed the memory of his delicious naked body in my head. Seeing his spectacular ass accidentally was a highlight and one I was keeping privately tucked away.

I should have felt terrible, invading his privacy like that.

But I didn't.

He was stunning.

Like someone had reached inside of my brain, picked all my examples of the perfect man and molded them into a living breathing one. Too bad the banging on the bathroom door rudely interrupted my ponderings on whether Nick was in fact a gift.

"Hey Jane, lover boy Larsson is hitting up your IG," Luke called through the door.

Social media wasn't something I was great at, Instagram, my typical fail. I preferred Twitter where I didn't have to take pictures of everything, leaving quirky antidotes instead of deciding which filter made my plate of fries look more delicious.

My eyes widened, quickly wrapping a towel around myself as I yanked open the door. "I thought everyone agreed I wasn't Jane. And I haven't been on Instagram for months."

Luke shook my phone in his hand. "Well you might want to tell him that."

"What are you even doing going through my phone?" I grabbed it, the screen unlocked and the app open.

He shrugged like it was no big deal. "It buzzed, I was curious."

"Well get uncurious." I held the phone against my chest.

Luke laughed. "Careful, you don't hit the camera and post an InstaStory of your tits."

"Thanks for the tip, ass." I dropped my hand, putting my breasts safely out of danger from accidental flashing.

With the towel wrapped around my body and my phone clutched in my hand, I power walked from the bathroom to the privacy of my bedroom. I closed the door, my damp back pressing against the wood as I heard Luke's laugh trail off.

He had the decency to give me my space, knowing full well I'd probably tell both he and Scully everything later, anyway. But in the meantime I was alone with a virtual Nick Larsson, standing almost naked in my room as I swiped my hand across the phone screen.

I'd assumed he'd eventually find me. If he'd missed my personal introduction when I gave him both my *first* and *last* name, it had conveniently been written on my story Scully had given to Dave. Figured it was only a matter of time before I'd get a call. Maybe an email.

Instead, he sifted through the web, possibly messaging a bunch of random Claires before he'd gotten to me. Knowing my last name wouldn't have helped, preferring to use the nickname my dad had given me when I was three.

ClaireBear.

That he'd gone to so much effort to track me down excited me. That was until I took a closer look at my account and realized my lameness and dumbasary seemed to be more responsible for his discovery than his impressive detective skills.

There I was, smiling widely on the set of *Crash,* the image I had chosen as my profile picture. And not that anyone else would

have known, but in my hand I held the script from the episode
where he'd played the bartender.

I thought I was being cute, posting the photo from the day
we'd met, saving it for prosperity so we could joke about it with
our grandchildren. Seemed like a really good idea at the time, now
not so much. I'd pretty much Hansel and Gretel'd him, leaving a
trail of breadcrumbs right to my door. Who needed to give the
man a phone number when past Claire had illuminated the path
like a landing strip.

The little red circle warned me of three private messages.

Three.

Because one, *hey, I found you,* wouldn't be enough; the man
needed more.

Lord, what the hell did he say?

My finger hovered, opening up the bubble to our private chat.
I hitched up my towel conscious I was mostly naked. "What am I
doing?" I laughed to myself. "It's not like he can freaking see me
through the phone." And to prove the point of how ridiculous I
was being, I let the towel drop and sat on my bed, naked.

> *Nice profile pic. ;-) You forgot to mention that when we first met
> you had been blond. No wonder I couldn't remember you. Honest
> opinion, you look better as a brunette.*

Okay, so maybe shucking the towel wasn't such a good idea.
The words on the screen made my skin tingle like he was looking
at me as he made his assessment. Still, I wasn't going to cover myself with my hands like a prude. And he was only saying my hair
looked better dark. It's not like he said, *hey you're hot, let's make out.*
And still, that he said anything at all made me excited.

The second message was a photo, and it took me about two
seconds to work out it was his front door.

> *Having trouble with my key, know where I can find someone
> who's handy with a lock.*

The third message was another photo, the contents not in any way ambiguous as I stared at a stack of papers that was very obviously a copy of my story.

You should know that I fought to the death for this. Okay, so not to the death—Dave is still breathing—but I did get a hangnail when I stole it out of his backseat. Looks like some interesting reading. Tell your friend thanks.

Great.

Just fucking great.

The ghost of Christmas past had decided to show up and taunt me.

And rather than ignore his messages—which would have been the smart thing to do—I decided to respond, trying not to swoon at how adorable and funny he was. Like the heart eye emoji exploded on my screen.

I was in big trouble.

Heeeeeeey, you found me! Surely you don't have the time to read all of that? Why don't I continue to save you and just tell you what happens?

It was a long shot, hoping he was only kidding about reading it. He must have dozens of scripts that needed his attention. Why would he read an unedited and unsolicited manuscript from someone he didn't even know? I wasn't even sure if he'd worked out I was the author yet, possibly using it as a conversation piece. And in any case, providing him carefully curated CliffNotes were a better option. At least then I could control the narrative.

I think my heart only beat twice before his reply flashed across the screen.

Sounds good, I like this plan. You free tonight? 7 work for you?

Terror and excitement jostled for position. He wasn't supposed to ask me out. *Was* he asking me? Teasing me? Luring me in for a trap when a blanket was tossed over my head like a hostage and I was shoved in a basement?

No.

He was curious and wanted the opportunity to judge while sober.

I bit my lip as I typed back, unable to help myself.

Sorry, plans. I have to travel the city looking for men who are passed out on their doorsteps and save them from themselves.

Fine, I'll be drunk and on my doorstep by 7.

Did the man type three thousand words a minute, how the hell was he able to respond so quickly? Barely a beat passed between when I'd hit send and when his new message popped up.

I tried to stop the stupid grin from spreading across my lips as my fingers hit the letters in response.

That wasn't supposed to be an encouragement.

This time there was a slight pause, and for a minute I thought he'd given up.

It was an invitation. You didn't seem to need one before, but I thought we might try something different this time around. :-P

God help me, if I thought I was grinning like an idiot before, there was no help for me now. I was almost tempted to say yes and lose myself in the fantasy. The one where he'd laugh off I'd been a love-sick fool who not only dreamt about him but put it all out there on a page as well.

I shook my head, reminding myself this was no fantasy.

Seriously I can't. I need to work. I'm reading scripts.

Part of me hated myself, angry I was denying whatever brief encounter we could've had. Sure, it was better this way, but I couldn't help but feel the disappointment. Ironically, disappointment was something I'd been dealing a lot with lately.

Yes, we already established that. You're reading one to ME. Do you want me to do the man parts? I'm good with man parts. ;-)

I laughed out loud, adding cocky to his list of qualities.

Sure, that wasn't a loaded sentence.

You really think "load" was a wise word choice. :-o

This man was going to be the death of me. If not literally, then definitely my career. I was contemplating playing hooky, tossing aside a script I needed to have read ASAP and go see how good he was with his man parts. But getting fired wasn't the only danger, there was still his impressive network I hadn't forgotten about. And yet . . .

If I agree to come tomorrow, will you let me get back to work?

I'm going to be a gentleman and let that one slide. But you should re read your last statement. Tomorrow sounds good, should I be drunk inside the house or outside. Which would make you feel more empowered?

Funny, charming, cocky, freaking adorable—all of which were not helping! Which was why I should stop.

I would stop.

Eventually.

Most men would think that a woman saving them would be emasculating.

I'm not most men.

OH.

MY.

GOD.

If I hadn't been aroused before, I sure as shit was after that statement. That towel I had tossed to the floor because I wasn't going to be a prude was swiftly picked up and wrapped around my body as I felt my skin flush. How could he do that? Turn me on like a light switch, and he wasn't even in front of me. Worse, his words weren't even spoken, they were just letters on a screen, and yet it was like he had leaned forward and whispered them seductively in my ear.

I thought about last night. How he'd touched me. How he'd moved his hands over my body and then pulled me down on top of him. How his lips had pressed against my skin.

And yes, he probably didn't remember any of it . . . but I did.

Be sober this time around.

Will you still put me to bed if I am?

I was going to spontaneously combust.
Burst into flames from a flirty text.
It wasn't even a freaking text; the man was sending me flirty instant messages via my underused Instagram account.
Well, that did make a better story to tell our grandkids.
Oh, for fuck's sake, I needed to stop.

Sure, and then I'll rob you right after. You are way too trusting.

There, humor. Because it was the best redirection I knew and there was no way I was going to answer that question seriously without a resounding hell yes!

If you wanted to rob me, you would have done it last night. See you tomorrow night. You know where I live.

My fingers fumbled a quick *okay, see you,* and then I tossed the phone aside. It was too dangerous to continue, not trusting myself, my mouth or my hands.

As I stood up and walked to my wardrobe, common sense

kicked in. He was a known flirt who had a wicked sense of humor, it wasn't like those messages *meant* what I thought they'd meant. He was playing around, being funny, because that was what he usually did and talking to me was no different or special than doing his laundry. In fact, he was probably doing his laundry while he was talking to me, that was how unaffected he was. Meanwhile, I was the one getting all hot and bothered over a few "cheeky" messages like I had never sexted before.

I was ridiculous.

And with that in mind, I pulled on some clean clothes and resolved to push any thoughts of Nick out of my head for the rest of the day. In fact, I was going to take a nap.

Wouldn't think of him at all.

Not even a little.

Okay, maybe only a bit.

A tiny, little, bit.

Fine.

I would be thinking of him.

CHAPTER #8

"HE KISSED YOU? Why didn't you mention this before? It should have been the first thing to come out of your mouth the minute you walked in the door. I thought we were friends." Scully narrowed her eyes, folding her arms across her chest like she was genuinely offended.

Luke joined in but with less venom and irritation, adding with a laugh, "No, the first thing she should have told us was he touched her ass."

"He didn't kiss me *or* touch my ass," I corrected them, wondering how dinner had turned into my cross-examination. "He was drunk, remember? He fell and pulled me down with him, there was nothing sexual about it." At least not on his part, on mine . . . well, that would just stay my dirty little secret.

Scully shoved a spoonful of mashed potatoes into her mouth, swallowing before continuing. "Still should have mentioned it."

As promised, after a solid few hours sleep, I had told Scully and Luke the whole thing. Not only the touchy feely slow dance before he lost consciousness but also how I ended up staying the night.

"So tomorrow's a date?" Luke asked, pouring me another glass of wine. I'll admit, the first glass had made the storytelling a little easier.

I shrugged, not really sure myself what it was. "He invited me to his house. Maybe he just wants to thank me more adequately."

"With his penis." Scully pointed her fork at me and laughed.

Luke pointed his fork at her belly. "Just wear protection or his penis won't be adequately forgotten nine months later."

"He's right," Scully nodded, "They tell you they'll pull out, but they never do."

"Guys! I'm only going to his house, I am not sleeping with him." I tossed my head back and laughed.

While I had no problem with sex for sex sake—this was a woman's world and we could do whatever or whomever the fuck we wanted—I was not going to sleep with Nick Larsson.

And not because I didn't want to.

If I thought that sordid dance between the sheets would remain without consequences, I'd probably arrive on his doorstep naked.

Okay, maybe not *naked* because I didn't really want to catch a public indecency charge, but strip the minute I walked in.

But I knew better.

While he might have *joked* he wanted me to put him to bed, there had been zero indication he had wanted me to join him. We'd already established he had a reputation for being a flirt, but he wasn't a manwhore. At least he didn't seem to be, so if he *was* screwing his way through L.A. like an 80's hairband, he was keeping that shit on the down low. And last time I checked, sex was still a two-person activity. I wasn't in the habit of begging or accepting sympathy sex—I still had some pride left.

Also, I still had grand notions of being successful in an industry he was currently kicking ass in. Pretty sure it wouldn't go well for me if it were revealed I was writing fan fiction and crushing on him like a teenager in heat. Didn't need the additional insult of people thinking I'd used him to climb the Hollywood ladder as well. I'd be laughed out of every job interview before I'd even get a chance to get in the door.

No, I would not throw away my dreams and wishes for a chance of a one-night stand. Because that would probably be all I would get with him anyway. One night before he found out I wasn't one of those beautiful people who'd seemed to be his friends. No, I was normal—fine, not *totally* normal—with a tendency to be neurotic. I got moody when I was on my period, cried at every sad movie no matter how many times I saw it, and when I wrote I got sucked into a world and needed to be alone. I didn't want to shatter the fantasy, either for him or myself.

"Look, I don't know why I'm going over there. But sex isn't it. If I'm lucky, he won't have read my story, I'll make up some bullshit on what it's about, and then convince him that last night's encounter was a coincidence. That I'm a travelling Mother Teresa, tossing out good deeds and building myself a stairway to heaven."

Luke lifted his wine, took a sip before lowering it to the table and spearing me with a sharp look. "Claire Becker, you are a fucking badass and one of the most talented people I know. If he reads your story and thinks anything other than *that*, then he is a dick. And not a nice dick either. A small, flaccid, ugly dick that no one wants."

"With genital warts." Scully raised her glass—filled with ginger ale instead of wine—adding with a smile.

I laughed, shaking my head as I responded. "Ewww, thanks for that image. Now I'm definitely not going to sleep with him."

And with my second affirmation that I wouldn't be having sex with Nick, Luke clapped his hands, giving me a round of applause.

"Awesome, now that we got that settled, let's finish dinner."

TRYING TO READ when your mind won't focus was almost

impossible, especially when what you are reading is bad.

I was trying not to be ungrateful, counting my blessing that my new job gave me the opportunity to pay my bills for another month. But the screenplay was terrible. Worse than that, it was fucking horrendous.

The storyline was boring.

The characters predictable.

And the writing . . . I'd read more interesting menus.

I wondered if that's what studios had thought when they'd read my earlier submissions, wanting to gouge their eyes out so it could all stop.

Putting down the screenplay, I pulled out my phone and flicked to my notes. I hadn't had a chance to read back what I'd written and wondered if my latest effort was more of the same.

Please God, let it be good I whispered under my breath as my eyes floated over the words. *Or at least don't let it be total shit.*

The air escaped from my lips as I started, following the opening directions and then to the dialogue, my heart racing as I slowly continued.

It *wasn't* shit.

In fact, it was so far from shit I was beginning to question whether I had been the one who had written it. Whether I'd been possessed—hey, crazy shit happened all the time—and controlled somehow.

Deciding that trying to focus on the small screen was giving me a headache, I transferred the notes to a Word document on my laptop. There I continued to read, making notes for myself as I went, each line encouraging me further.

OH.

MY.

GOD.

It was good.

It was *really* good.

I was really good.

Months of self-doubt and internal torment, believing I was destined to become another washed-up never was, bubbled up inside of me and I started to cry. I couldn't help it, sobbing on my bed like a moron as I tried to continue reading through the tears. And I felt the weight that had been sitting on my chest lift.

I took a breath, and then another, letting myself go as I fell backward onto the mattress, a laugh escaping from my lips. Whatever block had been there before was gone, and I was giddy with relief.

And with the pressure easing came a renewed sense of excited purpose as I sat back up on my bed again and started typing. My fingers didn't stop, flowing over the keyboard as the words poured out of me.

I was back, baby.

It was almost midnight before I'd stopped, my laptop propped up on a pillow while I sat on my bed. My preferred writing position wasn't textbook, but it was how I'd written every single piece of Nick fiction. It felt less structured that way, and less like work. Which reminded me . . .

Work.

That thing I needed to do in order to get paid so I could continue to eat.

While it had been exciting to play in my own sandbox like I used to do, I still had a responsibility to finish reading a script that some other person wrote.

Groaning, I packed my laptop away and pulled out the pages. I'd hoped that in the hours the script had been sitting ignored on my bedside table it might have gained some personality, or possibility even a plot. Either would do.

In an effort to further procrastinate—I'd rather jab pins in my eyes than continue—I grabbed my phone and started social media hopping. Flicking between my profiles and scanning my feeds for anything interesting.

One of the girls I'd gone to high school had recently been proposed to. She held her obviously manicured hand in front of her face to strategically show the ring but had tried to make the shot look candid. Because I know the first thing I thought about when I laughed was to daintily drape my fingers across my perfectly winged eye.

And yes, I knew I was being bitchy, but not because I was jealous. I was happy for her if that's what she desired; excited she had found a man she wanted to do the whole death-do-us-part thing with. It was the pretentious selfie I had the problem with. If I ever posed like that, I hoped one of my friends would beat the sense back into me. Hell, I'd probably beat myself.

I was still laughing at the thought when I went back to my private messages. No guesses as to which ones I was looking at. Maybe that was my version of a pretentious selfie, pretending I didn't give a shit as I reread every word and tried to decipher tone based on word choice.

He was definitely flirty.

And charming.

And sexy.

And playful.

Super hot as well.

Okay, so maybe I hadn't gotten that from word choices and more from his profile pic, but I figured it was only fair since he'd inspected mine that I repay the same courtesy.

What the hell?

At some point between me purging my soul like a mad scientist, and analyzing his command of the alphabet, I had missed that *NickLars* had started to follow me. And it would be totally rude not to follow him back. In fact, I was pretty sure proper etiquette *demanded* that I follow him back, and who was I to argue?

Also, since we were "following" each other, it wouldn't hurt to take a little look around his photos. To see if he staged his food shots, or posted exaggerated gym pics—all important stuff I should know.

Unlike my Instagram that had the grand total of ten photos—most of which were years old—his was bursting with material. Literally hundreds of photos—him with friends, him with his brothers, him looking so freaking delicious it made doves cry. And while the account wasn't something I hadn't occasionally checked out before—not like I stalked him, merely a causal peruse—this time around I felt like I had permission. Like our reconnection/friendship had given me the green light to go through his published moments with a magnifying glass. And it should be known that I was going to take full advantage of my newfound freedom.

It didn't take too long before I was countless clicks deep and about "three years" in when my finger accidentally clicked the heart at the bottom of the screen.

Shiiiiiiiiiiit.

Realistically, who didn't see that happening, it was basically the faux pas of every girl who had stalked a guy; a rite of passage I had yet to experience. And there it was, the cute little red heart underneath a photo of him holding an ice cream. Oh, and he was shirtless. In case there were any delusions, the focal point of the photo was the dessert in his hand.

"Shit," I cursed out loud wondering what my options were.

The way I saw it was I had three choices.

One: Unlike it and hope he hadn't been alerted to the original like and thus drawing more attention to it.

Two: Ignore it, bury my head in the sand and assume he must get so many notifications a day my harmless little heart would have gotten lost in the noise.

Three: Go ahead and like every single picture before and after, so my insanity plea will stand up in court.

Gah, all three kind of sucked.

Hungry? ;-)

The message flashed on my screen before I had decided which path I was going to take. Well, I guess that ruled out option number one. He'd obviously seen it.

There was no going back.

Yes actually, looks delicious.

The message loaded with so much innuendo I'd have blushed if I had any decency. But it was late, I was tired, and my judgment was clouded. Or at least that was what I told myself as I waited for his response.

On that, we agree.

What the hell did that mean? Did he misread my sexy Insta talk and assume I was talking about the ice cream? Maybe I hadn't been as obvious as I thought so I decided to try again, if only to see if I was capable.

Like an experiment.

I held my breath, typing out the words.

I wasn't talking about the ice cream.

Neither was I.

Like the phone was on fire, it dropped out of my hand and onto the bed. Whatever game I thought I was playing, he was a thousand times better. And I needed to know exactly what I was dealing with before I went over to his house.

Without fully thinking it through—because why the hell

should I start now—I sent him another message. Only this time around, there had been no words, only numbers—mine. Ironic considering he'd asked for it and I hadn't given it to him initially, but again, arguing logic seemed pretty redundant in the early hours of the morning.

He didn't even bother waiting, upping the ante as my phone lit with an incoming call.

"Hello," I answered casually, despite my heart racing.

"Up late?" I could hear the grin in his voice.

"Working." The one word my reply.

"You know," he took a breath, "I did offer to help you with work. What I said earlier, about my abilities. It wasn't just talk."

I shook my head.

A few hours ago, I'd decided I was going to play it cool. Apparently, playing cool also meant ending up on the phone with him. Oh, and this wasn't going to disintegrate into phone sex. I did have some self-respect left. "You know, since we were both awake and on the phone. I could go through the story now and save us both the time."

"Really?" He sounded surprised. "That's why you gave me your number, so you could cancel?"

My teeth played with my bottom lip as I rephrased it a million times in my head before I said it. "It's probably for the best."

God, I hated this.

I should have just gone with phone sex.

There was a pause, and for a second I thought he'd hung up. Not like he needed to keep having the conversation, especially when it probably wasn't turning out like he'd expected.

"Can you do me a favor, Claire?"

His words were slow, measured and calm.

"Huh?"

I pulled the phone away from my ear, wondering if I'd blacked out and missed part of the conversation. Or maybe this was where he asked me to do him a solid and not store his number.

"I said can you do me a favor?" he repeated and gave no more information than the first time he'd said it.

I shrugged, now curious as to what he was possibly going to ask for. "Sure, of course."

"Delete my number."

I FUCKING KNEW IT.

And still, part of me was disappointed. Ignoring the other part that dictated that it was what I had been expecting and what would make sense.

"I wasn't intending on keeping it," I lied, swallowing the hurt and trying to laugh.

"Good, now hang up, delete it, and I'll see you later tonight."

"Excuse me?"

He was talking in code, spitting out words for me to try to work out, like I was Robert Langdon and knew Di Vinci's secrets.

"If you are thinking of canceling, forget it." His usually flirty banter was gone, and in its place was all business. "And since you won't have my number, you can't. So I guess I'll see you tonight. I'll be sober and you'll tell me about this story. Seven sharp."

He didn't give me a chance to respond, ending the call before I'd even had a chance to say goodbye. And I couldn't work out if it was sexy as hell or if it made me mad.

A little of both.

Which was why I immediately called back.

"I thought I told you to delete it." He laughed, not bothering with the hello.

"I'm not deleting it, so there," I huffed defiantly into the phone. "And I'll see you tonight because I *want* to see you tonight."

"Good."

"Fine."

This time it was me who hung up, tossing the phone onto my comforter and smirking at it.

No one will tell me what to do.

I showed him.

I was *really* bad at this game.

CHAPTER #9

THE HEDGE THAT had tormented me the night before welcomed me like an old friend as I pulled up to the curb. It had just turned seven, and I had been nervous all day long.

There was no way to know how this meeting would go, but I wasn't going to sit holed-up in my bedroom, and not see how it played out. Getting out of my car, I moved to his stairs, climbing them deliberately with slow steady steps. Unlike the other night, there was no need to be stealthy. Not that I had done such a good job of it the first time, but still, I felt my confidence strengthen with each stride, walking right up to the front door ready to press the buzzer like a badass.

I was under no assumption that it was a date. Or that whatever the insanity was, would extend beyond the night. But that didn't mean I wasn't going to make an effort either. I'd borrowed one of Scully's designer outfits, a fitted black T-shirt dress she hadn't been able to squeeze into in months. It wasn't overly fancy, but paired with a pair of strappy heeled sandals it looked stunning. It also worked with my curves to give me a nice silhouette, playing on what nature had given me without making me look trashy.

My finger reached out with authority, pressing the buzzer as I waited for him to answer while my heart beat wildly in my chest.

It didn't take long, the door swinging open and Nick Larsson filling the gap. His eyes lingered over my body, moving down and then up before settling on my face. "Claire." My name sounding sexier every time he said it. "Please come in." He outstretched his arm, motioning to the hall inside his house.

I wasn't the only one who had made an effort.

He was wearing a pair of jeans that had no right to look that good, and a black button-down shirt that had been casually left unbuttoned at the neck and rolled up at the sleeves.

"Thank you." I smiled, grazing past him as he stepped to the side, my heels echoing off the wooden floor. "And so nice to see you on your feet this time. I'm so glad you followed my directions."

He laughed, following behind me to his living room. "Following directions is why they pay me the big bucks. But the other night wasn't the usual me, I was just letting off some steam."

"Really?" His response had me curious as I turned around, almost slamming into his chest. Close call. Not that it would have been bad to bury my face between his pectoral muscles, it actually sounded really nice. But I was intending to keep it professional, and I was pretty sure that crossed the line.

His grin widened as he glanced down at me. "You sound surprised? You expected a different answer?"

"No, I mean. I didn't really question, you know? I saw you and . . ." I stopped.

What was I saying, that I thought he was an alcoholic? No, of course I didn't. We'd all been there, had a little too much fun and needed someone to make sure we didn't puke in our hair. Some of us more times than we'd like to admit. Not sure why I would have expected more from him.

"Well, you didn't vomit on me, that was really considerate," I added, not helping the situation at all.

Awesome, could I be any more offensive?

His eyebrow rose, studying me as neither one of us moved, his expression completely unreadable. "Anything else I *did* or *didn't* do, I should know about?"

Wow.

There was I, stuck between a rock and a hard place.

Both of which had been his erection when he'd pulled me down on him on the couch.

And if that wasn't enough, the reminder of the rock-hard place was right beside me. Its black supple leather surface innocently standing near the coffee table, not at all looking complicit in what had happened last night.

"No." I swallowed, the air feeling thick and harder to breathe. "Everything else was fine."

His lips spread into a grin, tipping his chin toward his couch unaware of my fond feelings of his furniture. "Good, why don't you take a seat."

My butt answered before my mouth did, dropping to the soft leather, only this time without the heavenly weight of him against me. "So, about that story."

I had played out the possibility of throwing my body at him and trying to seduce him into oblivion, but we—me and what was left of my conscience—had already decided to be professional.

It *really* sucked doing the right thing.

He laughed, joining me on the couch. "Right to the point, okay, I like that."

Lord I hoped this was not an indication of how the evening was going to be. I thought it was fair that since I had shelved my plans of seduction, he should have the decency to do the same.

"Yes. We should get to the point." After all that's why I was there, right? Not like I was there under the pretense that he was interested in me, and that we were on some kind of pseudo date.

"You see, I wrote it. And it really wasn't ready for public consumption. So, I'd like it back, please."

That was the abridged version, and the one that made me sound less like a crazy person. And it wasn't a lie, the fact it was never going to be for public consumption didn't need to be mentioned at all. It was irrelevant. The important thing was that I stand up like a woman, admit it was mine and that he didn't have the right to read it. With manners of course, because there was no need to be rude.

Or something along those lines.

He pressed his lips into a tight line, his arm resting against the back of the couch. "If you're worried that I read it, you can relax. I haven't. You said you would tell me about it, so I thought we'd do a read through together."

Oh thank you, God.

It was like every single muscle in my body relaxed and if not for my spine, I might have melted onto the floor like an unattractive skin bag. The ease of tension made me spontaneously smile, fireworks of happiness bursting in my chest as I vowed to the universe I would take the gift it had given me and be the best person alive.

"Great." I tried not to leap into his lap and show my appreciation with a celebratory kiss. "Where is it?"

His smile dropped, his perfect plump lips—seriously, I bet they'd be fantastic to kiss—pulled into a pout. "Here I thought you were interested in me, but you only came for the story?"

He was joking.

He *had* to be joking.

Please, God, let him be joking.

"I-I." He gave nothing away, his eyes locked on me while I tried to think of something to say. "I thought you would be perfect for the lead."

What.

WHAT.

OH.

MY.

GOD.

WHAT?!

Those fireworks of happiness that had exploded in my chest, turned into an atom bomb the minute the words left my mouth. The force of the detonation was enough to stop my heart, at least that's what it felt like as I took a gasp of air and forced myself to stay upright.

Whatever I had "planned" to do when I had walked in, had been left on the man's front stoop. Because if there *had* been some plan, I'd have already been out the door, story tucked under my arm, commenting what a fine night it had been.

Instead I was undone by a pouty mouth and a pair of puppy dog eyes that I was positive were not respecting the rules of engagement.

Was it too late to call "no fair-sies?"

"You *are* here for me," his smile emitting another megaton watt blast, "I'm really glad to hear you say that."

Firstly, what the hell did that mean? And secondly, where did I go from the corner I had tossed myself into?

Okay, don't panic. I forced my lips into something that would pass for a smile. "I'm glad you're glad." I was panicking. "*So* glad."

If there was an opposite of glad, I was that—anti-glad, if you will. And I was about to take it all back, come clean completely and tell him the truth when he turned and looked at me and opened his mouth.

"You want to hear something funny?"

Lord I wasn't sure. "Of course, who doesn't like funny?"

Who answered a question with another freaking question? The whole conversation was a train wreck, and we weren't even an hour in.

"When I woke up the other morning, and saw you in my house, I knew you looked familiar." His finger tapped my nose, teasingly. "First I thought it was because we'd slept together, not *that* night, because like I said, I always know when I have sex." He rolled his eyes like it was the most logical thing ever. "But from before."

Okay, so maybe we could take honesty and put a pin it for a minute. I mean, I could always tell him later. Half an hour, tomorrow—there was plenty of time.

My eyes got wide. "We haven't—"

"Yeah, I know." He laughed, cutting me off. "I realized when I saw your picture from when we worked together." His eyes floated over my body making their way back up to my eyes. "I never forget a face."

God he was hot, looking at me like I was a piece of cake and he was desperate to have a taste.

"Well . . . it wasn't that much of a conversation," I stuttered, ironically not much better than the one I was currently having.

His brow rose, his tongue teasing his bottom lip with a quick flick. "You know, I was going to ask you out."

"What?" It shot out of my mouth almost as an accusation rather than a question. The need for more information making me want to break out into hives. "Ask me out when?"

When I was in his living room, camped out on the couch like a bum? Or when I had a bad dye job and dreams filled with delusion? Not that it mattered, I would have said yes either time. Hell, I'd say yes now if the offer was on the table.

Unless that was his way of putting it back on the table?

His hand moved to my hair, grabbing a loose strand and curling it around his fingers. "You really do look better as a brunette, which is insane considering how hot you were as a blond."

There was no noise, like a vacuum had sucked it out all the air and left a weird ringing in my ears. He wasn't serious; he *couldn't* be serious.

It was a joke, a laugh at my expense because he undoubtedly had read my story and thought it would be freaking hilarious to play with my emotions.

"Oh, you're an asshole." I shoved his hands from my hair, standing up and putting the distance between us that I should have kept all along.

Gone was the illusion of the sweet, charming, hot man with the body that defied reason and in his place was a cocky, arrogant piece of shit, who thought it would be funny to make fun of me.

Yeah? Well not today, sir.

He had the nerve to look surprised. "What? Why am I an asshole?"

"Why? Why?" I waved my hands animatedly in front of his face. "You really think I'm that dumb? That I would fall for your routine? Lure me in by being charming and sweet," *I had been so dumb*, "only to what? Hope that I dropped to my knees and gave you a blow job as thanks."

I was so mad, mostly at myself because I had been so caught up in the fantasy of him that I had forgotten I really didn't know him. And there were a million men like him in L.A., swiping left and right indiscriminatingly, treating women like menus and checking out before settling the bill.

"Whoa, I wasn't asking you for a blowjob." He held his hand up in surrender. "Is this because I mentioned your hair color?"

"It's not about my hair color, you ass." I pushed against his chest. It was a nice chest too, and I might have enjoyed it if I weren't so mad. "It's about you thinking I'm an easy lay because I—"

"Wait a fucking minute." He grabbed my hands, holding them hostage so I couldn't beat on his chest. Shame. It was making me feel better, to be honest.

"Do I want to sleep with you? Of course I do, I just told you how hot I think you are. But that isn't a fucking expectation, and I sure as hell didn't think it was going to happen tonight."

"What did you say?"

I stopped fighting against him. It was probably for the best because I had a hard enough time trying to move his weight when he was incapacitated, now he had all his faculties, I stood no chance.

His head lowered, leaning closer as he looked directly at me. "I don't expect you to sleep with me."

"No, the part about me being hot."

He laughed, the light hitting his eyes as he lowered my hands. "Why, so you can tell me I'm an asshole again?" He dropped his gaze following the lines of my body. "You're fucking stunning. Like I said, I remember you. You were smart and funny, and I'd hoped we'd have more time to hang out. But one of us definitely got hotter."

That was my line.

He wasn't allowed to steal my freaking line.

And also, holy shit.

"You *meant* that?"

"Claire, I thought when we agreed I was going to be sober, you would be too. Why would I say it if I didn't mean it?" He dropped his head, bringing it inches away from mine.

"I'm so confused."

With the anger dissipated, my hands decided it was time to get reacquainted with his chest. Man, it was a nice chest, so strong and tight.

So. Freaking. Nice.

"Can we assume that you fondling my chest is a good thing?" He glanced down at my hand. "Or do we need to explore more of this confusion thing?"

"You are really, *really* good looking."

"Thank you." A grin spread across his lips. "Which incidentally is the normal response when someone you're attracted to says that."

"Oh shut up with your *normal*." I pulled him down toward me, his lips fusing to mine.

He didn't argue, his hands threading through my hair and bringing me closer as he deepened the kiss. His mouth took more as I gave it to him.

"In case there's any confusion," his lips moved to my neck, his tongue trailing up to my jaw, "I'm *still* not asking for a blowjob."

My hands moved to his ass, grabbing it as I rubbed against him. "I thought I told you to shut up already."

He laughed, pushing me up against the wall so that I got the most out of my effort. "I don't remember you being so bossy. It's kind of hot."

And lord help me, I know we had established he wasn't asking for a blowjob but he was closer to getting one every single time he said something like that.

I knew I was going against everything I talked myself into. That I wasn't interested in Nick in anything other than to feed my creativity. That I didn't want to risk my career for a fling with a guy who could be with any woman he wanted. But I didn't care. All those problems would be there tomorrow and I would deal with them tomorrow.

Or the next day.

Or next week.

Basically any other time when he wasn't kissing me like my mouth was responsible for keeping him alive.

It was intoxicating, fantasy and reality intersecting in a craziness I couldn't have scripted even if I'd tried. And believe me, I'd scripted plenty.

He was into me.

Not a character I created, not a different, more improved

version of myself.

Me.

And if the world ended and this was the first and last chance I had to make out with him, I was going to take it.

Being sensible was for losers, and it had never done me much good, anyway.

Except . . .

"Wait." I pulled my mouth away from his while I still could. "I need to tell you something."

Nick's mouth wasn't as obedient, skimming the edges of my lips and teasing them to come back. "You can tell me later, I'm in the middle of something right now."

"No, no, I need to tell you now."

Oh, I wasn't going to tell him *everything*, don't get too excited. I still wasn't sure if my "usage" of him in the literary sense would be endearing, or creepy. It was a risk and would possibly put a stop to all the kissing forever. But I felt like I had to at least meet him half way.

"Tell me." A trail of feather kisses moved down my neck. And given how hard that was making it for me to keep talking, I wasn't sure he genuinely wanted to know.

"Okay, so the other night when I came here and found you. I wasn't really visiting a friend." I took a step back, there was no way I could multi task. It was either going to be kissing or talking. And I'd already committed to talking.

He laughed, shaking his head like he was amused. "I know, you were trolling the streets looking for men to save. You told me."

Ugh.

Things had been going so well too. He had admitted to liking me. And then kissed me. But I had to go and sabotage the whole thing. I swear, if I got a chance to kiss him again, I was going to keep my mouth shut. As far as talking went I meant, the other stuff with my mouth I would happily do.

"No, I mean I was looking for you."

"Specifically?" His smile hadn't disappeared, probably had gotten bigger if I was honest. "So it's not *random* men like you alluded to, huh? Well that just makes me feel even more special. How did you know I was drunk?"

Oh lord.

I bit my lip, bracing myself. "I didn't, I mean, I didn't until I was here."

Claire, this was why you couldn't have nice things.

"Is there a why you were on my doorstep? Or am I supposed to guess?" He tilted his head, waiting for my response. No anger, no suspicion, and no freaking idea how crazy I was.

"Ugh, it's so freaking lame." I took a deep breath, deciding I needed to just say it and move on. "I was trying to get my story back. Scully thought she'd given it to you, but had really given it to Dave."

"The chick from the X files?" His brow lifted, confused.

I chuckled nervously; I was really sucking at setting the record straight. "No, my pregnant friend."

"Ahhhh." The grin was back, a smug look of satisfaction joining it. "The mysterious pregnant friend that I was supposed to have met. Okay, so you were coming to ask for it back. And instead you ended helping me to bed."

I nodded, answering quickly. "Yes."

I figured that was enough honesty for one day, right? The main parts were there, there was no need to get caught up on pesky details like my intentions of breaking and entering. Especially since that had never happened. It was a hypothetical so technically did not need to be mentioned.

Yep, no need to tell him anything else about that.

He chuckled, "I'm not mad, Claire. If anything, I should be

thanking Mulder."

"Scully, and really please don't, you'll only encourage her. Also," my eyes cut to the couch, "we sort of touched."

"Again, going to need a little more information."

Seriously.

Why was I doing this to myself?

I hoped that my pain and suffering paid off in the future somehow. Because if I was making myself look like an ass for no good reason, I was going to be pissed.

I blew out a breath. "At first you used me to steady yourself and then I wasn't sure, and then you lost your balance and I fell on you. I didn't mean to be on you, but I was because I thought that was where you wanted me. And you were . . . hard. And we sort of touched. But I got off as soon as I realized."

Lord, for someone who wrote for a living, I'd jacked up that sentence in more ways than I could count. And not in an endearing way. I was like a seven-year-old with a recorder, playing music for the first time—cute in theory but mostly a nightmare.

His shoulders straightened, his chest rising then falling slowly as he stood completely still. "Come closer, Claire."

The lighthearted mood from before had evaporated, and if he was mad, he probably had every right to be. I mean, even though it was a complete accident, if the situation was reversed, I might be mad too.

I took a step forward. "I want you to know that consent is important, and I would never do anything—"

"Touch me." His eyes dropped to the front of his jeans. "You have my consent."

My hand reached out, sliding down his chest, moving to the waistband of his jeans and only hesitating a second before pressing against the bulge in his pants. If I thought he was hard the other night, it was nothing compared to how he felt right now.

My fingers moved against his fly, palming his length as lust heated in his eyes. I wanted to say something, to show my appreciation in case he couldn't see how much I was enjoying it. "This is really . . ." My body tingled all over. "Nice."

He reached down covering my hand with his, making it impossible for me to keep going. "Don't call my cock nice, Claire," he warned. "Or I'll stop you from touching it."

I smiled, bringing my mouth to his ear. "Your cock is *not* nice."

"You saying that is the hottest fucking thing ever." He took my mouth and claimed it, kissing me as he used his body for leverage.

One minute I was leaning against him, palming him while he watched, and the next thing I was pinned against the wall, with *him* rubbing against *me*. A hell of a maneuver and one executed like a boss.

It felt like a dream, probably because I'd had a similar one a million times, but it was no dream.

My body heated, undulating under his, as it craved more friction. I was on fire but I didn't want to be extinguished, preferring to burn and take him along with me.

"Yes." The moan escaped my lips as my fingers threaded through his hair, his mouth doing things to my skin I had never felt before.

It wasn't just his mouth that was making me feel things, his hand sliding up against my legs, pushing the hem of my dress up so he could settle between my thighs. My leg hooked up on his hip, palming his ass as the ridge of his cock hit me right where it needed to be. The slow and steady rock of his hips threatened to send me spiraling out of control.

It was too good, my synapses misfiring as my body became overwhelmed. We hadn't even taken our clothes off and I was about to come.

"Oh God, this is so fucking hot," I whispered, not sure if I was talking to him or myself, lost in the sensation.

He stopped, his talented mouth freezing mid kiss as he pulled away and grinned. "This was supposed to be a date, and as tempting as it is, I'm not going to screw you up against this wall. We should probably stop."

"Yes, probably," I panted, not sure I wanted to but knowing I should.

He nodded, his hands settling on my hips as he blew out a breath. "Okay, let's go back to the couch. I'll order us some dinner."

"Sounds good." My feet didn't move, wanting him to touch me a little bit longer as our eyes locked.

Reading my thoughts, he dipped his head back down, his smile widening. "Or we can keep making out for a little while longer?"

"Yeah, let's go with that."

Dinner could wait.

CHAPTER #10

I DIDN'T SLEEP with him.

We made out *a lot*, but that's as far as it went.

Hands stayed on top of clothes, lots of touching, and by the end of the night I felt like I was going insane, but there had been no sex.

I wasn't even disappointed by it, loving the sensation of my body humming from the way he held and kissed me.

The kiss he gave me at the door when he said goodbye was one of the best goodnight kisses ever.

E-ver.

I was still smiling from it when I woke up the next morning, floating through my kitchen like I'd recently won the lottery.

"Someone got laid." Luke straightened his jacket, putting his coffee cup in the sink. "He measure up to the fantasy? And when I say *measure*, I'm not talking in abstract."

My hand smacked him playfully across his chest. "Oh, stop it. We didn't have sex. We just kissed."

Luke looked horrified, shaking his head as he reared back. "You kissed Nick Larsson and didn't close the deal? What was wrong with him?"

"Nothing. He was perfect," I said so dreamily I'd become a caricature of myself. "But I don't want to rush it. Can you believe he remembered me from before our show got cancelled and was going to ask me out?"

I had had trouble letting it sink in, that when he'd met me, he hadn't thought I was an awkward dork.

"Of course he wanted to ask you out. You're stunning, and you have the brains to back it up. Why do you think I keep you around? You make me look better." Luke smirked, shooting me a wink before checking his watch. "And on that note, I have a morning meeting with a buyer." He gave me a quick kiss on the cheek and was out the door, ready to slay in a gray three-piece suit that was worth more than my car.

The next interrogation wouldn't be so easy.

"So tell me everything." Scully yanked on my arm after I hadn't noticed her ninja-like entrance. "And lead with the part where you've decided to call your first-born after me because we both know I was instrumental to your relationship."

I laughed, shaking off her grip as I turned to face her. "We're not in a relationship. We're barely even dating. And you haven't even named your child yet, so don't be naming mine." I playfully poked her in the belly.

"Psshh, stop trying to change the subject. Tell me things." She planted her hands on her hips.

I rolled my eyes, wrapping my arm around her shoulders as I guided her toward my bedroom. "Fine, but let me get dressed. I need to go meet with a producer today and turn in notes on a script I didn't finish. I'll probably be unemployed again before the day is out." And for the first time, I wasn't terrified about the prospect.

Scully sat on the edge of my bed, her hands clasped dramatically against her chest as I spilled details about our "date." While the initial intention of what it was had been ambiguous, the end was clear—nothing about last night being platonic.

Not that it meant he was suddenly my boyfriend, who knew if after a few more dates he didn't give me the thanks-but-no-thanks I'd been expecting from the start. Only time would tell.

"Awww Claire, I'm so happy for you." Scully pulled me into a hug, mentally probably choosing our wedding china.

"Let's not get too excited, I mean, nothing has really happened yet."

When it came to best friends, I was lucky in that I had two. Two equally wonderful, warm, loyal people who loved me unconditionally. And sometimes it made me feel greedy. But *one* of them had a tendency to jump the gun.

No prizes for guessing which.

"Ummmm, pretty sure making out with him all night counts as something. You have permission to get excited." Scully couldn't be reasoned with, and I didn't have time to argue.

I gave her a warm smile, gathering my things as I leaned against my doorjamb. "Thanks, now do you want a ride onto set or are we going to continue to talk about my evening?"

"We can talk in the car, I'm not done pumping you for details."

Scully usually drove herself, but I thought it might be nice to have company. It also meant I could continue the upbeat feeling until the last minute, dropping her off at her job before I went and lost mine.

Okay, so maybe I was being dramatic, occupational hazard when you worked in Hollywood.

Thankfully the drive wasn't all about me and Nick. Scully decided it would be a good time to inform me that she'd signed us up for birthing classes. In the absence of the douche canoe, I was going to be her birthing partner and took my role very seriously.

"You sure you want to take these classes, I haven't heard great things." I turned into Sun Studios, pulling into the employee parking lot.

Scully reached into the back seat and grabbed her bag. "Isn't that what I'm supposed to do? Have some woman who doesn't shave her armpits and smells of patchouli guide me through breathing exercises so I can squeeze a watermelon out of a hole the size of a lemon."

"You should write their advertising material." I winced, knowing the chance of us being thrown out before finishing the series of classes was going to be high.

She shrugged popping open the door as she thanked me for the ride. "I know there are going to be some natal-Nazis there, telling me that if I don't breastfeed this goober until he's going to college I'm going to burn in Mommy Hell." Scratch that, we were getting tossed out before the end of the first class. "But I want to try and do this right, Claire. I want to be a good parent. And if that means I need to sit through some woman named Moonbeam telling me I can get through the apocalypse of my vagina by listening to *Chopin*, then that's what I'll do. But make no mistake, if I need drugs, I'm asking for them."

I shook my head. "I want to know where the friend who once almost burnt the house down making grilled cheese went, and what you've done with her."

"She's still here, she just learned how to make grilled cheese without calling 9-1-1." She gave me a tight smile. "But I swear if you make me cry before I go into work, I'm going to kick your ass."

"Go," I groaned, looking at the time display on my dashboard. "I guess I need to go be a grown up too."

With Scully safely delivered to work, I headed to the producer's office, pulling into the parking lot shortly before nine. There was no point worrying about the outcome, which was why I affixed a smile to my face, grabbed the script and my notes and made my way to the reception.

"Ms. Becker, you can go ahead and take a seat, we'll be with you shortly." The receptionist directed me to a bank of couches where I was sure many a freak-out had transpired. Freak-outs usually happened when you had to sit around and wait because what else was there to do but think. And thinking wasn't always a good thing.

Like now, when I was "thinking."

The morning had been busy so there'd been no time for sending messages to Nick. I also didn't want him to think I was a needy parasite who wasn't able to function without constant messages, so I refrained from the good morning text I'd actually wanted to send.

It was too soon.

Conversely, Nick didn't message either, which made sense since it was less than twenty-four hours since he was sucking my neck. I mean, what could he possibly have to say in such a short amount of time? And unlike me, he'd recently come off a grueling filming schedule from the last six months, so was probably enjoying his summer break.

See what I mean about thinking.

Not always good.

Determined to spend the rest of my time constructively, I picked up a DIY magazine from the side table and flicked through the pages trying to teach myself how to refinish drywall. It might turn out to be a useful skill and my parents had always warned me that I should have something to fall back on.

"Ms. Becker, he's ready for you now," the receptionist announced right when I was learning about the correct consistency for the mud. Guess my future as a home renovator would have to wait a little while longer, the magazine tossed back on the side table.

Rising from my seat, I grabbed my things and followed her down the hall, the door opened as she paused just outside. My journey into the lion's den would have to be solo it seemed.

"Thanks." I nodded, stepping inside and closed the door behind me.

Carl Marconi was sitting at his desk like always, ignoring me as he scribbled on a yellow legal pad. "Take a seat." He didn't look up, his task clearly more important than the script reader in his office.

I folded myself into the worn fabric chair opposite him, waiting for him to finish his incessant note-taking before opening my mouth.

And I waited.

Marconi looked up, dropped his pen suddenly and then barked, "Talk."

"Mr. Marconi, I've prepared some notes we can go through. I did have some problems getting through the material," I started, wondering at what point I should mention I didn't actually finish.

He leaned back in his chair, his brow furrowed. "You didn't like it?"

"Well . . ." I tilted my head to the side. "The pacing was slow and the level of engagement was low. It would need some work, possibly with some new plot points and some additional character development."

"So what you're trying to tell me is it's boring and you'd give it a pass?" He didn't bother for an elaboration, drumming his fingers on top of the desk.

"I'm sorry?" I asked, wondering if he even cared that I never got to the end.

He shook his head in frustration. "I haven't got time for a book report, Ms. Becker. Just give me the bottom line, that's why we get other people to read these things before I do."

"In that case, that's a no from me."

I needed a buzzer, something to push so a big X lit up like a judge on a reality show. The power surge was incredible as he took back the script, tossed it onto a pile, and handed me another one. "Good, the script was garbage."

"I'm sorry?" I asked for the second time in only a few minutes.

He looked up, barely a smile across his mouth. "It was a bullshit script, a test to see if you would lie to me because you think that's what I want to hear. Ten people have read that exact script, nine of them told me that it was blockbuster gold. You're number ten. Congratulations. I'll expect another report on the new one soon." He went back to his scribbling, effectively closing our meeting and dismissing me at the same time.

It was a miracle.

Not only had I *not* been fired, but I had a new assignment. It was the best week ever, and it had only started.

The grin was almost bursting off my face as I strode out of his office, the new script clutched to my chest as I walked out the main building. I tossed my things onto the passenger seat of my car, gently placing my new assignment on top and actually fist pumping like an idiotic before starting the ignition.

Instead of being thankful for my good fortune, going home and getting started on my next read or working on my screenplay, I decided to message Luke and see if he could meet up with me for a mid-morning margarita. Scully was out for obvious reasons, and drinking alone, especially before noon, was never a good look.

My good luck continued, Luke agreeing to meet me in an hour at a bar called Heart and Vine. That gave me plenty of time to get there, my hand tapping on the steering wheel as I sang along with my stereo. Even the traffic didn't bother me, expecting at any moment motorists to leap out of their cars and sing between the gridlock like a musical.

It didn't happen.

Disappointing.

What wasn't disappointing was finding a parking spot right out front and being seated like a rock star the minute I walked in. I swear I needed to buy a lottery ticket or something, because stuff like that almost never happened to me.

"Hey, gorgeous." Luke gave me a hug, kissing me on the cheek before sitting down.

"Did you know Scully signed up for birthing classes?" I asked, placing our order for margaritas and lunch—see, not totally irresponsible—with our waitress.

Luke's eyebrow rose. "Really? Well better you than me." He grimaced. "I'll be the support crew outside of the room, a safe distance away from ejecting humans and vaginas."

"You are so full of shit." I shoved his shoulder. "You would be the first person in there if she needed you."

"Okay, fine, but I'd stay *away* from the business end." He smirked, adjusting his tie.

The waitress returned with our drinks, allowing me the opportunity to tell Luke about my continued status in the workforce while we drank. He cheered and then told me about a guy he was thinking of asking out, ordering us another round as our lunch arrived.

"Sooooooo." I twirled the margarita glass between my fingers. "How long should I wait to call him so I don't look desperate?"

Luke took a sip from his glass. "Why don't you take a picture of us and upload it your Instagram account, see if he calls you?"

I laughed, tossing a napkin at him. "Yeah, because playing mind games this early on is a *good* plan."

"You're right." Luke grinned. "One look at me and he'd know he would never be able to compete."

Besides, the aim wasn't to try to make him jealous. I only wanted to be able to call him when I wanted to and not feel like a loser. "Why do there have to be so many rules," I groaned.

"Since when do you follow the rules? You want to call him, call him." Luke rolled his eyes. "Invite him to lunch."

"What, no," I gaped, horrified.

If I'd thought sending a text message might seem needy, calling him and inviting him to lunch would be advertising myself as a five-stage clinger.

Not cool.

"Then finish your lunch and ignore him like you have been for the last five years," Luke deadpanned.

He had a point there.

Cursing myself, and not entirely convinced I was doing the right thing, I picked up my phone and scrolled to his number. If shit went bad, I'd just blame Luke or the margaritas.

"Hello," he yawned, his sleep-laden voice making him sound sexy.

I checked the time, making sure that lunch was happening at lunchtime and my cocktail drinking wasn't inappropriately early. Nope, it was twelve thirty, late enough to feel completely fine with our alcoholic additions.

"Hey, sorry. I didn't mean to wake you, I can call back," I offered, thinking I should have just obsessed about it longer like a normal person and not have actually called. That was the last time I was listening to Luke.

"Claire." My name vibrated off his lips. "What a nice surprise."

He could've totally been lying.

About the surprise being nice.

But that reality wasn't compatible with my good mood, which was why I chose to ignore it.

"Late night?" As ironic as it sounded, the question was in fact *not* rhetorical.

I left sometime after midnight but definitely before one. And while that wasn't super *late* by most people's standards, it didn't give him a lot of time to go ahead and make other plans that would facilitate the extra "late."

Unless he called someone else.

Another woman.

Who kept him UP.

I should have been a detective.

"Yeah something like that." He yawned again, giving me less than fucking zero to work with.

I could have just asked him to clarify, consequently sounding jealous, possessive and freaking crazy considering we'd been on one date. But as much as I liked to get my crazy out of the box—her legs having gotten a work out more than I'd like in recent times—I decided to act like a normal, rational adult.

"Well, if you aren't too busy, maybe you could join us for lunch."

Whatever reason I had for not inviting him previously was no longer valid, Luke raising an eyebrow as soon as the words came out of my mouth.

There was a rustling of sheets, his throat cleared as he responded. "I have a meeting later, so I don't have a lot of time. You out with Scully?"

He'd assumed that when I said "lunch with us" that I meant me and the only other friend I had mentioned. Made sense, he didn't have any other evidence to go on.

"Actually, no Scully had to work. I'm here with my other roommate, Luke."

Oh yeah, I went there. Not that I was intentionally trying to make him jealous, but I was in fact there with a man, and if I could use it to my advantage, when why the hell not.

Luke shook his head with a grin. "Nice, well played," he whispered as he took a drink from his glass.

"Luke, huh? Don't seem to remember you mentioning him."

"Well to be fair, we didn't mention much of anything last night."

Luke chuckled enjoying the show no doubt while I floundered around in Awkwardlandia.

Nick paused, rustling more sheets before he suggested, "Why don't you enjoy the rest of your lunch with Luke and then meet me tonight?"

"Sure, dinner sounds great." I glanced over at Luke like a deer in headlights.

I *wasn't* sure dinner sounded great because I didn't really know what I was doing. But, I wanted to see him—the curiosity of his late night tapping its foot in my periphery—so, good idea or not, we were going to be attempting our second date.

"Invite him over," Luke whispered, giving me a pointed look. "Scully and I want to be able to stare at him too."

"Actually, how would you like to come over to my place tonight?" My voice rose, sounding more on edge than I would have liked. "Seems only fair since I know where you live."

Also, if we had an audience there was less chance of dry humping on the couch and actually having a conversation. Like the one where he told me why he'd been up late.

"We can do that," Nick answered. "Let me know what time to be there and your address."

"Great. Okay. I'll send you the details. Talk soon," I rapidly fired, the conversation feeling like a piece of hot coal I was struggling to hold.

"Bye, Claire. See you tonight." Nick laughed and ended the call.

Luke shook his head, using the edge of the napkin to dab his mouth. "Claire, I don't know what the hell you think you were doing, but that was a hot mess. I've seen you with men before, I *know* you can do better."

"Ugh, I know." My head fell into my hands. "I was fine and then turned into a disaster, what is it about him that makes the wheels fall off my wagon?"

Luke shot me a glance. "Are we going down the list or is this more you thinking out loud?"

"Oh stop," I waved him off, "I've got to get home and find my game."

"Yeah, I should get back to work too. I've got a few vendors I need to check in with and a production meeting this afternoon." Luke checked his watch before pulling out a money clip. "Lunch is on me, but I have to run."

Leaving half the food on his plate unconsumed, he finished his margarita and left cash on the table.

"Great, now I look like a hooker." I mock sighed, wiping away the fake tears from my eyes as I clasped my hands dramatically to my chest. "Because I didn't have enough self-esteem issues today."

Luke could barely contain his grin, walking around to my side of the table and leaned down to give me a hug. "We both know that if you *were* a hooker, Claire, there's no way I'd be able to afford you. Enjoy the rest of your day and check in with me later if you need a kick in the ass."

My arms wrapped around him, giving him a quick hug back. "Yeah, yeah. Go back to work," I groaned, waving to him as he left the bar.

I looked back down at my plate, picking up my fork and continued to eat. After I finished I would head home, go through the new script, text Nick, decide on what I was going to cook for dinner, and then think more about what possibly could have kept Nick up all night.

It seemed to me that I had quite the schedule for the day.

CHAPTER #11

AUDREY RYDELL WAS a writer's assistant on *The Blue Line*, the show Nick was currently starring in. A hungry thirty-two-year-old, she was not only gorgeous—I looked her up online—but incredibly smart. And judging by what I found on the web, she was earmarked to co-write some episodes next season. The showrunners even bragged about how talented she was, giving her high praise I'd have killed for.

Not sure if it made it worse or better knowing that praise was earned, the talent they spoke of, staring me in the face. What I had failed to realize when leaving Marconi's office was that my next read was going to be an original work from *Mrs. Audrey Rydell.*

And yes, she was married, which only made the situation slightly better. Her French model husband was hot by anyone's standard, and she seemed like she had it all. Which meant my earlier suspicion about her wanting Nick was clearly wrong, or at least I hoped it was. She couldn't be talented, beautiful, with an amazing husband and get Nick. That shit would surely not be fair.

Fending off further jealousy of everything she had that I didn't, I turned my attention to her screenplay.

I couldn't have hated her even if I'd wanted.

It was cleverly written, brilliantly paced and had a great hook. I'd literally been unable to put it down. And even if I delved into the bitchiest, meanest, most vindictive part of my heart, there was no way I could find fault.

Thank God, hers hadn't been the first screenplay I'd read.

Weird that I'd had preferred to suffer through the last one, taking comfort that as bad as I was, I wasn't *that* bad. It had given me time to find my rhythm, and for me to find the love in what I did. It had been missing and I wasn't sure I'd ever get it back. And now that my mojo was back, and I was confronted with her brilliance, I didn't automatically want to go drown myself in a tub of double choc-chip and apply for a McDonald's drive thru job.

But now, well it just made me want my own success more.

I was as capable, as talented, and as hungry as Audrey or anyone else. There was no reason why I couldn't have what she had.

No, fuck that.

I didn't want what *she* had; *my* destiny was epic-level awesome and there for the taking. I just had to reach out and grab it.

The rest of the afternoon was great. I managed to clean the house and shop for groceries and still made it back before Luke and Scully got home from work. The concern that clouded my mind of Nick's late night hadn't been resolved, but I was excited to introduce him to my friends.

That, and I got to see him again. Because even though I was feeling happier and more confident, I was still sort of lame.

I just no longer cared.

"If he asks about the manuscript, what am I supposed to say?" Scully was pacing nervously in my room, not ecstatic that she hadn't been given enough time to get our stories straight.

The story—the one that had started the whole mess—had been shoved to the backburner. I assumed it was still in Nick's possession, but I was of the firm belief that if I didn't bring it up, he'd probably forget about it. Besides, who had time to remember something as insignificant as a stupid story when you had a budding new relationship to take your attention?

Besides, his show had *just* gone on hiatus; his focus would be on having a regular schedule and not having a five a.m. call time.

He hadn't mentioned it, so I hadn't either, and if we waited sufficiently long enough, it would be unimportant.

That was the plan, and for now, it seemed like a good one.

"He won't ask, and if he does, change the subject or fake a contraction or something." I pulled my hair into a ponytail as I finished getting ready. "Ooooooh, I know, pretend you have baby brain and you have no idea what he's talking about."

"Sure, why don't I just wander aimlessly around the living room and stare at him blankly like English isn't my first language," she deadpanned.

I threw my head back and laughed. "Okay, point taken. No need for the theatrics. And judging by the amount of time Luke has spent in the bathroom, I don't think it's you I'm going to have to worry about."

On cue, Luke waltzed in, his hair still wet from a shower, wearing a pair of dress pants and a business shirt without a tie. "He's straight," I reminded him, narrowing my eyes.

"I know he's straight, I'm not trying to *turn* him." He shot me a grin. "But he also has hot single male friends, not all of them hetero. I'm all about using the opportunity."

"Didn't you just mention some guy you wanted to ask out at lunchtime?" I reminded him, the conversation still fresh in my mind.

He leaned across using my mirror to fluff his hair. "Yeah, that's not happening. He's moving to Vegas at the end of the month, and I hate that goddamn place."

As important as Luke's future dating life was, we didn't have any more time to discuss it, the knock at the door getting our attention while we were all still gathered in my room like a PTA meeting.

"Best behavior," I hissed at them as I shoved past and ran to the front door. That second Red Bull had not been a wise choice, my heartbeat racing as I went to welcome him.

I pulled open the door, casually leaning against the jamb. "Hi."

Nick's lips edged into a grin as he moved closer. "We going to go inside, or do you want me to kiss you out here? Doesn't bother me either way, but you know I have a thing for you and doorsteps."

Lord.

It was like he had special powers, the ability to make women swoon into a puddle within seconds.

My arms linked around his neck and tugged his body toward me as my lips met with his. "I volunteer as tribute."

Kissing Nick was new and yet it felt soooooo right I had to remind myself that I actually hadn't done it that often.

I'd scripted it on a page a hundred times at least, mentally choreographed every hand movement and touch, imagining exactly how it would feel, smell and taste with the man himself. But no matter how good of a writer I believed myself to be, those carefully thought-out moments weren't a fraction of how amazing the real thing was.

"Excuse me." Scully cleared her throat nosily, gently nudging past, forcing us apart. "Sorry, baby brain. Makes me forget my manners." She turned around to face Nick, her grin wide. "Hi, you must be Nick."

"And you must be Scully." He slung his arm around me while he held out the other. "I've heard a lot about you."

"Really?" She looked at me sounding genuinely surprised. "If I was dating him, I wouldn't be talking about other women."

I rolled my eyes, spinning her around and gently pushing her inside. "We should get you off your feet, you look so tired."

I was going to kill her.

The first time Nick Larsson was inside my house, and he was going to be an accessory to a crime. Anyone else see a pattern? Should probably get a lawyer on retainer.

"Nice place." Nick laughed as he followed us inside, ignoring Scully and her comment about other women.

In my living room was another disaster waiting to happen, Luke standing near the couch looking like a GQ model and giving us both a grin. "Hi, I'm Luke."

"Nick."

They exchanged handshakes like two businessmen from rivaling firms—smiling, polite, but sizing each other up like they were wondering who had the bigger cash roll in their pants. Although I suspected their reasons were very different.

Luke retracted his hand, tipping his head in approval. "Good to meet you, can I get you a beer?"

"Yeah, that would be great, thanks." Nick's hand moved to my hip.

Had to admit, I sort of liked this game.

Luke might have prayed at the altar of cock, but flaming drag queen, he was not. He didn't throw around "darling" or snap his fingers like they were punctuation marks when he spoke. And if he didn't tell you that touching boobs made him nauseous, you'd never know. He dressed well, groomed well, loved sports, and knew his way around a socket wrench. But he solidly and undeniably loved the D.

Nick also dressed well, groomed well and loved sports. As for the socket wrench, I had no idea, nor did I care. And if the way he touched my boobs last night was any indication, he really, really liked them. And while I hadn't taken a survey, I was ninety-nine point nine-nine-nine percent sure he preferred what was between my legs than his own.

See, same, same, but different.

But from the look Nick was giving Luke, I was positive he didn't know that they played for different teams.

It wasn't like I could declare, "he's gay" without being both offensive and insulting. My sexual status wasn't announced when I entered the room, so neither should his. Which was why I kept my mouth shut.

Luke excused himself to go get drinks while Scully, Nick and I got situated. We took the couch while Scully took an armchair opposite us. At some point I was going to have to go into the kitchen and attempt to cook something without starting a fire, but I wasn't ready to leave Nick unattended yet. There was a danger of fire in the living room as well—Scully, the only flame required.

"My brother Dave tells me you were at my wrap party." Nick dove right in, taking the conversation exactly where I hoped it wouldn't go.

Scully beamed, nodding like one of those bobble heads you mounted on the dashboard. "Yeah, we were bored at ours. Yours was way more interesting. Next time we'll gate crash from the start, just don't tip off security."

"Your secret is safe with me." Nick winked, his hand moving to my thigh.

The move caught me by surprise, but I didn't flinch. While I hadn't been sure if PDAs were kosher or if we were playing it low key, we weren't exactly hiding our involvement. The *extent* of the involvement—well that was the five million dollar question.

Luke returned with three beers and non-alcoholic sangria for Scully, handing them out before settling into the other armchair next to her.

"Luke, did you join Scully at the party the other night? Can't remember seeing you there," Nick asked, taking a sip of his beer as he relaxed into his seat.

That had to be a trick question.

He didn't remember seeing *Scully* there, and she was hard to miss. Which meant his question was a fishing expedition for something else.

Luke's smile slid slowly across his face, tipping his beer in my direction. "If you're looking for extra names to add to the watch list, you'll find none here. Both Claire and I had other plans. But from what we heard, it was an interesting night." He tipped his beer toward Scully.

Thankfully Nick was still looking at Luke and Scully so he didn't see my eyes bugging out, the strength of my ocular nerves solely responsible for holding them back in.

Because as much as we hadn't been with Scully that night, he was well aware of what transpired. Namely, he'd been the one who'd helped me carry Nick into the bedroom, something I still hadn't mentioned. It was too late now, the time for that little revelation having come and passed the morning I'd left his house.

"I should probably start dinner, feel like helping me?" I asked Nick knowing it was safer to have him see my incompetence in the kitchen than leave him with the uncertainty behind.

Nick rose to his feet, not needing the tug on his arm I had ready for extra encouragement. "Of course." He took another sip from his beer. "Lead the way."

He wasn't far behind me as I strolled out of the room, the eyes of my two best friends following us out.

"What do you need help with first?" he asked, wrapping his hands around my waist and turning me around to face him.

My sanity, I was tempted to answer.

"Well, to be really honest, I *suck* at cooking. The last time I attempted to make something from scratch, we all ended up in the emergency room."

Food poisoning was never fun, especially not in front of a guy you had secretly liked forever.

Nick laughed, giving me all his attention. "I'd like to skip any emergency rooms if we can help it. Maybe you should let me cook."

His offer was not only sweet, but downright tempting. While I'll admit it was embarrassing, I could screw up scrambling a couple of eggs, my talents lay elsewhere. As for Nick's talents, well we were only starting to see the full extent of those.

"I was just going to order Uber Eats and palm it off as my own," I answered honestly. "Or bribe Luke, he's the best cook out of the three of us."

"Yes, Luke. Tell me about him. He and Scully . . . together?" He tilted his head to the side, his tone in no way accusing.

Not sure I would have been so calm, especially since I had been sort of jealous of his friend Audrey before I knew she was married. And she didn't even live with him. Because *that* made sense.

"No. Not only no, but hell no." My hands rubbed over his chest. "We're all just friends—close friends—but no one is romantically involved with anyone else."

"They're not my type." Luke's voice came from the doorway, his eyes on me and Nick as he walked slowly toward us. "And by *they*, I mean women."

"Wasn't implying anything, I was just curious." Nick held his hands up defensively, looking a little surprised by Luke's admission.

Luke didn't seem annoyed, if not amused by it. He nodded, leaning back against the counter as he folded his arms across his chest with a grin. "Yeah, you and every other guy who's walked through that door before you. But we're friends, *good friends,* and I love both Scully and Claire like my own family. Which is why I'm here, with all the love in my heart, to ask that you *don't* cook for us. And man, if you have any self-preservation, you will back me up on this."

Nick laughed. "She did mention the last time she cooked you

guys ended up in the E.R."

Luke pulled his face into a grimace before turning to me with a grin. "Which was a disappointment because I'd been praying for the morgue."

"Looks like a job for the men then." Nick nodded to my roommate, releasing his hold on me. "You should probably go back to the living room and talk about world domination while Luke and I get dinner ready."

Luke laughed. "Fast learner, but it's my kitchen, so my rules. You game, Larsson?"

"Rules were meant to be broken." Nick brushed a sweet kiss against my lips. "And I have a sordid history with them. So, the question is, are *you* game?" He eyed me hard before turning back to Luke.

Luke shrugged, his eyes ping-ponging between us. "Sorry is that directed at me, or is this some sexy word play I'm supposed to ignore?" He grinned, tossing a tea towel at both of us.

I caught the tea towel, using it to fan myself as I laughed. "Not sure who it was directed at, but it was really hot. So hot."

"Go objectify me behind my back like a regular person." Nick pulled me in for a hug.

"Fine, fine. I'm leaving." I gave him a quick squeeze before backing away from the door. "But you should be warned, we'll— probably more so Scully than me—will be eavesdropping and listening to everything you both say."

"You'll be listening just as much as me, Claire. Don't pretend you won't," I heard from behind me, her voice closer than it should have been if she'd not been doing exactly that.

"Enjoy." I saluted them both before sliding out of the room, Scully grabbing me around the arm as I'd cleared the doorway.

"I like him. He makes you smile, is good looking and he's offered to cook. We should take him hostage and keep him forever."

I was only half sure she was joking.

The idea did have some appeal, especially considering how happy he seemed to make me. While I knew he wasn't the sole reason things were improving for me professionally, it was hard to deny the coincidence. "Yeah, I'll put him in a gilded cage and stare at him fondly as I work. Think of how amazing my screenplays will be."

Scully shivered as she shook her head. "Okay, when you say it like that, it sounds creepy. I guess you just date him like a regular person."

God I hoped so, hoping that our relationship—did what we were doing even qualify?—would last longer than my previous ones. I also hoped that if/when it ended, that it did so amicably. I really didn't want have a reason to hate him. Especially not now, when I'd found out he was still just as charming, funny and good-looking as when I'd first met him.

No, we had to be friends forever.

Okay, maybe *that* was even creepier than the gilded cage idea.

I think I needed help in more places than just the kitchen.

CHAPTER 12

LUKE AND NICK had bonded while they prepared us a feast of Moroccan lamb and couscous. I didn't even know we'd had items in our pantry to make anything that fancy, but it turned out that Luke had shopped on his way home too. I'd like to think it was because he had become inspired, voices calling him to action like saints to a miracle, but I knew it was mostly because he knew he'd have to save my ass or we'd end up ordering pizza.

Nick had also added to his resume, having apparently been as proficient in the kitchen as my roommate. Not going to lie, the thought of him cooking for me while I looked on in adoration without fear of salmonella poisoning was sexy as hell. Crazy what was a turn on these days.

And in addition to being a culinary genius—anyone who could negotiate the disorder and turn out anything resembling a meal was a master in my eyes—he and Luke had a lot in common as well.

Their conversation was easy, a mutual respect flowing between them as they sat next to each other. And Scully—who was sitting beside Luke—had become his biggest fan. Not only was he making sure he addressed and included her in the conversation, but he'd also made her a mocktail, combining seltzer water, lemon and berries.

His sister-in-law, Tia, was expecting her and Eric's first child and apparently she loved the combination of fizz and berries. I tried not to hyperventilate that I was having a conversation with a man about pregnancy and he hadn't run screaming from the house. Most men looked at Scully like it was something contagious, and they were suddenly going to awake with a screaming kid and a child support payment.

And so, the list of Nick's attributes grew, setting the bar ridiculously high for future men for not only me but Luke and Scully too. Okay, so we had *all* become his biggest fans.

After dinner was done, he offered to help with the dishes, insisting even though I had said it wasn't fair since he'd helped cook. Although it did become pretty clear as to why he was so anxious to help once he'd gotten me alone in the kitchen. I think we got more soapy water and bubbles on each other than we did on the plates. It was after three unsuccessful attempts at actually getting the dishes clean that I mentioned we had a perfectly functioning dishwasher. Which was great because I didn't have to divide my attention anymore, cleaning up the kitchen and moving to my bedroom shortly after.

Scully had already gone to bed, she had work early the next day and was losing the battle with narcolepsy while sitting on the couch. And Luke proved how awesome a wingman he was, excusing himself too, citing some bullshit work he needed to do in his room. While I loved that Nick got along with my friends and they adored him, I was anxious to spend some time with him alone.

Not sleeping with him had been a terrible idea.

Horrible.

And I was determined not only to see if he lived up to what I'd imagined in my mind, but unwrap more of his layers.

It was clear that what I thought I knew wasn't all there was, and I was desperate to get to know him better.

"Just so you know." The door closed behind us, my body pressed to my bedroom wall as I kissed him, his hand moving to my breast. "That blowjob you weren't asking for last night, probably going to happen tonight."

He laughed, his teeth pulling against my bottom lip. "All because I cooked you dinner? Or was there something else that won me favor."

While kissing him against the wall was hot, getting him on my bed was my objective, tugging his arm to lead him where I wanted him to be. Nick lowered his ass to the mattress, watching me as I followed, pulling him down further so we lay side by side.

"So many things." My body shifted, rolling on top and straddling him. "But I don't want to be distracted by listing them right now."

His hard ridge lengthened underneath me as I rocked against him. "Not that I'm complaining but that doesn't feel like a blowjob." His fingers locked around my hips, guiding me.

Slowly and as seductively as I could manage, I lowered my lips to his ear and whispered, "If you build it, they will come."

Nick erupted into laughter, his body shaking as he pulled himself up and rested against the headboard. "You're quoting 'Field of Dreams' to me while you ride me?"

"You want to stop?" My mouth pressed against his neck, sucking gently against his skin as I smiled. "I'd hate to have ruined the mood."

His hands around my waist tightened. Lifting and then flipped me onto my back before covering me with his body. "You didn't ruin anything. And we're not stopping unless *you* want to."

I shook my head; I definitely did not want to stop.

Nick caught my gaze, kissing me as my body hummed underneath him. "Good, because I don't want to either."

Given permission, my hands moved to his ass and pulled him

closer. I wanted more, the friction he was giving me, a tease of what was to come. He didn't hesitate, grinding harder against me through our clothes as we kissed.

"That feels so good," I moaned against his mouth, wondering how much better it would be naked but wishing I didn't have to stop to find out.

His hand went between us, under my shirt and pulled at the lace cup of my bra. My eyes closed, getting lost in the sensation as his fingers pulled against my nipple.

"The morning I woke up to you in my house," his kisses moved down my neck, heading toward his hand, "I thought about doing this. About taking off your clothes and kissing you exactly like this."

"Okay." I nodded, knowing that I probably would have protested for about a second before I would have let him.

His tongue swirled around my exposed nipple, making my skin tingle. "Just okay?" He moved to the other, pulling down the other side of my bra and splitting his attention between the two.

I had no idea what he was asking.

I'd heard the words so I knew he'd said something but as to what that had meant, was a mystery. And I was fine with that, happy to live in my ignorant bliss if he kept kissing me the way he was.

"More." My back arched, lifting off the mattress. "More kisses."

He chuckled against my skin, unhooking my bra and pulling it off along with my top. My skin pebbled, tiny dots rose as his finger trailed along my torso in a leisurely descent to the waistband of my jeans. He hesitated, watching me before he undid the button and then the zipper, pulling it down agonizingly slow as his eyes stayed locked on mine.

"Kiss. Me," I gritted out, pulling him back toward me as our mouths crushed against each other.

My hands decided it would be a good time to take over, less graceful than his had been as they fumbled with his pants.

Completely by touch, I had his pants undone and pushed down to his hips before he took over, helping me the rest of the way. The team effort meant I could turn my attention to his shirt, cursing my fingers weren't moving quickly enough as they undid the buttons and finally freed him of it.

I'd seen him topless before but being able to touch him made it so much better. Hungry hands clawed at his skin, feeling the strength of his muscles flex under my fingertips as we stripped each other naked.

We were completely bare, a pile of clothes dumped beside us as we touched. I wanted to know every inch of him, running my fingers along his body and exploring him like he was a piece of 15th century bas-relief. I knew *nothing* about art, but I could tell what was under my fingertips was a masterpiece.

If I thought the journey of discovery was my own, I was mistaken as his hand slipped up my thigh, hesitating before going any further. And if my mouth hadn't been so busy kissing him, I would have demanded—no begged—that he touch me. But I didn't want to stop. Instead I kept my lips exactly where they were, wrapping my hand around his and moving it to in between my legs.

We both groaned, the heat almost unbearable as he slid in a finger and pumped twice. I was slick, burning alive as my hand left his—he was doing *totally* fine without my help—and grabbed his cock, his length pulsing as I jerked him.

My fingers strained around his girth, moving up and down his shaft while he fingered me. I'd felt him before, with my hands and against my body but not like this—completely bare with unrestrained access.

"Fuck," he groaned, his jaw tightening as I continued the glide of my hands. I could make him come—just like that—and the power was intoxicating.

His eyes closed, then opened again as he regained control,

tearing my hands away from his cock and lifting them above my head. "I know I should probably wait and ask you if you're sure. Because that would be the right thing to do, and when it comes to you, I want this to be right. But I am fucking struggling right now not to be inside of you."

I pushed against his hands, my body straining and desperate to be touched. "Being inside of me is the right thing to do."

It was too soon.

I knew it, knew we had barely been dating, hardly knew each other, and sleeping with him would probably not be a good idea.

But I didn't care.

He didn't hesitate again, letting go of my wrists and moving further down my body. Spreading my thighs with his hands, he settled between them, licking me with the entire length of his tongue before plunging a finger back inside. "You're so ready for me, Claire." He groaned against my skin. "So ready for me to be right here."

His thumb circled my clit as he added another finger, his eyes on fire as my center rocked against him slick and needy. It felt so good, but I wanted more, wanted to feel him deep and look into his eyes while we drove each other insane.

My body trembled, heat inching up my skin as he licked and sucked me, just begging for the release. I didn't want to wait anymore, almost kneeing him in the face as I turned and leaned over the edge of my bed.

"Claire, what are you—"

"Condoms," I breathed out, hanging off the side with stretched out fingers, retrieving the shoebox I kept under my bed.

While most people had a condom or two tucked away in their purse or in the top drawer of their dresser, I had an entire shoebox filled with condoms, lube and other helpful paraphernalia hidden under my bed.

He glanced down at the box before looking back at me, probably wondering why I had a *doomsday prepper* amount of protection in my bedroom.

"When Scully got pregnant, she didn't want me—" I started to explain, his fingers pressing against my lips and silencing me.

He shook his head, reaching across to the box, picking up a condom and tearing it open. "You don't need to tell me or anyone else why, let's just both be eternally grateful that it's there."

"Yeah. Sounds good to me." *Scully was so getting a gift basket of all her favorite things tomorrow.* "Let's be grateful."

He smirked, showing how *grateful* he was as he rolled on the condom, my eyes glued to his hand as he did it. He gave himself an extra tug, making sure the latex was secure as he shifted back on top of me. His knees pushed open my thighs as he edged the head of his cock against my core and rubbed against it.

I.

Was.

So.

Freaking.

Grateful.

"Claire."

My name on his lips was the most perfect thing I'd heard, each letter rung out like a chorus sung by angels. Or maybe it wasn't my name I'd heard at all, my breath coming out in a rush as I felt him enter me.

He was slow and gentle, taking his time to ease into me as my body adjusted. Never once did his eyes move from mine, watching me the entire time as his hands stayed locked around my hips.

"You feel so good." He thrust all the way in, lowering his head and kissing my collarbone. "So good."

It might have felt good for him but it felt *amazing* for me, my hips lifting off the mattress and joining in with him in the slow rock. "I told you this was a good idea."

He drew out, thrusting back into me and then holding still. "Your idea was a blowjob, this idea was mine."

We didn't get to discuss whose idea it was, and to be honest I didn't really care. The slow-and-steady he'd started, tossed out the window as he proved how much of a *good idea* it was.

My body had a mind of its own, my hands clawing against his back as my legs wrapped around his waist. He seemed to like it too, the change in position giving him more leverage so he could drive deeper inside of me.

Each drag of his hips got faster and harder, the "yes", "more", "please", "don't stop" coming from my lips also picking up the tempo.

"You're fucking gorgeous." He bit gently against my shoulder. "And you're driving me crazy."

He was telling me.

My body was so primed for explosion I wasn't sure if I was going to come or black out, my skin tingling as he edged me closer to oblivion. He knew I was close, his eyes widening as my fingernails dug into his back.

"Make me bleed, Claire," he dared me through gritted teeth. "I want to feel it and don't hold back."

I couldn't have even if I tried, the surge of energy taking over my body as every muscle inside of me tightened and then . . . let go. My teeth bit down on my lower lip to stop myself from screaming as he continued to move, teasing each tremor out of me like extra credit.

"Yes, yes," he groaned, thrusting harder and faster as the pleasure continued to roll through me. I wasn't sure it would ever end, tiny vibrations tingling all over my body.

My grip on him tightened, my fingernails biting into his skin as I panted against his mouth. "Make me feel it too."

And I didn't have to ask twice.

With one final drive he found his finish, covering me as he pulsed inside of me. His body was hot and slick with sweat as he shuddered against me and he'd never looked more perfect as he did right at that moment.

I'd seen him on magazine covers, on billboards, and countless hours of television. But as he lay above me—his body glistening and his hair a mess—it was by far the best version of him ever. And sure I was probably biased, buzzed from sex endorphins and still a little surprised we had sex in the first place. But he was without a doubt the most beautiful man I'd ever seen.

"You think your roommates heard?" He kissed my shoulder, lifting his weight off me.

I shrugged, too blissed out to care. "I've had to listen to both of them, it's about time they had to deal."

I failed to mention that both were probably proud—sure that didn't sound gross—and glad I threw caution to the wind and took a chance.

"Oh really? Well I don't care if you don't, but if you ever want to get loud, remember, I live alone." He kissed me again this time moving his mouth back to mine. I liked it there; those lips of his were very talented.

"Are you going to stay?" I yawned, desperately wanting the answer to be yes.

He rolled onto his back beside me, pulling the covers on top of us. "Umm yeah." His eyes went wide, pretending to look shocked. "You were just going to use me and kick me out? I feel so cheap."

I laughed, snuggling up to his side and loving how well we seemed to fit. "Well, there is that *whole* box of condoms. Might be fun to see if we could put a dent in that stash, so you should probably stick around."

"So what you're saying is, it's my duty to stay." His arms

wrapped around me and drew me in closer.

"Feel we owe it to each other."

He looked up at the ceiling, taking a deep breath as he whispered, "Thank you."

I playfully poked him in the chest, shaking my head. "You want to see what else is in the box besides condoms?"

A smirk spread across his lips. "Oh hells yes."

CHAPTER 13

IT HAD BEEN a while since I'd woken up beside a warm body.

My last boyfriend got up early to run—I never understood the compulsion—so even if he did spend the night, I usually was alone when I opened my eyes. And before him . . . well, it was safe to say that I had never really *wanted* to wake up beside someone.

I liked all the men I'd ever slept with, but never loved any of them. I knew it at the time too, assuming that maybe after a while, stronger feelings would develop. But when I realized I preferred waking up alone, I *knew* it wasn't and wouldn't be love.

With Nick, I *liked* the feeling of his body pressed against mine, holding myself still as I absorbed the sensation.

"Good morning." His voice was rough, all jagged masculinity and sleepiness that made my skin instantly heat.

We'd done things last night.

Lots of things.

And not all of them had been sexual.

I felt my lips turn up in a smile, my body practically radiating as I nestled in closer. "Good morning."

I had always been attracted to him, even all those years ago before he was uber famous. There was something about him that went beyond his looks, a sincerity in his smile that was captivating.

"Should we pretend like I'm going to leave, so you can ask me to stay?" He kissed my shoulder, a smirk playing on his lips. "Or can we cut straight to the part where I fuck you in the shower?"

I laughed, his cockiness sort of endearing. "How do you know I'd ask you to stay? Some of us have to work you know, Nick, so maybe I don't have time for shower sex."

He opened his mouth in shock and whispered, "No time for shower sex? Who even says that?"

Nobody.

Nobody said it, especially when you had the hottest man alive in your bed and he was promising to deliver orgasms. But I did have to work, and losing my new job so soon would definitely suck.

"Maybe we could have quick morning sex instead?" I suggested, not willing to just kiss him goodbye and push him out my door. "I have at least forty pages to read today and make notes."

He grinned, his hand traveling seductively down my body. "Ah yes, the mysterious script you're reading you can't tell me anything about. You know, I could always torture the information out of you?" His head dipped, lowered his mouth to my nipple and he sucked. His teeth grazed against my firm peak sending my body into overdrive with a flood of arousal.

Oooooh.

He.

Was.

Good.

"I'll never tell. Never," I moaned, trying to concentrate on anything else other than what his mouth was doing.

"Fine, your call," he chuckled against my skin, "torture it is."

Five more minutes of his delicious mouth on my body and I'd tell him the name of the script, as well as the synopsis and character notes. Not only would I volunteer the information, but enjoyed my interrogation and begged for more.

"How well do you know Audrey Rydell?" I asked suddenly, the question leaping out of my mouth before I had a chance to stop it.

I hadn't meant to mention her name, the fact that it had been *her* script I'd been trying to keep a secret made my mind wander as to their still unknown connection.

"Audrey?" He lifted his head, huffing out a breath of frustration, no longer interested in my torture. "She's married, don't believe everything you read."

Ooooooh that wasn't a response I was expecting.

"I hadn't read anything." Okay, that was a lie; obviously I had read her work. Maybe, I'd misread the situation and talk about work wasn't only off limits for me but for him too. Guess that was fair, too bad it made me feel like shit. Like I'd imposed where I wasn't wanted, pulling myself away from him as I felt him cool toward me.

He shook his head, not allowing me to go. "Shit, I'm sorry, Claire. I didn't mean it like that, I'm just sick of the questions. Everyone assumes we're having an affair, but she's a talented writer and we're looking for a project to work on together. That's it."

"Nick, you don't need to explain. I mean, we don't even really know each other that well." We'd seen each other a few times and slept together, hardly constituted a relationship. He certainly didn't owe me anything, even if I did want to know.

"No, I don't *need* to explain but I want to." He kissed my shoulder, holding me against his body. "It's just work. She has some awesome ideas and I'm excited to see what she comes up with for us. She's easy to be around."

That he was talking about her in the professional sense didn't help. God, how pathetic was I that I wished he'd said all of that about me? Because deep down I guess I'd hoped that we'd have the chance to work together too. Having him embody the words I had written.

"You're not saying anything." Nick lifted my chin, studying me closely. "Why?"

And even though he was probably more than capable of fooling me with his brilliant acting ability, I could tell his confusion wasn't for show. He genuinely didn't know. How could he? Not like he could peer inside my mind and know what I wanted.

"I just hope I get the opportunity to work with you too someday," I answered wistfully, knowing it probably made me sound like a loser. "Or anyone," I added with a laugh, my effort to sound less pathetic failing miserably. "Anyway, I'm sure you guys will find something awesome to work on. Maybe sooner than you think."

The script I was reading didn't immediately point to Nick as a lead, but I didn't doubt he was capable if given a chance.

"Oh really?" His interest seemed piqued. "What do you know?"

I bit my lip, trying to sound playful. "You might have to go back to torturing me."

A sly smile edged across his face. "Just remember, Claire. You asked for it."

IT WAS BY far the most productive I'd been in months, if not years. I was not only working on my own screenplay—ecstatic at what I was producing—but I had won even greater favor with Marconi. I had binge read my last job, sending him a glowing report on how much I loved Audrey's script. My notes had apparently pleased him, sending over another script via courier and asking me for feedback.

And Nick, well, he was an unexpected surprise.

"What's your family like?" he asked, pouring wine into a glass as he checked on dinner.

I hadn't really planned on spending every night with him, intending to play it cool as I tried to figure "us" out. But being with him just felt so good and I hated to deny myself. Besides, he was almost impossible to say no to.

"Great." I smiled, the thought of them always making me warm inside. "I had a great childhood, two parents who loved each other and two siblings who thought I was amazing. They moved when I was in college, and after I graduated, I just decided to stay here."

"Yeah, must have been hard though. As much as my brothers piss me off, I'm glad they're around. Not that I'd tell them that." He laughed.

It was weird talking about his family like they were just a normal family. I mean, I guess they *were* just a normal family, but it was still sort of surreal.

"It's hard sometimes, but we talk on the phone and I go back and see them. Plus, I have Luke and Scully, trust me, they *more* than make up for it."

He grinned. "Yeah, I like your friends."

"Oh really?" I wrapped my arms around him, pulling on the dishtowel he had slung over his shoulder. "Should I call them? Invite them to dinner?"

His hands dropped to my waist, tugging me closer to his body. "Nope, I want you all to myself."

"Why?"

"Because I'm selfish," he said with no apology, his grin widening.

What did that even mean?

"Well, you might not always feel like that," I leaned in and whispered. "Sometimes—not a lot but—I have a tendency to be a little crazy."

He threw his head back and laughed. "I was kind of counting on it. I like your kind of crazy. It keeps me on my toes."

"That's a good thing?" I wished I didn't need to ask, assuming that everything he said were flowery complements, but there was only so much delusion I was willing to entertain.

"Hell yes, it is. You're real, and so freaking refreshing I honestly can't wait to hear what comes out of your mouth next. As much as I like your friends, I like *you* better."

"Because I'm the *right* kind of crazy." I used the dishtowel I still had in my hands and flung it at his arm.

"Yeah, you are. So let's make a deal, I'll feed you and while we eat, we can discover more about each other."

My heartbeat accelerated, the thought alone making me giddy.

He was sooooooo nice.

Not just to look at, but genuinely *nice* with a good heart. And boy did I want to "discover" more.

I wanted to know it all.

"You've got yourself a deal."

I think it was easier when he was just the hot dude I'd met five years ago, or the famous hot dude I lusted over. And yet . . . there wasn't a chance I was walking away.

CHAPTER #14

"SO, I NEED to tell you something."

That was never how you wanted a conversation with your boyfriend to start, especially if it wasn't you who was the one saying it.

"O-kay." I lowered myself onto his couch as I tried not to panic. It had been a place of such fond memories, surely it wouldn't let me down now. Especially not when we had two of the most outstanding weeks ever.

I'll admit that I was tentatively waiting for the other shoe to drop, knowing that things had been going too well and yet, I couldn't stop myself from enjoying it.

And of course, Nick was amazing—all the things you could want in a boyfriend multiplied by a million. And then there was the added bonus that he got along with my friends and they loved him. I hadn't had a chance to meet his yet, but that was because I had to work, and when we had free time, we were sort of busy a lot.

What? Like I was going to turn down sex with Nick Larsson.

His hand reached out to mine, locking our fingers in a gesture that would have otherwise had me excited. "Remember the night you came over and we were supposed to go over that script Scully had given to Dave?"

"You mean the night I came over and we ended up making out like a pair of animals in heat, that night?" I asked, the memory of it forever burned in my brain. It was our first official date, something I wasn't likely to forget. Like ever.

"Yes, and after you left . . ."

Oh God, he was going to admit he called someone else for a booty call not realizing we were going to be permanent. I knew I should have pressed him the next day when he'd admitted to being tired, damn me for being so loved up that I decided to trust him.

"Look, whatever it is, I just need to know the truth. Please don't lie to me." It was tempting to say it was in the past and I didn't want to know, live in happy oblivion and ignore it. But now it was out in the open I would obsess about it. The thoughts would eat me alive as I imagined whatever he'd done as the worst-case scenario.

"After you left, I picked up the script and read it. I had only been meaning to flick through because I was curious, but once I got reading, I wanted to finish."

Oh thank you, God.

As far as indiscretions went, this was by far the best.

I wasn't even surprised, assuming he'd eventually pick it up to see what it was about anyway. So, no, the shock hadn't sent me reeling into a panic that I couldn't comprehend, because honestly, I was amused he'd waited at all.

Who was going to have a document—regardless of what's written on it—in their possession penned by the person they were swapping bodily fluids with and *not* read it? I wouldn't have even needed the last caveat; just *in my possession* would have been enough. I'd have flipped through the pages of that bad boy so fast anyone would have thought I was a speed-reading prodigy.

In any case, even though I had theoretically buried my head in the sand, it was something I knew would have eventually been dealt with.

"It's not a script, it was . . ." *fantasy musings about you of which I have at least ten others tucked in a plastic tub like the dead body that had been my career at the time.* Yeah, probably best if I didn't say that.

" . . . It's a story, something I was tinkering with and hoping to use in future ideas."

The sweet spot for any script was one hundred and twenty pages. At approximately one page per minute, anything longer than that was given serious side eye unless you wrote the next Schindler's List. My tales of *Nick and Blaire* didn't need to adhere to the standard because it well . . . it wasn't a script.

He took a breath, seeming to measure his words. "Can we discuss it?"

Something else you didn't want to hear unless it was coming out of your own mouth. Discuss what? Whether or not I was going to seek an insanity plea during the proceedings for the stalking charge he was going to level at me? Or if I'd be willing to sign an NDA as his parting gift as he sailed out the door? Or maybe he wanted to discuss the misrepresentation of the "Blaire" character, disappointed that I didn't have her stellar attributes, namely her perfect body and "together" life? I wasn't sure he could argue false advertising since he wasn't my target audience but who was I to judge?

I groaned, closing my eyes as I buried my head in the crook of my arm. "Can we go back five minutes to when I could pretend you didn't read it? There really isn't anything to talk about. It was a rough first draft, that at best had been self-edited, and at worst had so many typos and grammatical errors it was debatable it was even English."

I had a process, and my hands and brain worked at two different speeds, which sometimes got me into trouble. Go ahead, cast whatever dirty aspersions you want, they were probably valid too.

"You think I was worried that there was a comma out of

place?" Nick laughed, tugging my arm down. "Claire, I picked it up because I was curious, but I read it because it was good. It was really good. It was funny and entertaining and had a really great storyline."

Okay, so that was all positive stuff but I was sensing a but; there was always a *but*. And he hadn't even mentioned the most obvious issue; that I had basically written a fairytale that included him and me. And all *before* we were dating because that wasn't at all weird.

"Just say it." I shook my head, thinking of how fondly I would remember our time together. It had been more than I'd expected, so there could be no disappointment.

He looked at me confused, tilting his head to the side. "Say what?"

"Gah, you're going to make me do it? Come on, Nick, you're supposed to be a gentleman. Go ahead and tell me how freaking creepy it is that I wrote about you."

I left off the "and me" part because A. it was assumed and B. well it sounded worse with the addition. And while there wasn't a lot I could say that would make it any better than it was, I was sticking to the age-old defense that dictated that you never admitted more than you had to. Yes, no—brief and concise—that would be what would set me free.

Failing to admit the obvious even though I had plainly spelled it out for him, his brow knitted in confusion like he couldn't see what my problem was. "Ummm, you know that screenwriters write screenplays with actors in mind a lot, right? Tarantino, Woody Allen, Kurt Sutter—do you want me to keep going?"

I scoffed, "Well, Tarantino and Woody Allen—"

"Okay, yeah. Those two were bad examples." He laughed knowing if he was trying to point out how "normal" it was, those two weren't great pieces of supporting evidence. "But Sutter is solid, and what about Francis Ford Coppola?"

"You're comparing me to the guys who created 'Sons of An-archy' and 'The Godfather'? I'm not sure if you are trying to make me feel better or join me on the crazy train."

Maybe I was just *really* good in bed. My vagina had magical powers that had Svengali'd him so that he was willing to lie to my face. While it was far-fetched, it was easier to digest than being compared to Francis Ford Coppola.

Jesus.

A good self-esteem was one thing, out and out delusion was something completely different.

He grabbed my face in his hands, holding me still as he looked into my eyes. "Claire, I'm just saying screenwriters do it all the time. I'm honored you wrote it for me."

Oh. Wait. A. Freaking. Minute.

He thought I wrote it *for* him.

As in, he *inspired* the character, which technically was true.

As in, I wrote a story, envisaging him as the lead and tailored my "screenplay" for him.

Well if that wasn't the very definition of what I'd done, then I didn't know what was. The reasons behind it didn't matter, and he hadn't even asked what those reasons were. Who cared? No one did. No one asked Francis Ford Coppola, I bet. Who knows, maybe Frankie boy had been trying to score a date too.

"You *don't* think it's weird?" I asked again, reinforcing that I thought it was and giving him the opportunity to rethink his life choices.

He brought his lips to mine, kissing me hard as his thumb skated against my jaw. "I'm fucking flattered beyond measure."

I was going to cry.

There was a scenario I hadn't even bothered to hope for be-cause it was too fantastical to even dream. My fan fic had not only been misconstrued as a serious story, but the man who was the object of the fantasy believed that in fact, he was merely the inspiration for the character. And not only that, but he liked both his representation, and the story as a whole. I couldn't have even written a *script* that convincing, and that was supposed to be my job.

Oh God, I hoped I didn't die suddenly in my sleep or something. It would be so cruel to have escaped what could have been one of the most catastrophic events both professionally and personally, only to get hit by a bus or something like that.

"Wow, I'm just . . . Wow." I was honestly speechless, unsure of whether I should be thanking him or be embarrassed. "That's really great."

His lips spread into a grin. "I'm glad you feel that way, because I sort of gave it to my agent."

"What the actual fuck?"

I had meant to think it, continue with my internal pondering as I had been safely in my own head, but it had wheezed out of me all the same.

Not that I could be mad at my mouth, because seriously, *what the actual fuck?* How could my fortune have turned so quickly on a dime? All that awesome stuff we'd been celebrating was now circling down the toilet as I watched on, unable to do anything but wave it goodbye.

My lungs burned as I tried to suck in air. "You gave it to your agent?"

I think getting hit by a bus would have hurt less. It definitely would have left less mess and be easier to explain.

"Claire, isn't that the point of writing it? For it to be turned into a movie?" His brow furrowed, looking at me like it was freaking obvious.

Oh my God he was serious.

My chest constricted in what was probably an anxiety attack with my heart beating so fast I was guaranteed to blow out a rib or two. "Your agent is Jeremy Levin."

It wasn't a question because I knew *exactly* who his agent was, and he was a huge asshole. Granted the words agents and assholes were kind of synonymous, it was not helping my cause that the particular agent asshole combo in question was the very man who I'd queried a year ago. Not only had he turned me down—rejections something I was used to—but he had told me he'd prayed for blindness so he'd never have to read shit like mine again.

Nick nodded, still not seeing the problem as he added, "Yes, my agent is Jeremy Levin. I gave it to him last week, he read it."

I was mistaken. It wasn't a bus that would take me out but a freaking tank.

"Listen to me." I grabbed his hands trying not to show him how much I was freaking the hell out. "Jeremy hates me, this is not a good thing. I probably should have brought this up, but I didn't see the point. I mean, it's not like it's important because why would it matter." I barely took a breath, trying to get it out as quickly as possible. "But I queried Jeremy about a year ago. Not that it had anything to do with you. And to be honest, I didn't even know he was your agent at the time—"

"Claire, take a breath." He grabbed both my arms, holding me still and forcing me to breathe. "Jeremy can be a prick but he knows Hollywood and he likes making money. He loved your story."

"What the actual fuck?" This time I had absolutely meant to say it, pushing my hands against his chest as I reeled from the shock.

Nick laughed, grabbing both my hands and holding them hostage above my head. "Let's lay off the shoving just for a minute so I can tell you the rest of it. He read it and he loved it, said that it obviously needed to be adapted, but once it was a workable script he'd be interested in shopping it to networks and studios."

It wasn't possible.

There was no way Mr. You-write-so-shit-I-want-to-poke-my-eyes-out had said that about me. There had to be a mistake, or some kind of misunderstanding.

"Does he know I wrote it?" *Would he even remember me after a year?* "My name was on it, and he isn't under some delusion that some other famous person wrote it, right?" Because I would rather have the asshole agent tell me he changed his mind than believe someone else was responsible for my work.

"Of course your name is on it, who else would I have told him it was?" he asked, tilting his head to the side, curious as to why I was questioning his integrity.

Uh-uh busted.

Firstly, why I believed he liked the script and wanted to help me, there was a part of me that was worried his opinion was clouded. We were sleeping together, and no matter what anyone said, it changed things.

I didn't want for him to have skillfully misrepresented—with all the best intentions—who actually wrote the damn thing. It was one time where bait and switch would surely backfire, and I already had enough personal demons to fight without being laughed out of the building when Nick realized he'd been thinking with his penis and not his head. Not the thing I could exactly ask though was it?

"Because he isn't a fan of my work, and I don't want you sticking out your neck for me only to have it blow up in both our faces," I responded trying not to sound defensive, the attempt not great. Hey, it was the best I could do considering what I had to work with.

"Regardless, he knows *you* wrote it." He chose to ignore the mention of probable doom and continued. "He even told me to get you to call him and set up a meeting."

"Jeremy Levin wants *me* to call *him?*"

Now that had to be bullshit. You didn't call Jeremy, you were fucking summoned, and even then he didn't give you his phone number.

"Well, he wants you to call his assistant Jessica, but she'll set up the meeting." He smiled, because he knew the difference.

He wrapped his arms around me, his body engulfing me in a hug. "This is a good thing, Claire. Why are you freaking out?"

He was right. There certainly was the possibility that it was a good thing, and things had definitely been better in the last couple of weeks. I had listed all the ways my luck had changed and how wonderful my life was. So, it was perfectly reasonable to assume the run of luck would continue, catapulting all the awesome into out of this world outstanding.

I was being paranoid.

It was a *good* thing.

"You just caught me by surprise. I wasn't expecting it." I laughed nervously. "I wished you'd asked me before you'd given it to someone else."

His lips curled to the side as his brow rose. "If I'd asked, there'd be a chance you'd say no. Better to ask forgiveness than permission."

"Really? You're going to plead ignorance as a defense? You know I would have said no because I didn't even want *you* to read it," I huffed out, pretending to be mad. I'll admit it was difficult, probably because he was so goddamn charming.

He nodded, his hands settling on my hips as he grinned. "That's a fair call. And I probably deserve you being angry at me right now."

"Funny, you look too smug to be sorry." I laughed, the man was also adorable, which was making any anger I might have felt difficult.

"Because I'm not sorry."

"You're impossible." I rolled my eyes, shoving gently against his chest.

He grinned wider, knowing exactly what he was doing. "Impossible to be mad at, right? Don't fight it, Claire, you know I'm a lover, not a fighter."

If there was any chance at all, any hope that I could be angry, it evaporated when he unleashed those gorgeous puppy dog eyes. There wasn't a woman alive who could resist him or them, and I was no different.

I shook my head, burying it into his chest. "You are a bad man, Nick Larsson."

"I promise you," he whispered into my hair as he chuckled. "That I only did it to help, I know this is what you want. And yeah, maybe I have a vested interest because I want to play the lead, but I wouldn't waste my time if it wasn't an amazing story. It's really that good, Claire, and if I can put it in front of a few people and help you get recognized, then I'm not going to apologize for that."

Well then.

Now I was the one who felt like I should apologize.

I lifted my head, looking up at him—the risk of the puppy eyes be damned. "You're right, you are impossible to be angry with."

And suddenly his eyes weren't the biggest threat in his arsenal, the crooked grin spreading across his lips, by far more lethal. "I'm just getting you the meeting, the rest is going to be all you."

"Even if he likes it, he'll probably want me to change it. They are going to tear it apart." The words fell from my lips as our gazes locked, my vulnerability on full display.

He shook his head. "No one will tear it apart, trust me, Claire."

"I do trust you. But this story . . ." *Was personal* "Is important to me. I want it done right, I want it treated with respect." *And I wanted to be treated with respect*, I didn't say the last part, leaving it just for me.

"Look at me." He lifted my chin, his thumbs cradling my jaw. "I know you want it done right, and it will be. You've earned this, Claire. Trust me, no one will railroad you."

"God." I shook my head, barely allowing myself to believe that there was even a possibility of it being optioned let alone becoming anything. "I have to be the one to adapt it."

He nodded, his smile returning. "Of course, who else is going to do it? And I can't wait to see how amazing it turns out."

"Okay, you can stop now. You're already getting laid, no need for overkill."

His grin got wider. "If I knew sexual favors were on the table, I'd have done it sooner."

"You're going to be my undoing." I didn't even try to hide it, knowing there was very little I'd be able to do to resist it. To resist him.

Man, I was falling so fast, it scared the shit out of me, and yet, there I was doing it anyway because it felt so right.

His hand lifted my chin, cradling it as he dragged his thumb along my jaw. "We'll undo each other, together. It will be more fun that way."

Somehow, I didn't think we were talking about the same thing.

Too bad I was in too deep to care.

CHAPTER #15

"NOW TAKE A long cleansing breath, all the way out, feeling the tension exit your body as you exhale."

A loud rush of exhales followed as Pru—her name hadn't been Moonbeam after all—wandered around the room. Her voice was calming, the soft and steady cadence up and down each syllable making you want to go to sleep.

"You're not breathing properly," I whispered, rubbing Scully's back as I encouraged her through another fake contraction.

She blew out, puffing out her cheeks as she rolled her eyes. "It's breathing, if I wasn't doing it right I'd be dead."

"In and out, nice and slow." Pru's voice wafted from behind us.

"Sounds like what got you into this mess." I snickered, biting my lip as I suppressed the laugh.

Scully wasn't so disciplined, chuckling before jabbing her elbow back and landing me right in the ribs. "Stop it, we're supposed to be serious."

When I had agreed to come with Scully to birthing classes, we knew it was going to be out of both our comfort zones. But as her due date crept closer, she was starting to freak out, and we'd hoped that the class would help her relax.

But it hadn't worked out that way.

If anything it was doing the opposite, making her feel even less prepared and more overwhelmed, watching all the happy couples around her with their shit seemingly all together.

"That's it partners, keep rubbing their backs." Her voice droned from behind us. "Birth is as much of a state of mind as it is about your body, and it is natural to need support. Take it, reach out and accept it, because when the time comes, it's easier if there is someone there with you."

I felt Scully's body stiffen, her smile dropping as she continued to breathe.

Pru circled the room, nodding gently as she moved between the couples, her footsteps getting closer to us. "Awww, so much love in the room. Babies are created in love so it's important they feel your connection. Partners, make sure you keep holding our precious mommies. So much comfort is transmitted by touch, let them feel your support."

Yeah, probably not what you want to say to a woman who hadn't seen the other party responsible in months.

"Ignore her, she's clearly been smoking weed," I whispered in Scully's ear, hoping like hell we could move back to breathing.

"Ladies, you are bringing into this world the miracle of life. It's not only your bodies that will change, but your life will forever be altered."

"Get me out of here." The words sounded strangled in Scully's throat as her eyes started to water. "Please, I need to get out."

Without another word, I rose to my feet, holding out my hands and helping Scully to hers. I grabbed her water bottle and her oversized bag, the exit only a few feet away. The other couples turned around, eyes on us as Pru came over to investigate. "Is everything okay?"

"Everything is perfect." I stood in front of Scully giving her a minute to collect herself as I discreetly popped off the top of the water bottle and used the large bag as cover. "It's so great, all the love and Zen, I'm feeling so relaxed."

Pru beamed, clasping her hands against her chest. "Oh, I'm so pleased. The way you got up in a hurry, I thought you might be leaving."

"Oh, we *are* leaving unfortunately." My fingers squeezed against the plastic, the bottle aimed at my crotch leaking and forming a large wet patch on my yoga pants. Ugh, it was cold, the water soaking through and making the fabric stick to my skin.

"You see," I leaned forward trying to look suitably embarrassed. "I felt so calm and relaxed that I accidentally peed myself." I moved the bag, revealing the full extent of my shame. "One minute you're fine, the next minute . . . well, we've all been there, right ladies." I winked at the swollen-bellied sisterhood on the floor who nodded their head in sympathy. "Anyway, we better go. Thanks so much."

I dragged out Scully, her tears no longer threatening to fall now that she was laughing at me.

"Don't say I don't do anything for you." I closed the door behind us, walking down the hall toward the main door.

Scully chuckled, waddling to the exit and then stepping outside into the night air. "You couldn't think of a better excuse than peeing your pants?"

"It worked didn't it?" Although, it probably wasn't my wisest choice, the drive home in wet yoga pants not one I was looking forward to, but sometimes you just had to do what you had to do.

"Thank you." She hugged me, her voice getting wavy.

The pregnancy emotions weren't anything new or anything to be ashamed of, but I knew it was bugging her. The feeling of being out of control was something I had been through, though for a vastly different reason. And I could understand her not wanting to have her breakdown in public, wanting to control what she could when her life was changing so drastically. Yet another thing I could relate to. And if I had to let a bunch of strangers think I had incontinence issues to protect my best friend, then so be it.

I hit the keyless lock on my fob, my headlights lighting up as the locks disengaged. "Let's get home, put on pajamas and watch television."

"That sounds amazing." She sighed, walking to the passenger side and hopping in.

Other than being uncomfortable in my "pee" pants, the drive was really nice. We hadn't spent as much time together lately—Nick getting most of my attention—so it was good to laugh and talk.

"I'm so wet, I can't wait to get out of these pants." I pushed open our front door, tossing the keys onto the side table."

"Really?" Nick smirked as he rose from his seat on the couch. "Words every man wants to hear."

Luke scoffed, "Speak for yourself. This man wouldn't."

"Hey." I closed the gap between us and gave him a hug. "Did we have plans tonight?"

We'd spent almost every night together since the night I crashed on his couch, but when I told him about Scully's baby class, I assumed I'd be spending the night alone.

"Nope, no plans. I was on my way to visit Eric and figured I'd stop by and say hi to Luke." Nick lowered his head, dropping a kiss on my lips.

Luke grinned, tipping his head to the coffee table where two partially empty bottles of beer sat. "That's right, Claire. He came to see *me*."

"Oh yeah?" I looked curiously at Nick, grinning. "Well, Scully and I were just going to watch television so don't let me interrupt your bromance."

"Hey, Scully." Nick waved, looking down between us before frowning. "Wow, your pants really are wet."

"Long story, follow me into my bedroom so I can change, and I'll tell you about it." I pulled on his shirt, yanking him toward my room.

"Remember your breathing," Scully called out after us.

Nick shut the door, moving his hands over my body as he kissed me. "I'll call Eric and cancel."

"No, don't do that. You should go. I'm sure your brother is looking forward to seeing you."

Of course I wanted him to cancel, to spend the night with me like he had the other nights, but I knew he shouldn't. Things had gotten so intense so quickly and it was probably for the best that we slowed down.

Without asking, he lifted my T-shirt over my head and tossed it to the floor, his hands next going to my pants. "I really don't care."

Initially the plan had been to go into my room, change out of my clothes and tell him about my day. And I wanted to hear about his day too, find out what inspired his impromptu visit. All of those things had been important, or at least they had been until he kissed me.

My fingers fumbled with his T-shirt, tearing it off him while I kicked off my yoga pants. His kisses continued, trailing down my neck as he scooped me up in his arms and laid me on the bed.

"God, you're beautiful." He lifted my arms above my head, running his fingers along my skin. "You have no idea how freaking crazy you make me."

"I can guess. Making people crazy is a specialty of mine." I laughed, pulling him down on me.

While his hands were all over me, I was still in my underwear and he was mostly still clothed. He made no effort to further undress me, his lips taking a dip down my neck to the swell of my breasts.

"You know this is easier when we're naked." My hands tugged at his pants. "We can be quick."

He raised his head, bringing his forehead to mine and rested it against me. "I don't want to be quick with you."

The way he looked at me gave me goosebumps, my skin tingling as he hovered above me. I felt beautiful, precious, important, but most of all, wanted. I liked the way it felt, warming my body from the inside.

"We're not going to have sex are we?" I asked, running my fingers along the strong muscles of his back.

"Trust me, I want to, but that wasn't what I was here for." He pushed himself up, kissing my nose as I shuffled up the bed.

He turned, grabbing his T-shirt and pulled it back over his head. "I'm really bad at this, you know? The 'relationship' part of the relationship."

"What do you mean?" My arms folded across my chest, suddenly feeling cold.

"I mean, I feel like all we ever do is hang out together at your place or mine. I think somewhere along the line, I forgot how to date."

It was true that since we'd been together, there hadn't been a lot of typical dating behavior. Dinners had either been at my house or his, with our evenings spent holed up in a bedroom. But I understood it wasn't so easy for us.

"Nick, it's okay, really, I understand. You're you and I'm . . . well, I'm me. And we just can't date like a regular couple. Not unless we want it documented by the press."

"Claire, you know eventually there are going to be photos. Who cares, we're not doing anything wrong."

It was easier for him, he'd been in the spotlight for years. Not only with his own fame, but following in the footsteps of his famous brothers too. But for me, well it was different.

"You know what they will say, right? That you could have done better."

It wasn't insecurity—okay, not entirely insecurity—but the spotlight we were going to be under wasn't going to be pretty. It didn't bother me that his previous girlfriends had included models and actresses, or that by most people's standards, I wouldn't measure up. But *he* would need to answer those questions, justify why he'd rather be with an average nobody than a stunning, whatever-her-name-was.

"See, that is where you are so wrong." He shook his head. "And exactly what I wanted to avoid. I do *not* want you to feel like that."

I grabbed his hands, squeezing them in mine. "It's not your fault. Trust me, I'm happy just being with you. I don't need to announce it to the world."

My life was fantastic, and I didn't feel lacking. Nor did I feel like I was hidden away. If anything, I felt like I was the one using him, commandeering so much of his time when he could have been out and being seen. Not to mention how much happier I was when I was around him, my life had never been as great. And while he wasn't the only reason, he was a large contributing factor.

He took a deep breath, running his hands through his hair. "I need to tell you something about the night we met."

"O-kay," I answered hesitantly, not sure what else there was left to say.

"I was drunk, *really* drunk. I'd done so many shots at the bar, I'd lost count." He laughed, probably remembering that he could barely stand when I found him. "I'd spent the last six months filming and I was exhausted. I'd come home every night, tired, to an empty house. Or if I did bring a girl home, it was an empty fuck."

His words stung even though they didn't mean to. I knew he'd been with other women, and he had owed me zero explanation. I had a past too and we couldn't be held responsible for what we did before we were together.

My hand reached out to touch him, needing him to know

that whatever he'd done didn't matter. "Nick, I never judged your lifestyle."

"Well, then you'd be the only one." He laughed, his voice devoid of humor. "Everything I do is talked about. What I wear, what I drive, who I sleep with. And you know, I really didn't care. I was too tired or too busy to notice. I mean, I didn't want to be a prick, but if I had to be surrounded by people I really didn't care about then why not just get hammered? And during the hiatus I'd do whatever the hell I wanted to. No one cared anyway, right? I mean fuck it, these assholes don't pay my bills, why do they get a say in my life? But as I sat at that bar with my friend, I realized it was all so empty."

His beautiful brown eyes fixed on me as he took another breath. "That was the first *real* conversation I'd had with someone other than my family in so long, I'd forgotten how much I missed it. No women, no interviews, no assholes trying to get their pound of flesh—just two dudes at a bar—drinking, laughing—and I felt more free and happier than I had in months. And then I came home and *you* were there."

"I don't understand." My eyes squinted, wondering how I fit in. "I mean, I had no idea you were dealing with all of that. And trust me, I was just as bad as all those other assholes, believing you were living a charmed life."

"No, you *weren't* and *aren't* like those assholes. You are amazing." He took my hands and kissed my knuckles. "And my life is good, trust me, I know it sounds like I'm complaining but that isn't what I mean to say."

As much as I liked the idea of being on a pedestal, I sure as hell didn't deserve to be on one. He'd been my fantasy, conjured for inspiration; I wasn't the angel he thought I was. "Nick, I—"

"How many women would have spent the night at my house and wouldn't have taken photos? Or stolen some shit to keep as a souvenir? Or posted on their social media they were with me?"

I didn't answer, the thought of doing any of those things hadn't even crossed my mind. Granted I had other sins to repent for that night, but taking advantage of him while he was vulnerable wasn't one of them.

He looked at me and continued. "Of the women I've dated in the last few years, all have been transactions. One way or another. But you're different. I don't want to just sleep with you, Claire. I want to *be* with you."

My body shivered and not only because I was in my underwear, his words making a lump form in my throat. "I want that too."

"Well good." He smiled, looking pretty pleased with himself. "So, why don't you get dressed, and come with me to my brother's house."

"Nick, I would really love to." *Who wouldn't want to go meet the family of a man who'd just said the nicest things ever.* "But I promised Scully we'd hang out and I don't want to be that person who dumps her friends when she's with a guy." Not to mention how emotional she'd been. I mean, I'd pretended to pee my pants for God's sake so she didn't *have* a breakdown. I didn't want to turn around and be responsible for the next one.

"You can go," I heard through the door. "Luke's already gone to the store to buy me cookies, so you've been replaced, sorry."

I shook my head, getting off the bed and yanking on a bathrobe before opening the door. There she was, unapologetically standing on the other side, not even trying to hide she'd been eavesdropping on our private conversation. "You were listening?"

"Don't be mad at me, I'm pregnant." She tried not to smile. "And I was only concerned, making sure if you needed someone to verify that it wasn't real pee, that I was available."

"Really? You were concerned? It wasn't that you have a problem keeping out of my business?" I put my hand on my hip trying to sound angry when really all I wanted was to laugh.

"Remember you love me," she squeaked, pulling a face.

"You sure you don't mind if I steal her?" Nick came up behind me, circling his arm around my waist.

Scully waved her hand, "Pfft, take her. Besides, it will give me time to find out what you and Luke were gossiping about."

"Yeah, what were you talking about?" I turned in Nick's arms to face him.

He laughed, tilting his head to Scully. "You know she's only trying to distract you."

"Or you are?" I pushed lightly against his chest.

"I'll tell you all about what we spoke about in the car." He kissed my lips. "Let's go meet my brother."

CHAPTER 16

IT WAS THE quickest I'd ever gotten ready for a date in history. Then again, my date wasn't usually sitting on my bed while I got dressed.

Nick watched with interest as I pulled on a pair of skinny jeans and top, his hands reaching out and touching me which slowed down the process. My hair was a lost cause, with no time to wash and blow it out, I threw it into a ponytail, put on some makeup and called it a day. It was not my best work, but I was too worried about meeting Eric for the first time to worry about what I looked like.

Not only was it our first official date, but the first time I'd been in Nick's car, a silver Mercedes coupe. It was sooooo much nicer than my regular looking Toyota, the leather seats cushioning my body as we drove to Eric's house in the hills.

We chatted in the car, me telling him about the disastrous baby class and my subsequent distraction when we needed to make a hasty exit. Nick laughed, impressed at my commitment to the cause, telling me he'd come to visit Luke hoping he'd get to see me before he had to go to his brother's. Apparently getting me to come with him had been the plan all along, his visit not so much impromptu and more calculated than first thought. He'd even told

Luke, recruiting him to help if the need should arise. But in the end, I hadn't needed much convincing, just knowing Nick wanted me to be with him, reason enough to go.

"What did you tell them about me?" I asked, waiting for the front door to open. I wasn't sure if Eric was the kind of person who did it himself, or outsourced that kind of work to a butler.

"I told them the truth, that you followed me home one night and I wanted to keep you." He smirked, giving my hand a squeeze.

I turned, punching him in the shoulder. "I really hope you're kidding."

"Hey!" The door swung open, a very attractive and pregnant brunette standing on the other side. "You made it, come in."

"Thank you." I stepped inside, clutching Nick's hand tightly.

Tia Larsson was a woman that needed no introduction. As the wife of Nick's eldest brother Eric, and a successful columnist, she was a fixture on Hollywood guest lists. It wasn't a surprise we'd never met; all those lists she was on, I wasn't, but I had looked forward to the pleasure.

"Little brother." Eric stepped out into the hall, ruffling Nick's hair. "I was beginning to think you weren't coming."

"That's my fault, I was at birthing classes and needed to change."

Tia and Eric both stopped, their eyes widening as they looked at me and dropped their gaze to my flat stomach.

Awesome, because it wasn't awkward enough meeting his famous family for the first time, I had to make it sound like I was knocked up.

"I'm not pregnant, my roommate is," I added quickly, Nick's grin doing absolutely nothing to help the situation. "Hi, sorry, I'm Claire." I stuck out my hand, hoping someone would shake it back.

"I'd have left them on the hook longer," Nick mock whispered, Eric accepting my handshake as he elbowed his brother.

"Pleased to meet you, Claire, I'm Eric. I'm not sure what you see in him but we're grateful for the charity." He gave me a blinding smile.

"They're both as bad as each other. You should see when the rest of them are around." Tia squeezed in, taking her turn at introductions. "I'm Tia, and I married into this crazy."

Eric and Nick both laughed, slapping each other on the back like what Tia said was the most hysterical thing ever.

"Sweetheart," Eric purred. "There's a drawer in the bathroom vanity with about a thousand red lipsticks that would argue you were crazy before you got here."

"It's not a thousand." Tia rolled her eyes before turning back to me. "And all of them were necessary."

"I accidently bought twelve eyeliners once." I shrugged, my habit of late night online shopping responsible for a few questionable credit card statements. "My finger hit both the numbers when I was checking out, and I didn't notice until the charge went through. I had one for each month, turned out to be a pretty good year."

Tia opened up her arms, smiling brightly. "Welcome home, Claire. You've found your people." She engulfed me in a warm hug, her swollen belly taking up most of the space.

"Tia, you can't have her." Nick tugged at my arm, pulling me against him. "I found her first."

"Awww baby," I cooed as I patted his cheek. "You'll always be my number one, but you have to learn to share."

Nick kissed my neck, grinning against my skin. "She said she likes me best."

Tia and Eric lead us to the backyard where they had a stunning outside area. We ate snacks and drank wine—Tia sipping the fruit concoction like Nick had made Scully—as we chatted in the warm night air.

Eric and Tia were both wonderful, making me feel welcome

as they asked me about my work. They seemed genuinely interested, Eric asking questions about the screenplays I'd written and the studios I'd worked with.

Naturally Nick mentioned the one I'd "written" for him, dissecting the plot and breaking it down for his brother and sister-in-law.

"Sounds great, are you writing full time?" Tia asked, refilling my wineglass. It was my third, and it was definitely making the conversation easier.

I thanked her, taking a sip of the crisp Chablis before continuing. "I'm working on something new. Edgier, but I'm really enjoying the process."

Nick rested his hand on my knee beaming with pride. "She won't let me read it yet, but I'm sure it's going to be amazing."

"You're only saying that because I'm your girlfriend," I giggled. "And this time around, you aren't getting a look until it's done."

He shook his head, smiling smugly. "Or I can just get Scully to get it for me. You should know by now I always get what I want."

"How far along is your roommate?" Tia asked, her hand rubbing her belly.

"Almost eight months, how about you?"

"Twenty-six weeks." She looked over at Eric. "We're really excited."

Even if she hadn't mentioned it, one look at both of them and you could tell. I was sure they were going to be great parents, while Nick was obviously destined to be the cool uncle. The kind that bought the kid a drum kit when they were eight, and then beer when they were eighteen.

I took another sip of wine. "I'm excited too. For Scully. I mean, of course it's *her* baby, but it feels like all of ours too."

And I was definitely the cool aunt. Maybe Nick and I could go drum kit shopping together, that would be fun. I bet he'd make a great dad too.

Whoa, where the hell did THAT come from?

I didn't know if he wanted kids.

Hell, I didn't even know if *I* wanted kids.

Maybe all those pregnancy hormones in the birthing class had gotten to me, no wonder Scully was so desperate to get out of there.

Warmth spread across my skin either from the wine or the thought of having Nick's baby, but it was definitely time to go.

"We should probably head home." I rested my glass on the table, sliding my hand into Nick's. "I'm sure Tia must be exhausted."

He nodded, rising to his feet as I stood. "Of course, and I don't think Tia is the only one who's exhausted." He caught me trying to suppress a yawn.

"Sorry, long day." I laughed, feeling a little light headed.

Tia and Eric walked us out, and we said our goodbyes. They asked us to come back and their invitation sounded so sincere, I accepted without even asking Nick. I liked his family, and I was relieved that they seemed to like me too.

My head lolled to the side as Nick started the engine, smiling at him as we drove down Eric's driveway. "You are so getting laid tonight."

"Why do you think I'm taking us to my place?" He winked, turning onto the main road. "I want you to be as loud and unrestrained as you want."

My hand dropped into his lap, brushing against the front of his pants and found him already hard.

"You should drive faster."

WE'D BARELY MADE it inside the door when I clawed at his pants. I blamed the Chablis, my body hot as I alternated between stripping him and myself as I giggled against his chest.

"You want to go to the bedroom?" he asked, trying to control my octopus arms as I managed to free him of his pants. "Or not." His eyes widened as I thrust his cock into my mouth.

I groaned, feeling it hit the back of my throat as I hollowed out my cheeks and sucked him hard. His fingers gripped my hair and pulled tight as my hand joined in the rhythm, sliding up and down as I picked up speed.

"Fuck, Claire," he gritted out, his jaw tense as the muscles in his abdomen locked.

I nodded, doing my best to indicate that I indeed wanted to be fucked but was unable to say the words. My mouth was busy, and I wasn't in the mood to stop.

His eyelids lowered, watching me on my knees in front of him, and I saw his total submission. If I'd asked, he'd have given me the deed to his house, my fist around his hard length tightening as the surge of power made me feel invincible.

"You're killing me." He closed his eyes, his gorgeously toned chest rising and falling with each deep breath. "Beautiful, you're going to make me come."

I didn't stop.

Moving my mouth and hand harder and faster, I watched him fight to maintain control. Every single muscle in his body tensed, the need vibrating through him like a tuning fork.

"Jesus, Claire," he bit out with a curse, his eyelids sliding open as he locked his gaze with mine, his hot load spilling down my throat.

I took everything he had, watching as his body shook until he pulled his cock from my mouth with a pop.

"Were you thinking about it all night? Or just on the drive home?" He sunk to his knees in front of me, his hand slipping between my legs.

"Since I came home and we made out in my room," I moaned,

feeling his fingers slick as they slid inside of me.

I'd wanted him then, wanted him to take me on my bed before we'd left my house and the anticipation had only made it worse. By the time we'd made it through the night, my body felt like it was going to explode, needing to be touched by him.

"I thought about this," his thumb circled my clit as he brought his mouth to my breast. "Thought of how much I wanted to taste you." His tongue swirled around my stiff peak, gently closing his teeth around and pulling.

"Oh." It was my turn to close my eyes, losing myself to the sensations as my body relaxed.

"Lay down for me," he whispered, guiding me back as his mouth kept busy. His lips moved to my other breast, sucking and teasing while he fucked me with his fingers.

The carpet gave way underneath me, tickling my body as I opened for him, his tongue swirling its way down my stomach.

"Nick." My back arched as his mouth made contact with my hot center, his tongue giving me a languid lick while his fingers didn't stop.

It didn't matter that it was on the floor, in his living room. The way he was worshiping me with his mouth and hands made me feel like I was lying on a bed of the finest silk sheets, surrounded by a million pillows.

My hands threaded through his hair, grinding my hips as he brought me closer. "Yes, baby. Oh, that feels so good."

I was so close, teetering on the edge as he continued mercilessly with his mouth, pushing in his fingers as I exploded on this hand. My body trembled, waves of pleasure echoing through me as I panted on the floor.

"Don't move," he growled against my thigh, reaching down to his pants and pulling out a condom.

He tore open the pack, sheathing himself in latex before

pushing into me in one hard thrust. My body opened for him, slick and ready, as he drew back and then pushed back.

My hands slid up his chest as he settled between my thighs, his hard cock driving into me as he lifted my leg for leverage. "I loved being in your mouth, but feeling you tight around my cock was where I wanted to be."

I didn't disagree, rocking against him desperately as my body tightened. Chasing the wave of my last orgasm, the sensation inside me built. Higher and higher—tingles radiating from my core and rippling out along my arms and legs.

"Yes!" I moaned, gripping his corded arms and holding on while he plunged into me. Harder and deeper, each drive of his cock sent me closer to oblivion.

"You're so close," he breathed out, maintaining the rhythm while I writhed underneath. "I can feel your pussy squeezing my cock, begging it to come."

White light hit me, my body splintering apart as I came in a rush. He followed right behind, pulsing inside of me as we screamed out, our voices echoing off the walls.

He kissed my shoulder, rolling off me and tucking me in close. "Just so you know, I don't usually fuck on first dates. I'm really hoping you'll still respect me in the morning." His grin was infectious.

"That *wasn't* our first date," I laughed, jabbing him in the ribs. "And technically you didn't take me out, we went to your brother's house."

He reared back in mock shock, covering his mouth with his hand as he whispered. "You mean we had sex *before* our first date? I feel so cheap."

"Our *first* date was breakfast while you were hung over," I reminded him, that morning feeling so long ago.

So much had happened in such a short amount of time. Who knew that ultimately we'd end up together. And not just as a one-night stand, *together*, together. Not even my stories—where I was guaranteed to get the guy—came close to how magical it had been.

His brow furrowed looking slightly concerned. "Wow, I was such a cheap bastard. I'm going to have to do better. You know I'm good for it, I've been told I'm charming."

"You are *so* charming." My arms circled around him, inching even closer. "But I don't need fancy and expensive dates."

"And I don't want to hide you," he warned, a grin creeping along his lips. "You think we can find a compromise? You be seen, as my *girlfriend*, and I'll still buy you shitty breakfasts."

I was so gone.

All he had to do was smile like he was doing now, and I'd have agreed to anything. Add to that he didn't want to hide our relationship? Well, that just lit a fire in my chest that I was positive could burn us both alive.

"I'll go anywhere with you." It was the only answer I could give, meaning every single word with every single one of my breaths.

His brow rose, his smile spelled out the trouble he knew he was capable of. "Oh anywhere, huh? You probably shouldn't have said that, you know I'm going to take that as literal."

I didn't argue, didn't try to put sanctions on the *anywhere* I'd freely agreed to. It was too late to change my mind anyway, the path I was on had already been dictated by my heart.

"You can take that any way you want."

"How about I just take *you* instead? Come on, beautiful, let's go to bed."

CHAPTER #17

"YOU KNOW THIS is fucking ridiculous, right?" Luke sighed, shaking his head as he looked out the windshield. "Though the last time we piled into my car on a mission, you ended up with a hot, successful boyfriend so maybe there's hope for us yet."

"It's not ridiculous, we're being supportive. And if you were interested in a hot, successful boyfriend, then you should stop dating fuck-buddies who are only after a fling," Scully called from the backseat, being more honest than Luke probably would have liked.

He pegged her with a hard stare in the review mirror, the "I'm pregnant," coming soon after as the road passed by in a blur.

Maybe Luke was right; it was ridiculous.

My hands gripped the seatbelt, the uneasy feeling churning in my stomach. "I should cancel this meeting."

"No," they answered in unison, the first time they'd agreed on something since we'd gotten into the car.

Like Nick had suggested, I'd called Jeremy's assistant and set up an appointment. I figured what was the harm, with the probability of him being able to meet me anytime soon remote. Not how it turned out though, with Jeremy having a late afternoon vacancy two days after the phone call which was about two weeks sooner than I'd expected.

There had been no time to prepare, either accepting the appointment and hoping for the best, or turn it down knowing there might not be another chance. Both options terrified me, but I wasn't going to say no. Not when it presented me with the first real chance to open a door I had been knocking on for a very long time.

"You're right, you're right. I can't cancel." My hands wrung in my lap as I tapped my foot impatiently. "It's going to be fine, he probably won't even remember me."

Nick had been ecstatic that I had gotten the meeting so fast, expecting—like I had—it would take a week or two. He'd also offered to come with me for moral support and wait outside until I was done. It was incredibly sweet and also incredibly tempting, but the whole idea was that I did this on my own. If Jeremy saw Nick he would assume that I was a loser who couldn't hack it on my own. Then I'd torture myself by believing the only reason he'd be nice to me was because of Nick.

No, I had to go it alone, which was why I politely thanked him for the offer but told him I'd be fine and promised to call him right after.

But there was no way I wasn't enlisting the help of Scully and Luke, both of them needed to stop me from freaking the hell out.

"Claire, who cares what Jeremy thinks of you? He's just one agent in a sea of agents. You can't spit in this town without hitting one," Luke offered, trying to be reasonable.

Scully nodded in agreement, adding encouragement from the backseat. "Not to mention he mainly represents actors, he probably wouldn't know a decent screenplay if it bit him on the ass."

I knew they were trying to be helpful, and while the man was an arrogant prick, he wasn't incompetent. "He sees *decent* scripts all the time, he didn't get rich and successful by not being good at what he does."

We rolled to a stop in front of Levin Murphy Talent Agency a little before four. Initially I had asked both Scully and Luke to be on standby, knowing I'd need to talk to someone on the ride over. I'd planned to conference call them, hoping the chat would help with the anxiety as I drove myself there.

Then, in a strange coincidence—and one I didn't buy—Luke's afternoon meeting was cancelled, leaving him free for the rest of the day. And in what was an even bigger miracle—again, they weren't fooling anyone—Scully's schedule got changed, also giving her the afternoon off. Such a serendipitous turn of events that no one could have predicted and so obviously orchestrated it was ridiculous. But with the wonderful turn of events it was decided that we—the three of us—went to my meeting together. Luke would drive so I could go over any last-minute notes in the car and Scully would join us because there was no way she wasn't coming for the ride.

And I was so thankful I could have cried.

"We'll go to a coffee shop nearby, text us when you're done. We'll come back and pick you up." Luke left the car idling as he waited for me to get out.

Scully grabbed my shoulder, leaning forward in her seat. "But you can call us if you need backup. We'll storm his offices like a military coup."

"This child is destined to be born in prison." Luke sighed as he shook his head. "She's going to nail it, impress the pants off of him and then we're taking her out to dinner. Claire can pay since she'll be earning more cash than both of us."

My heart squeezed, feeling so incredibly blessed to have the best friends in the whole world who had so much faith in me. I had no idea what I'd do without them. Hopefully, I'd never find out, giving them both a friendly hug before I exited the car.

I stepped out onto the sidewalk, waiting until Luke's Lexus disappeared before pulling out my phone and rereading the message from Nick.

> *I'd wish you good luck, but I know you're not going to need it. You should call me the minute you're done. It will make me feel important and feed into the God complex I'm working on. ;-) Knock them dead, beautiful x*

It hadn't changed from the last three thousand times I'd read it, my eyes misting over when I got to the word beautiful. Unlike a lot of guys, Nick never called me babe, preferring to use my name. *Beautiful* was new, making me grin like an idiot at what was probably an off-the-cuff endearment. But to me it was special, and no one would tell me different.

Gah, I was tragic.

Giving myself a firm talking to, I left my loved-up feelings on the sidewalk and made my way to Jeremy's office. Jessica, his assistant, welcomed me, offering me a seat while I waited.

"Claire Becker?" Jeremy walked out, at exactly four-fifteen, adjusting his jacket as he waited for me to answer.

I stood, fighting the urge to run my palms down the front of my skirt as I held out my hand. "Hi, it's a pleasure to meet you."

He accepted the shake, holding his office door open and he directed me to enter, closing it with a heavy thud behind us.

"Nice to meet you too, glad you could make it." He pointed to the chair in front of his desk, not bothering to wait as he sat down on his. "Nick tells me you're a screenwriter, but this isn't a screenplay."

My butt had barely hit the chair, the lofty stack of documents I hadn't seen in a while dumped on his desk as he tapped it with his finger.

I'd been tossed into the lion's den, any hope I had of easing in with friendly pleasantries was left at reception with his assistant as we got down to business. I swallowed, taking a breath and refusing to show fear.

"It was a story I was hoping to adapt. Sometimes it's easier for me to flesh out the ideas in long-form before I craft them into a workable script."

He seemed surprised, the corner of his mouth lifting the tiniest bit in what I hoped might have been a smile. In any case, I was taking it as encouragement, sitting up straighter as I waited for his response.

"Yeah, well, it definitely needs some work, but I think you've got something solid here. Good ideas, and very marketable. Best bet would be to pitch it to a network."

"Err . . ." *Was he offering to represent me?*

He hadn't said that in so many words, but if he wasn't, then why was he wasting his time talking about where to pitch? And at the risk of looking like a moron, I needed to know for sure. "I'm sorry, but are you interested in acquiring the rights to my story?"

Jeremy leaned back in his chair, the slight curve of his lips spreading into a full-blown grin. "Oh, I see where the humor from the story comes from. You're actually funny." He laughed, tilting his head back in amusement. "That's great, really great."

"Great," I echoed, still no more enlightened than I had been a minute ago when I asked. "But you still haven't said."

He leaned forward, still chuckling as he looked at me. "Yeah, I'm interested. No offense, but there isn't an agent in this town who is going to invite you to their office just to turn you down, so I just assumed you knew."

"Well, I didn't want to presume anything." I tried to remain calm, my heart beating a million miles per second. "All I really knew was that you'd read it and you liked it."

"I do, and I like you." He waved his hand around before stroking his chin. "And I see what Nick sees in you. Pretty, talented, and you seem smart which is always a good thing. Not sure how the two of you dating is going to work out, but that's really none of my business." Delivered with a completely straight face like he'd just run a credit check. "The important thing is that we all make money, right?"

I coughed, trying to clear my throat. "Money?"

While I was out-of-my-mind excited at the prospect of actually *selling* a script, his words made me uneasy. Was it some elaborate plan to see if I was using Nick? Trying to leverage my relationship to get further ahead? Even though I hadn't been the one to suggest it, it could have easily been a test.

"No, it's not only about the money." I leveled him with a stare. "At least not to me."

Jeremy rolled his eyes, not even bothering to hide his irritation as he groaned. "I swear to God these Larssons are like a virus. You've only been with him for a few weeks, right? How the hell do they infect people so fast?"

"I'm sorry, what?" I leaned in closer wondering if I hadn't missed the part of the conversation where what he was saying made sense.

"The it's-not-about-the-money bullshit." He threw his hands up. "All you creative types who want to hold on to your personal integrity. What the hell is up with that? Can't we all just do what we've got to do and be ridiculously rich? What have you got against money?"

I laughed.

Couldn't help it, the noise bubbling up my chest and out of my mouth. "This is *just* about money? Do you remember me at all? You've read my work before and you hated it. Pretty sure you said you'd rather never be able to read again than read another word I'd written."

Psychosis had set in, saying the words out loud just making me laugh harder.

He looked at me like I'd clearly lost my mind and at that point he might have been right, eyeing me up and down. "Of course this is about money, do you know how many of my clients bring their girlfriends, boyfriends, pet Chihuahuas in here looking to get them jobs? This isn't the local outreach center and I'm not a charity. So if you're here—in front of me—it's because I think I can make money. I don't care who you're dating, what steaming dog turd you wrote last time, or if you wear a Howler monkey as a scarf, that's between you and whichever sucker PR firm you hire." He pushed away from his desk, shaking his head as he stood. "What I do is make sure everyone keeps working and we're all getting paid." He spread his arms out wide. "That's it."

While it did reaffirm what an asshole he was, it did make me feel better. Knowing that I had earned my place honestly and not because of anyone pulling strings. And as long as the asshole was honest, then his moral choices were no business of mine. So in that, we had something in common.

Wow.

How awesome had my life gotten?

"Good to know." I bit my lip, trying to stop myself from grinning. "Although I will tell you that it kind of makes you sound like a pimp."

He shrugged as if weighing my observation. "My wardrobe costs more and I get invited to better parties."

"You do dress better." I nodded to his suit that was probably worth more than my car.

"Thanks." He smirked, straightening his tie. "So, can we talk contract terms, or do you want to remind me how much I hated your earlier submissions?"

I didn't hesitate, squaring my shoulders as I looked him in the eye. "I want to be the one who adapts it. It's important that I'm part of the process."

He leaned back, his grin widening. "Oh, so the whole doe-eye,

I'm all about the creativity was just an act, huh? Now we start with the demands?"

"You said you wanted to negotiate contract terms, I'm negotiating." My brow rose, not allowing my gaze to break. "Are we going to do this or not?"

"Sure, let's see what you've got."

"HI," I BREATHED into the phone, unable to contain my smile. "Have any plans for tonight?"

Nick chuckled. "That depends. You going home to change or keep that skirt on? Very hot for teacher, I like it a lot."

My head whipped to the side, knowing he must be somewhere he could see me. "Where are you?"

I felt arms grabbing me around my waist and pulling me against his body. "Right here," he said in my ear, his voice no longer on the phone.

My hand lowered, my phone tossed into my bag as I twisted in his arms. "I thought I told you I was doing this alone."

I didn't even try to sound mad, wrapping my arms around his neck as I gave him a huge hug.

He lowered his head, giving me a kiss while trying to look sheepish. "Have I mentioned how terrible I am at doing what I'm told? We can call my mother and she can verify, I am literally the worst."

"So terrible." I kissed him, freezing the minute our lips touched and taking a step away.

Shit.

While we agreed we were going to take our relationship public, there hadn't been a test drive yet. I was still neck-deep in work, splitting my time between reading and writing. And our big reveal—a party Nick was invited to—wasn't until Saturday.

He pulled away, looking at me with concern. "What's wrong?"

"Do you see any cameras?" I looked around, half expecting to see a zoom lens peeking out through a window like a sniper.

"Who gives a shit if there are?" He shrugged, cozying up closer as his arms went back around to circle me. "Did you want me to spin you around, so they can get you from a better angle?"

He grinned, thoroughly amused by my head bouncing around like a meerkat.

"I'd hoped the first paparazzi photo of me would be of my face, and not of your hands on my ass." My head tipped to the side, drawing attention to his hands that were very much on my ass.

"I hate it when they do that." He squeezed my ass and grinned. "Maybe I should do this instead."

I was no longer worried about my ass, his mouth crushing mine in a kiss that left no doubt as to what we were to each other. My lips parted, letting him stroke my tongue with his as his hands pulled me in closer. Man, if anyone was taking photos I hoped I got copies.

My fingers threaded through his hair, making out with him on the street like a pair of deviants as I forgot what my protest had been about in the first place.

"I need to call Luke and Scully," I mumbled against his lips trying to catch my breath.

He bit his lip, shaking his head trying to look coy. "I relieved them of their duty a few minutes ago. I saw them at the coffee shop across the road and told them I'd bring you home. But we're going to *need* to actually go back to your house. Only way we could convince Scully to go was if I promised we'd go straight there."

"Pretty presumptuous aren't you? Kissing me on the street, dismissing my ride home. What if I didn't want to go with you?"

He gave me a nonchalant shrug. "Then I guess I'd have to eat the cupcakes all on my own. Baked goods are only for passengers."

"You have cupcakes!" I looked around spying his silver coupe parked against the curb slightly up the road.

"Well, I wasn't going to show up with a bunch of flowers, how predictable would that be?" His arm snaked around my waist, his words hot in my ear. "Plus, with cupcakes, I get to lick the frosting off your lips, so I was really only thinking of myself. It's best you know upfront how selfish I can be."

He wasn't the only selfish one, I was pretty greedy myself and I had no other intention than getting into his car with or without the cupcakes.

"I like you selfish, should we get into your car or should we flirt a little more on the street?"

"Ooooooo, tough choice." He looked as if he was giving it some serious thought. "Why don't you get into my car and we can flirt in there. Then you can also tell me how the meeting went since I texted Jessica half an hour ago and she refused to answer me. You'd think with my brother dating her she'd have more loyalty to the family. Poor Dave, I'm going to have to insist they break up."

I laughed, tugging on his arm as we headed toward the car. "Okay, let's get you home before you can do any more damage."

With more PDA than I was usually comfortable with, we walked to his car and hopped in. It was amazing how easy he made me forget, the idea that someone might have been watching us the furthest thing from my mind as he started the car and drove away.

I told him about Jeremy and his plans to pitch it to a network. He was drawing up a contract for me to sign that I would hopefully have by the end of the week. Of course, that meant I also had to find a lawyer, there was no way I was signing anything without someone else going through it. The whole thing was surreal and slightly overwhelming, ironically the same way my life had become.

"I have a lawyer I can recommend," Nick suggested, his hand linked in mine as he drove.

He didn't need to tell me who he had in mind.

There were five Larsson boys in his family, three actors, Eric, Dave and of course Nick—all of which I had met—and two in law, both of which I hadn't. One was a certified badass who apparently made Jeremy look like a nice guy—Nick's words not mine—and the youngest still in law school.

"Hmm." I tapped on my lip. "Are you suggesting your brother, Roman? Thanks, but I think I've had my fill for intimidation for one week."

He barked out a laugh. "Roman isn't intimidating, he's an arrogant pain in the ass, but he is a really good lawyer. Don't tell him I said that, I'll deny it."

As much as I would love to use Nick's pain in the ass—I still bet he was intimidating—albeit awesome lawyer brother, I was already neck-deep in gratitude. There was also part of me that wanted to do it on my own, something I'd been doing for a long time, and didn't want to feel like a damsel in distress.

"Thanks, but a friend of Luke's is a lawyer. I used him once before so it's probably easier if I just give him a call."

If he was offended, he didn't show it, shrugging it off as we arrived at my house. "But even though I'm not retaining his services, I'd still like to meet your brother though, and the rest of your family sometime." Assuming they wanted to meet me. God, I hoped they liked me. Maybe we should hold off a little longer, introduce him to my family first. Yeah, that was a much better option. "And maybe we can go see mine in Colorado? My mom is going to come visit when Scully has her baby, so if we haven't had a chance before then, at least I can prove I'm not an orphan."

His thumb brushed along my jaw as his eyes filled with sincerity. "I would love to go with you to Colorado to meet your family. We should make time before I start filming again."

Oh. God.

I think I loved him.

Not falling, but certifiably and genuinely in love with him. Him.

Nick, the guy I'd met five years ago but had finally gotten a chance to know.

Not a character from a television show, not a fantasy I'd built up in my head. But *the man*—perfectly full formed, with nothing I'd want to change.

"Nick, I—"

I hadn't had the chance to finish the thought or the sentence when my front door opened and Scully came waddling down the stairs. She had some serious speed for someone who was growing a life form, prompting Nick and I to quickly get out of the car.

"Slow down, you're going to trip and fall." I managed to grab her around the arm.

Nick was on the other side, making sure she stayed upright. "Scully, I'm afraid I have to agree with Claire on this. I don't think running down the stairs is a wise choice."

"You were supposed to bring her right home." She pointed accusingly at Nick. "You are on my shit list."

"Babe, it was peak hour traffic in Los Angeles, we got here as soon as we could," I tried to explain, the drive taking a little longer than expected. Not that I had noticed, just being with Nick and talking making it seem like the minutes had flown by.

She waved her hands animatedly. "Psh, I don't care about reasons, tell me what happened."

"Fine, but let's go inside and talk like civilized people." I gestured toward the door.

"Okay, fine," she agreed, glaring at Nick like he was somehow responsible.

As Scully slowly climbed the stairs back up to the front door, he laughed leaning into me. "Something tells me this conversation is going to be a while. She looks mad."

He was right, but however long and drawn out Scully's interrogation was going to be, it was still easier than deciding whether or not to tell Nick that I was in love with him.

I smiled back, slipping my arm through his, hugging his body. "It's okay, there are worse things in the world."

Like him not loving me back.

"Either way, I'm going to get the cupcakes from the back seat." He kissed the top of my head. "Today was huge, and we needed to celebrate."

The day had been huge in more ways than one.

CHAPTER #18

EVERY SINGLE TIME I went to say something, I chickened out.

It wasn't the right time.

And why did it need to be said anyway, it wasn't like *not* saying it would end our relationship. It wasn't going to fall apart like *Whoville* if I didn't make enough noise. Everything was great, and I wanted to keep it like that.

Jeremy had given me a contract I could barely understand, so I gave it to Luke's friend, Tyler. He practiced corporate law, spending more time in a boardroom than a courtroom, but could navigate the legalese like Jacques Cousteau. He wanted some of the verbiage tweaked, which the Levin Murphy lawyers readily accepted, so it was conceivable that very soon I could be holding an option for my screenplay.

Okay, so maybe *soon* was optimistic, and with even a successful option there was no guarantee anything would see the light of day anyway. But I was happy, and happy people didn't see things as impossible. Instead they saw endless possibilities, my career only being one part of it.

The screenplay I'd started writing the first night in Nick's house had also been finished. I hadn't broached the subject of selling it yet, wanting to fine-tune it before anyone read it. But even in its rough first-draft form, it was probably the strongest piece of work I'd ever written.

"That dress looks terrible." Scully sat on the edge of my bed, thankfully not critiquing my wardrobe choice for the evening as she spoke on the phone. "The episode calls for a gown for a gala, she isn't going to wear something she picked up at JC Penny."

Unlike whatever dress Scully was talking about, mine had been purchased from a boutique on Beverly. Not a single department store in sight.

"You people are color blind, it isn't candy apple red, it's vermillion. And it doesn't change that it looks like shit." Scully huffed into the phone. "Okay, fine, then find someone else if you know better."

She tossed the phone onto my bed, her body collapsing with it and what looked like utter defeat.

"Everything all right?"

"No." Her body curled up into a ball as a sob escaped her lips. "I'm pretty sure I just quit my job."

Scully had been determined to work until the day she went into labor. Luke and I had joked that the baby was probably going to be born in a trailer in a studio back lot because she hadn't shown any signs of slowing down.

"I wasn't ready to go," she sobbed into her pillow. "I'm not ready."

And if I thought her tears were for the job she may or may not have resigned from, then I wasn't a very good friend.

"Babe, it's going to be fine." I rubbed her back in tight circles. It was one of the few things I'd picked up from the birthing class before we made our hasty exit, never to return again. "They didn't deserve you, and you should have told them to take a hike months ago."

The network had been passing her around like a whore at a

gangbang, knowing at some point she would need to leave and not wanting her committed to any one show. I highly doubted she would miss erratic schedules and rotating crews. What she was going to miss—and what she wasn't ready for—was the perceived loss of herself.

Something she'd worked hard for—her career—was going to have to take a backseat. And while there wasn't a doubt in my mind she would love that baby with every ounce of her being, part of her was going to mourn the loss of her old life.

"You look so beautiful, Claire." She wiped her tear-stained cheeks, snuffling as she turned her head to get a better look. "You're going to have the best time tonight."

Her hiccupped words tugged at my heart, and I felt like the biggest piece of shit alive. I'd been so preoccupied with Nick and the new job that I'd checked out a little with her. And she needed me more than ever.

There was a knock at the door before it opened, a well-dressed Nick filling the space. Head-to-toe black in tailored mastery, he oozed sexiness and style with an ease of unpretentious flare.

No wonder I'd been distracted.

He looked like a God.

But I wouldn't let that be an excuse—not any more.

The debut appearance of Niclaire—our couple name as I'd imagined it—was going to have to be postponed, the apology ready in my throat when he stepped into the room and went straight to Scully.

"Hey, Scully." He knelt down beside her on the bed. "You need more time?"

"No, it's fine." She blew out a breath. "She's all yours, have a great night."

Nick looked confused, furrowing his brow before looking between us. "You're ditching us? Wow, you know I've won an

Emmy, right? You can at least pretend to be impressed. I'm hurt."
He palmed his chest with so much drama I wasn't sure he wasn't
gunning for his next one.

She laughed, rolling her eyes as she shuffled to sit up. "You
know your celebrity doesn't work on me, what are you even talking
about?"

She wasn't the only one confused, the what-the-what responsible for my lack of participation in the conversation.

"I forgot, *Dave* is your favorite." His lip curled into a sneer at
the mention of his brother, adding a shake of his head. "If you
two conspirators had your way, *he* would have usurped my next
staring role. Nice try sliding it to him, instead of me. Lucky for
you, I'm forgiving."

If his *explanation* had been supposed to enlighten us, then I
hadn't followed. It was only supposed to be the two of us going
out, but I did love that he was attempting to make Scully laugh.
He might not get to go out with me tonight, but he was getting
a blowjob later.

"You're forgiving me?" Scully scoffed in disbelief.

"Well, okay, since you asked so nicely. But you'll need to get
changed and put on something decent. I still have a reputation to
uphold and some people *are* impressed by my celebrity."

"Changed for what?" Scully echoed my thoughts.

"Well, you didn't think Claire and I were going to go out in
the wild without an entourage did you? I need people—lots of
them—around me at all times so I feel important." His lips spread
into a grin.

My heart burst.

Shattered into pieces, overwhelmed by his consideration and
kindness and it was more than I could take.

I wanted to leap off the bed, into his arms and tell him I loved
him, only stopping the words just before they came out.

I didn't want it to be a reaction; to have him think the feeling was out of gratitude. I was grateful, but I loved him for so much more than that.

"What do you think, Scully?" I squeezed her hand. "You want to come out with us and help me make Nick look good?"

She glanced at Nick, her eyes filling with tears she tried to blink away. "Are you sure? I don't want to be the third wheel."

"I absolutely want you to come, and to be honest you kind of owe me. It would round out the apology and prove that you are indeed genuinely sorry."

I was going to cry.

So incredibly touched and grateful that I wanted to throw myself at him and cover him with kisses.

"Well, I *do* want you to accept my apology." Scully tipped her head to the side as if considering it. "So, I guess, I am sort of obligated to come."

He shrugged. "I'm not too proud to take obligation. Is that a yes?"

"Yes!" Scully lifted her hands in the air in celebration.

"Well, go get ready then. Tell Luke I expect him to come too, he was complicit and therefore guilty as well and needs to make amends. But he's not allowed to dress better than me," Nick warned, keeping a straight face the entire time.

Luke appeared at the doorway at the mention of his name. "What are we doing?"

"Heading out." Scully tugged at his arm. "Come help me find something to wear and I'll tell you all about it."

Luke didn't argue even though I knew he already had plans. He—like Nick—decided to put the need of a friend in front of his own.

He looked over at me, a knowing glance passing between us, and then tapped Scully's arm. "Just let me make a phone call and we'll do whatever you want." Luke tipped his chin to Nick and then let Scully lead him away.

"You are the most wonderful man alive." I wrapped my arms around him and kissed him.

Nick's body accepted my weight, holding me close as he smiled against my lips. "Because I'm arrogant? Or because I won an *Emmy*? Let's just say all of the above and cover all our bases."

I didn't answer him, preferring to give my response via the appreciation shown by my lips. He seemed to find this acceptable, shutting my bedroom door shut with his foot and pushing me up against the wall.

My hands ran along the front of his shirt, his firm muscles flexing under my touch as we deepened the kiss. His eyes were hungry, loaded with the promise of what he wanted to do but the heart that beat underneath my hands was full of something else.

"Thank you," I whispered against his lips. "Inviting Scully means a lot to me."

"She's a friend, and we take care of our friends, right?" He brushed the hair off from my face.

I nodded, the emotion in my throat as I looked up at him. "Yeah, we sure do."

LIT—THE CLUB WE were at—was *not* aptly named. It should have been called *muted light* or *almost darkness*, our eyes requiring a few minutes to adjust to the dim interior lighting.

There had been a few photographers at the front asking Nick who I was, but he just put his arm around me and led me inside. The flashes in my face were disconcerting, but I was more worried about what words they were going to write to accompany the photo. Ready or not it was all in the open now, and as nervous as I'd been, I couldn't make myself regret people knowing we were together.

"See, it wasn't so bad." Nick had bought the group a round of drinks, joining us as we sat on a red leather banquette.

Scully accepted her orange juice, grinning as she relaxed into her seat. "It's probably because you're not *that* famous. I mean, if Eric were here, or even Dave, we'd have to call the LAPD just to clear a path to the door."

I loved that the little game she was playing with Nick distracted her from the anxiety she had been feeling at home. Tonight, she was given a small reprieve and Nick would happily play along with her, even at the expense of making fun of himself.

"I think you're better looking than Dave," Luke deadpanned, taking a swig of his beer.

"Well thank you, Luke." Nick clinked his beer with his new buddy, smirking at me and Scully. "You have an excellent eye."

Luke nodded, adding with a smile. "Eric, well, he has that blond, Viking thing going for him so that's tough to go up against."

"Couldn't have just left it there? I take back my statement about your taste." Nick laughed, turning his attention to me and kissing my neck.

I could feel eyes on us, people looking, possibly some discreetly using their phones to take a photo. But I didn't let it bother me. I was too busy being loved up, openly kissing a man that I'd dreamed about for years to care what anyone thought.

"Want to dance?" He nodded to the dance floor. Or at least where it would have been if it weren't packed with gyrating hot bodies.

I slid off the banquette, standing and knotting my fingers with his as I gave him a little tug. "Sure, I did offer to go anywhere with you. The dance floor seems like I got out of it pretty easy."

"That's right, you did say anywhere." He grinned as he joined me on his feet. "I really need to take better advantage of this open-ended clause."

We left Scully and Luke to enjoy their drinks as he let me lead him to the dance floor. He wasn't more than half a step behind, his hand on the small of my back as we weaved through the sea of people.

He brought his mouth to my ear, his voice competing with the music. "Have I told you how beautiful you look tonight?"

"A couple of times, but I don't mind hearing it again. You look pretty delicious yourself." I licked my lips, running my hands down his strong arms.

"Easy there, Claire." He pulled me against his hard body, holding me still with his hands on my hips. "Not a lie, I will take you right here and not give a shit who's watching."

"Oh really?" I grinded against him. "Well that would make an interesting story."

His hand moved up my spine and wrapped around the base of my neck. "I love how you think I'm joking." He kissed me hard.

Our bodies crashed against each other in a heated mess, the music thumped in the background while flashing lights washed over us in intermittent waves. Deeper he pulled me into the crowd so we were caged in. Arms and legs moved either side of us in time to the music, but in the sea of madness it felt like we were alone. No one could see what he was doing with his hands, his fingers skating against the hem of my dress and inching their way up.

As they climbed higher, teasing at the edge of my underwear, I held his gaze daring him to keep going. I wasn't some delicate little wallflower whose reputation needed to be saved, and I wanted to be touched.

By him.

Right then.

His eyes scanned my body like he was reading sacred texts, moving his finger deeper underneath the scant fabric and rubbing against my naked skin. Desperately wanting him to push inside, I moved against his hand as I circled my hips. He continued to tease me, brushing his finger and thumb against my clit as I felt myself get wetter. He felt it too, smiling in satisfaction as his strokes got a little faster.

My breasts tingled inside my dress, begging for his mouth or his hand but got neither as I rubbed myself against his chest. The friction made my nipples pebble, instantly amplifying what was happening between my legs.

It didn't matter we were out in public surrounded by people, I wanted to tear off my clothes and ride his hand, and make him finish by sucking his cock.

"Do it," I begged, grazing my teeth against his neck, needing more than what he was giving me.

He shook his head, seeming to enjoy watching me beg as he smirked. "Uh-uh, not yet."

Faster he moved his hand, my body so hot and slick it ached. He circled, teasing my entrance with his fingertips, giving me the tiniest bit before pulling them back.

"Please," I panted, legs starting to shake. "Please do it."

He didn't.

Instead he continued his slow and delicious torture like a sadist, making me feel like I was caught between heaven and hell until I thought I would go insane.

And then, when *he* was good and ready, he pushed inside.

It was like a bomb had detonated.

My body crumbled, his arm around my waist holding me up as I came hard on his hand. Waves of pleasure ripped through me as I pulsed against his fingers, barely able to keep my legs from going out under me.

"Yes," I cried out, my voice eaten up by the noise around us as he steadied me, keeping his hand right where it was until the last of the tremors were done.

"I did try and warn you." He slowly slid his fingers out while his other hand stayed locked on my hip. "And I don't make idle threats."

I giggled against his chest as my body continued to tingle. "If you were trying to teach me a lesson, you failed miserably."

"You think?" He tilted his head to the side, a sly smile playing on his lips as he lifted the fingers that had been inside of me closer to his mouth. "Or do you think every time you see this hand and my mouth tonight you're going to think about what I just did to you." His lips closed around his fingers and sucked them clean.

His head nodded, pulling his fingers out as he brought his mouth closer to my ear. "Yeah, I'm going to enjoy watching you, knowing you feel the heat between your legs and imagining me there."

I had no comeback, with the closest thing to a reply I was able to manage being a noise that sounded more like a wounded animal than a human. I couldn't even be mad, in awe the man had given me one of the best orgasms of my life and we hadn't even been having sex.

He kissed me again, my body melded to his as he guided us off the dance floor. "Want to go to the bathroom and freshen up?" He beamed with pride.

"Yes, but expect retribution. Lots of dark corners around here." I gave him a grin over my shoulder and pushed opened the bathroom door.

I heard his laugh before it closed, making my cheeks heat. He was a drug, and I was addicted, and there wasn't a thing I wanted to do to change that.

Still dizzy from the buzz, I quickly used the facilities and washed my hands. I didn't even bother looking in the mirror, not caring how I looked when I stepped outside.

"Hey." Nick kissed my neck, his hand gravitating to its usual home on my hip. "Let's go back and see how Luke and Scully are doing. We'll look for dark corners along the way."

My body leaned back into him, enjoying his touch and remembering what he'd done only minutes before. "Sounds like a great plan."

Like two lovesick teenagers, we walked back to where we'd left our friends. We were grinning like idiots, probably tipping off everyone who saw us as to what we'd done with our time away.

Scully was going to have a field day.

Or maybe not.

Instead of a smug best friend, a pale and worried one was sitting in her place. Luke was holding her hand and not looking much better.

"What's wrong?" I asked, racing to her side. "Is it the baby?"

Her eyes widened as she squeezed my fingers. "I don't know, I don't know what's going on, but I feel really weird."

Trying not to panic—fine, I was panicking—I strained to remember everything I'd read in that stupid baby book. Wasn't it too soon for labor? "Okay, are you having a contraction?" I asked, rubbing her back like Pru had instructed.

"I don't know. I don't know what the hell they're supposed to feel like," Scully bit back almost taking my hand with her as her eyes filled with fear. "And stop touching me, it's making it worse."

Yeah fuck you, Pru, and your show them love and support.

"Let's head to hospital just in case," I suggested, making sure the only thing I held was her hand. She seemed to be okay with that, so until told otherwise that was the extent of my *comforting touching.*

"Oh my God!" Scully let out a scream that was heard even over the music, the fear in her eyes replaced by full-blown terror.

If she hadn't been having them before, I was pretty sure she was having a contraction now.

Her face turned red as she held her breath, my hands grabbing hers as I calmly—okay, it wasn't calm—told her to, "Breathe, Scully."

So maybe Pru wasn't *totally* full of shit.

Good to know.

Luke and Nick went either side of her, supporting her weight as she tried to stand. She swayed, the seconds feeling more like hours as I waited for it to pass.

"Fuck that hurt." She rubbed her belly, slowly straightening. "Now get me the hell out of here before this poor kid is born in a club."

CHAPTER #19

WE'D TAKEN TWO cars to Lit—Scully had ridden with Luke and his Lexus, and I had gone with Nick and his Mercedes. But that configuration wasn't going to work again.

With Scully refusing to let my hand go, and Nick insisting his car was faster, the three of us jumped into the Mercedes, bound for the hospital while Luke followed behind.

The drive was tense. Nick blew through the speed limit while I tried to make sure Scully didn't hyperventilate in the backseat. I might have seemed calm, but I didn't take a full breath until Scully had been admitted.

Luke gave a hug first to Scully and then to me, tipping his head to the door. "I'll be in the waiting room. If you need anything, I'll be right here."

"I'll be there too." Nick gave Scully a smile before putting his arm around me. "Let me know if there is anything I can do."

I nodded not really having the ability to think straight as the nurse closed the door behind them.

"Okay, sweetie, we're just going to have a look." The nurse talked Scully through as she did an internal exam, her voice calming and reassuring as she asked questions.

"I'm too early, right? We need to wait longer." Scully shook her head, gripping her belly like she had the ability to stop it.

The nurse smiled, writing notes on her chart. "Thirty-two weeks isn't ideal but if this little one wants to come out, we'll be ready. Best thing you can do is try and relax, and let us see what's going on."

How was that woman so calm? My best friend was about to have a baby early and we hadn't even packed a hospital bag yet. I hoped that when Scully eventually asked for drugs, she could get some extra for the help. It was going to take a lot more than kind words for me to be able to relax.

There were more questions, more exams and a couple more contractions, Scully crushing my hand through every single one until we finally got to see a doctor.

"We're looking good, Scully." He snapped off his latex glove. "No sign of fetal distress and haven't dilated too much yet which means we have a chance of trying to slow you down. We're going to give you some meds to attempt to slow the contractions and also give you a corticosteroid to help the little one's lungs in case we go early." He turned to the nurse, giving her instructions as she adjusted Scully's IV.

"And that will make it stop?" I asked, hopeful we could keep the little guy in there a little longer.

He gave us a polite smile. "Hard to say. Sometimes we can slow it down by hours, sometimes days. In other cases, it makes no difference. But even if we need to deliver, we've got an outstanding NICU and an amazing team ready to spring into action."

Scully thanked him, putting on her best brave face as he walked out the door. "I should call my parents. My mom is going to freak the hell out, you know she isn't great in a crisis."

She wasn't wrong there. While her parents were great, loving their only child beyond measure, they were also the most high-strung people on the planet. Which was the reason why *I* was her birth partner and not her mother.

"Scully, you don't have to do anything you don't want to do. We can hold off calling them if you want, the main thing is keeping you calm." Something we weren't going to be able to do if her parents were around.

"Maybe we'll wait then?" She looked at me, almost as if seeking permission.

"We can wait, there's plenty of time." I glanced at the clock and saw it was almost midnight. "I'm going to go out and send the guys home. Will you be okay by yourself for a few minutes?"

She nodded, and after reassuring her I wouldn't be far, I slipped out of her room.

"How is she?" Luke and Nick both asked, standing the minute I walked into the waiting room.

I gave Luke a quick hug before settling into Nick's arms. "Pretending to be brave but freaking the hell out."

"And you?" Nick asked as he kissed the top of my head.

I laughed. "Pretending to be brave but freaking the hell out."

We moved back to the chairs, sitting down while I brought them up to speed. With no real news, there was no reason for them to stay. I, on the other hand, wouldn't be leaving.

"Yeah, I'm staying too," Luke insisted, folding his arms across his chest.

Nick's grip around me tightened. "I'm here as well."

"It could be days, you can't camp out here indefinitely." Not sure when I became the voice of reason, but whether I wanted the job or not, I'd been tasked with it.

"Fine, we'll take shifts then." Nick didn't leave any room for debate.

Too tired to argue and knowing it wouldn't do me any good anyway, I gave them both a gentle shrug. "Well, can someone go get me something else to wear?" I looked down at my fancy dress and heels, not really hospital material. "Maybe pick up some things for Scully?"

"Make me a list," Luke offered. "I'll go to the house, get whatever you need and then stay here tonight. Nick can take over later in the morning."

"And I'll wait with you until Luke gets back, just in case you guys need anything in the meantime," Nick added, the plan as good as set in stone.

I mumbled an okay, knowing it wouldn't matter if I didn't agree anyway and said a goodbye to Luke with a promise I'd text him a list.

"Come here." Nick opened his arms, and I collapsed into them, loving the feel of his arms around me.

"I love you."

I'd mumbled it into his chest, a halfhearted effort to conceal what I was still too nervous to say. Not because I wasn't sure that was how I felt, but because I was positive the timing wasn't great. But I'd put it off for as long as my heart would let me, my mouth finally giving into the peer pressure.

My attempt to fly under the radar sucked, with the minute the words had left my mouth, Nick pulling me away from his chest— where I was perfectly happy to stay—and looking down at me.

"Did you just tell me that you love me?"

Was it too late to change it to something else? Pretend I said, "I love shoes" or "I love blue." It was the color of the dress I was wearing; conceivable it would be something that I love.

"Yes," I answered, my mouth and heart deciding to be on the same team.

His fingers curled around my chin, lifting my head and forcing me to look him in the eyes. "Do you want to say it so I can hear it this time? Kind of jealous my pecs got all the action." His lips spread into a grin.

Man, that smile did it to me every single time.

It was a shot right between the eyes, blinding me and making me stupid all at once.

"Well, I think you heard it pretty good the first time, and I quite liked saying it to your pecs. Maybe they're the real ones that I love."

I was such a liar.

He knew it too, shooting down my bullshit with another one of his blinding smiles. "That would be a shame since *I'm* very much in love with *you*."

Whoa.

What?

"Say it again."

Unlike me, he hadn't mumbled, saying the words with conviction as he looked at me without flinching. But even though I'd heard him clearly the first time, I needed him to say it again.

"I love you." He said it again without hesitation, his lips curling on the last word.

"I love you too." It came out so fast that I was positive he was going to ask me to repeat it.

"I know, my pecs told me." He laughed, leaning in while he stage-whispered. "Don't trust the bastards, they're only out for their own interests."

It was such a relief, the weight lifting off my shoulders in finally admitting how I felt. And had we not been in a hospital, with my best friend in preterm labor, it might have been perfect. But the reason I'd been unable to stop myself from saying it was *because* he was here.

Right beside me, even though things weren't perfect.

"I should go." I cringed, knowing it was probably the least romantic thing I could have said.

Hey there, I love you, and now I have to go, and to think I wrote for a living. I really could have found some better words.

He brushed his mouth against mine. "I know, go back and be with Scully and don't forget to let Luke know what you need. I'll come get you when he gets back."

If I could have split myself in two, I'd have happily done it. Wanting to stay right there in that room and go be with Scully. But that wasn't a choice, which meant I had to go.

"I love you." I wanted to say it a million more times before I left. I figured now I had broken the seal, it made sense to get more mileage.

"You need to go." He gave me another kiss, this time deeper, his tongue and mouth saying everything that he wasn't.

That he wished we had more time, but he loved me anyway.

I laughed, this time it was me who pulled back. "Okay, we both suck at this game. I'll see you soon."

This time I meant it, turning around and walking out the door.

And sure, I looked back over my shoulder, giving him a smile before I disappeared around the corner. I didn't even care how cheesy it seemed.

"You're back." Scully yawned, her eyes struggling to stay open.

"We gave her a sedative as well, figured if she can get some sleep it would be good for everyone." The nurse gave me a warm smile, checking the printout on the fetal monitor attached to Scully's belly. "You've got a strong one in there." She nodded, approving of the peaks and valleys that snaked on the page. "Just like his or her momma."

Scully yawned again, this time her eyes losing their battling and closing. "Thank you," she mumbled, resting her head against the pillow. Her breathing slowed as she seemed to relax.

The nurse went to the chart and added some notes, looking at me as I continued to stand.

"Why don't you take a seat in the recliner? See if you can't get some sleep too while she's resting."

I didn't think sleep was even a possibility even though I was exhausted, but I loved the idea of getting off my feet.

"Thanks."

I waited until she left the room and then pushed the recliner as close to the hospital bed as I could get it. It wasn't easy—the thing weighed a ton—but once I had positioned exactly how I wanted it, I let myself fall into its lofty cushions. It was actually really comfortable; maybe sleep wasn't as impossible as I'd thought.

Scully was either asleep or very close to it. The lines on her face smoothed with each steady breath, the swishing noise from the fetal monitor becoming louder in the silence.

I leaned closer to her belly, using the opportunity to have a heart-to-heart with my little niece or nephew—Scully had never wanted to find out—and make sure they knew what was going on.

"Hey, you haven't met me yet, but I'm your Aunt Claire." I glanced up at Scully, looking for any movement. She hadn't even blinked since she closed her eyes so I figured it was safe to continue.

"Okay, so your mom is taking a nap, which is good, so we can chat just the two of us. Anyway, so I know you're in a hurry to come meet us all, and trust me we can't wait to meet you too. But if you can, just try and hold out a little while longer. We need you big and strong, so you can play that drum kit I'm going to buy you on your eighth birthday. Just act surprised when you get it." I laughed. I was totally going to buy it too.

"So try and hang out another few days or even a week, and when you're ready you'll get to see everyone. I promise you, you are going to have the best life." That was probably one of the easiest promises I was ever going to make, my eyes tearing up a little knowing how much love he or she had waiting for them on the other side.

"Okay, why don't we all try and get some sleep, and I'll check back on you in the morning?" I wiped away a stray tear and took a deep breath. "Sound like a plan? Awesome. Oh, and by the way." I paused, taking another look at Scully and making sure she was still asleep before I continued. "I told Nick that I loved him, and he said he loved me back. But don't tell your mom, she'll be planning our wedding and gunning for a playmate for you."

Scully giggled, a sleepy eyelid sliding open. "You told him?"

"You know once this baby is born your get out of jail free card is gone." I rolled my eyes, only mildly annoyed with her. I really should have known better.

She leaned down cupping her stomach and smiled. "All the more reason to stay in there little one, we need to find out more of Aunt Claire's secrets."

I shook my head, giving her a stern look. "You should be resting."

"If I close my eyes will you tell me everything?" She yawned, sliding her eyes closed.

I took a deep breath, slowly blowing it out. "I'm in love with him, Scully. Not like infatuation, I'm talking the real deal."

He was so much more than I could have imagined, the connection deeper than I thought. It wasn't only about how he made me feel, but how uncomplicated it all was. In the mess that had always cluttered my life, he was a spot of calm. And I loved that he wanted nothing from me other than me.

No strings attached.

Just me.

Her eyes stayed closed as she tried to smile. "Claire, I'm so happy for you. And I'm happy for him too because let's face it, he is getting one hell of a woman out of this deal."

"You're only saying that because you're my friend." I pointed out the obvious, me feeling like I was getting a whole lot more out of it than he was.

"No, not because I'm your friend." Her eyelids rose slowly as she focused on me. "But because here you are holding *my* hand when you just told the man of your dreams you loved him."

I squeezed her hand, the choice one I would make every time. "You need me, of course I'm here. I'd never leave you when you need me."

"And that's why *he* is the lucky one. Because he'll have that too." Her voice got wavy as she cleared her throat. "But if he ever hurts you, Luke and I will probably kill him."

I laughed, shaking my head. "Just make sure you don't get caught, okay."

"Please," Scully scoffed. "We're like professionals now."

Not sure I agreed that she had the necessary skillset to avoid prosecution, but what I didn't have any doubt of was how much she'd meant what she said.

Not killing Nick, or at least I hoped not.

But that she had my back.

Just like I had hers.

And Luke's.

And now Nick's.

God, I hoped he had mine too.

"Get some sleep, Scully." I swallowed, fatigue overcame me as I laid against the recliner. "We've still got a long way to go."

And that was true for both of us.

CHAPTER #20

SEBASTIAN DYLAN SOUTHERLAND was born at thirty-seven weeks with a scream that rivaled a hurricane.

He'd held out, just liked I'd asked him to, for another five weeks.

And I'd never cried as much as when I saw his perfect little face nestled in the arms of his momma.

Scully had been an absolute warrior, not complaining once about being stuck in a bed for over a month, and delivering her son with the strength that would make Thor jealous. She didn't even flinch when her well-meaning—but slightly crazy—mother demanded she call the baby daddy. Instead she stayed strong, reminding her mom that she hadn't moved, changed her number and it had been the deadbeat's *choice* not to be involved. She wouldn't stop him from seeing his son if he wanted, but she'd be damned if she was going to beg him. She'd rather take her placenta and serve it as hors d'oeuvres before she cut that man some slack. And there wasn't a day where I wasn't still in awe, feeling beyond lucky that I got to be a part of it.

And life—life was as perfect as that little boy.

Don't get me wrong, those five weeks in between hadn't

been a picnic. I'd spent so much time in yoga pants, missing meals, working with a laptop on my knees that I almost thought I'd time travelled back to college.

Adding to the chaos, the press had dug up every single horrible photo of me that had ever existed. It seemed just a few photogs were enough to cause a frenzy with news of our relationship causing a stir. Predictably they mentioned how plain I'd been, how surprised he'd shacked up with someone so "ordinary." Had I not had the worry of Scully and Sebastian to distract me, it might have really hurt. I still didn't feel great about the things that were said, but I was currently too busy to give it the attention.

And Nick had been wonderful.

It wasn't every day that you got thrown headfirst into a crisis courtesy of your brand-new girlfriend. He had no problem telling the press he was blissfully happy, and they needed to back the hell off. And whenever I mentioned some stupid article I'd seen, accompanied with another unflattering photo of me running to the store for diapers with unwashed hair and yesterday's clothes, he'd shut me down and tell me how beautiful I was and how much he loved me.

It couldn't have been easy, feeling like he constantly had to defend his new relationship. Not to mention that the closest he'd gotten to sex in almost a month was some fast and furious make out sessions while I was doing the laundry and a cheeky hand job in the bathroom while Scully slept a few feet away. Yes, it probably wasn't my proudest moment, but a girl had to do what a girl had to do.

Many men would have cut their losses and pulled the ejection handle, possibly with a *"call me when things go back to normal"* parting gift. But he didn't. He not only stayed at the poker table, playing the hand I'd dealt him, but he doubled down. He brought us hot dinners, ran errands, made calls, and helped Luke build the crib all without one word of complaint. No eye rolls, no passive aggressive remarks and no pressure at all, telling me that he loved me and everything was fine.

Clearly he was auditioning for sainthood.

He might not be the first Saint Nick, but he would definitely be the sexiest.

"Are you going out?" Scully had laid down Sebastian for a nap, appearing in my doorway in a fluffy pink bathrobe and ready for bed despite it only being seven p.m.

I nodded, adding the last lashings of mascara to my eyes as I turned around. "I feel like it's our first date again. Luke is staying home though just in case you need help."

"I don't need a sitter you know." She rolled her eyes, popping her hip to the side. "Besides, my plans include getting as much sleep as I can between feeds, so I'd be shitty company even if you were home."

"Well, as exciting as a nap sounds." She wasn't the only one who'd been sleep deprived. "I'm spending the night at Nick's." My head tipped to the overnight bag at my feet.

Ever since Scully had returned from the hospital, Luke and I had been home making sure one or both of us was around to help. And while Nick had spent a couple of nights tucked up beside me, most of the time—okay, all of it—I was so tired that we just fell asleep. In fact, I was pretty sure he'd forgotten what it was like to have sex with me, and probably had lost interest after seeing me in the same worn Tee for the third day in a row.

"Bring condoms," Scully warned, watching as I collected my purse.

My stomach fluttered, excited like it was going to be our first time. "What do you think is in the overnight bag? Who needs clothes?" I laughed, giving her a hug. I was only half kidding, hoping the three jumbo boxes I'd stashed in there would be enough. It had been a while, what if he genuinely didn't want to?

"Do you think he still . . ." I stopped, wondering if I was over-thinking it. I mean, he'd never said he didn't. He was just being patient, giving me space and time because I'd been so busy with first Scully's pregnancy and then the baby.

I was doing more than overthinking it.

Scully tugged on my arm using her new mommy voice. "If you even dare suggest that Nick is no longer interested in having sex with you, I'm going to kick your ass."

"We're not supposed to swear anymore, remember?" I tried my own mommy voice, which was nowhere near as convincing.

She laughed, folding her arms across her chest giving me old-school Scully attitude. The combo of sass and authority was actually slightly intimidating. "Seb is asleep so I can say *ass*, especially when you're acting like one."

I shrugged, not convinced we hadn't accidently fallen into a really good platonic friendship. Sure, there were those make out sessions *and* the hand job, it wasn't like I gave my other male friends those. Nor did I spend time with them in bed just hugging them.

So many nights I'd fallen asleep, listening to him tell me all the crazy stuff he'd gotten up to with his brothers. His mom must have been a goddess, raising amazing, strong men who also had hearts.

Nick had also learned all about my family too, and even though he hadn't met them, I just knew he'd love them.

God, I hoped it hadn't been too much too soon. Between the press attention and everything else, we had either the most amazing relationship ever, or he was my new best friend. I didn't want to imagine a world without him; he was so deeply ingrained into my heart.

"Well I guess I'll find out tonight. If he hands me the remote when I suggest we *Netflix and chill*, I'll take it as a sign I need to buy a vibrator."

The fact I wanted sex so much pissed me off a little. Not that there was anything wrong with sex, in fact, sex was a healthy and normal part of a good relationship.

But he was being such a *good* man, not doing anything that was overly suggestive. And there I was, wondering how long I should wait to get naked after I walked in the door.

I'd turned into a nympho.

"Go, get out of here," Scully groaned picking up my overnight bag and handing it to me. "Go have hot dirty sex with your hot boyfriend."

I huffed, pretending to be annoyed. "Fine, if I must."

Grabbing my keys and saying goodbye to Luke, I got into my car and drove to Nick's. It had made more sense than him coming to pick me up, especially since I was staying the night.

My body hummed with nervous energy the whole time I was driving, keeping myself distracted by singing *Lady Gaga* songs. You want irony? Try listening to "Paparazzi," and keeping a straight face.

And if I thought I was anxious on the drive over, pressing his buzzer almost sent me into a full-blown panic attack.

What the hell was wrong with me?

Nick was my boyfriend, and we loved each other. We weren't some shallow sexual fling.

But gee, was that man as hot as hel—"Hellllllloooo." My eyes almost burst from their sockets, trying not to drool on his doorstep as I stared at him.

Holy.

Freaking.

Shit.

If he had plans to sit on the couch and watch television, he had not dressed appropriately. Because standing in front of me in all his six-foot-whatever hotness was Nick Larsson in a pair of worn blue jeans and not much else.

Bare feet, no shirt and a smile that said nothing platonically, his arms braced either side of his door like he was giving me a show. I had to fight the urge to scrounge through my purse to find a dollar, reminding myself that wouldn't be polite. Not that I should be worried about being polite when my tongue was washing his front doorstep.

"You want to stand there and ogle me some more or do you want come inside." A smug grin spread across his lips.

"I want to *come* everywhere," I said with zero shame as I lifted my chin off the floor and threw my arms around his neck.

I couldn't be next to all that hot toned muscle and not touch it, my hand brazenly trailing down his chest as whatever concerns I had were left at the door.

"Good to see we're on the same page." He pulled me into his arms and lifted me off the floor. "I've missed you."

His mouth was on mine less than a second later, kissing me like we might never kiss again.

My back hit the wall as his tongue stroked mine, feeling his hot body press against me with unambiguous purpose.

"Nick," I breathed, his tongue deciding my neck needed the attention. "Shut the door."

He grinned, letting me slide down the wall until my feet hit the floor. "I constantly seem to have a problem with that door, good thing you showed up when you did."

He grabbed my overnight bag still on his stoop, tossing it on the floor before shutting the door.

"Now, where was I?" His hands moved back to my body, touching me all over as his mouth went back to my lips.

Clawing at my dress, his fingers finally found the zipper, pulling it down and pushing it off my shoulders so that it pooled at our feet. It was only fair since he was wearing such few clothes, which was why I also kicked off my heels as we continued to kiss.

Lifting me off the floor like he had when I'd arrived, he pulled me against his body and carried me to his room. I could barely breathe, the anticipation building inside of me as he laid me down on the mattress.

With a quick flick of his finger my bra was off, my breasts coming to attention like he'd given them an order. Nodding in approval, he lowered his lips and sucked one of my puckered nipples into his mouth while his hand palmed the other.

He alternated using his mouth and hands, touching my body all over while I struggled to reach his jeans. Don't get me wrong, I would have loved to have laid there and let him give me an orgasm with absolutely no penetration. It wouldn't take long, just a swipe of his thumb on my clit and I'd be picking up what was left of my brain cells off the floor. But I was greedy, wanting to feel him hard and knowing it was only for me.

Twisting around from under him I was able to reach the waistband of his jeans, my fingers wasting no time in undoing the button and lowering his zipper.

It felt like I was trying to jump rope drunk, trying to push down his jeans while his mouth made its way down my body.

"Get naked," I demanded, unable to concentrate on anything other than the flick of his tongue as he licked me through the fabric of my panties.

He chuckled, covering me with his mouth as he blew hot air against the lace.

"Ah." I arched my back forgetting what I'd asked him to do.

Pants.

I wanted him to get rid of them.

Clearly he wasn't to be trusted, continuing his own agenda while he ignored mine, I peeled my body away from him and flipped him down on the bed. Well, it wasn't so much a flip as it was a shove, only able to be achieved because he'd been taken by surprise.

And that was exactly what I intended to do.

Take him.

Yanking at his jeans, I pulled them and his boxer shorts down and off while he looked on in amusement. I kneed open his legs, taking his thick cock in my hands and stroked it.

He edged up onto his elbows, his eyes hooded with lust as watched me take him into my mouth, lollipopping him while jerking him off.

I loved his hot gaze on me, the control he was trying to keep simmered underneath as I pleasured him with my tongue.

He pulled his cock from my mouth and hand, moving to his knees in a rush. With a decisive jerk, he hooked his thumbs into my underwear and pulled them down my legs. The air hit my bare skin first and then it was his hand, his fingers coated in my slickness, while my core burned with need.

"Claire, I'm going to fuck you." His voice so raw, it vibrated through my body.

Oh my God, yes.

I moaned, the only thing I could manage as he grabbed a condom from his nightstand and put it on. There was no time to enjoy the view, pulling me onto all fours as he steadied me with his hands on my hips.

He plunged into me, the invasion filling me so suddenly I gasped out loud, pitching my body forward.

"Please, more," I begged, not wanting him to be gentle. "Don't stop."

And he didn't.

Driving in hard behind me, he reached down fingering my clit, gaining more power and speed with each commanding thrust. "Let me feel how much you missed me," he continued. "Because I sure as hell missed you."

My body shook as the orgasm tackled me from behind, radiating through me like a sunburst. I couldn't hold my weight, feeling my body fall toward the mattress as rivulets of pleasure echoed through me, his hands locking around my waist to keep me upright.

And with one final thrust, he was right there with me. Both of us falling, his body crashing down on mine as he pumped into me, giving me exactly what I wanted and needed.

"I'm crushing you." He tried to roll off, his chest plastered to my back as the mattress compressed under our weight.

I shook my head, loving the feeling against my skin and begging him to stay. "No, please. I need to feel you."

He slid out of me, flipped onto his back, taking me with him and laid my torso on his chest. His hand caressed me as we panted on the bed.

"Well, that was interesting." I laughed against his skin unable to suppress my smile.

"Wow, *interesting*?" he scoffed. "I think you need to reevaluate your choice of words."

I was about to agree, list a million adjectives that I was sure wouldn't be sufficient, when he kissed me. Not desperate and hard like when I arrived, but slow and soft, taking his time with each pass of his lips.

"I love you," he mumbled against my mouth. "I don't think I told you enough these past weeks."

I shook my head wondering how the hell I got so lucky. "No, you have been amazing, I couldn't have asked for more. And I love you too."

We stayed like that for what felt like hours—kissing, touching, caressing—reacquainting our bodies as we spoke in hushed voices. And I felt myself awash in a serene calmness I'd never felt. All those concerns—about him, me, us—just melted away. I had been waiting for the drama, expecting that no one had a right to be this happy, but maybe it *was* possible. In that moment, it sure felt like it was. And I was so eternally grateful to have found a man who got me on every level.

At some point we fell asleep, both of us waking in a tangle of arms and legs, not wanting to be apart even while we were unconscious. If I had any doubts in my mind, they no longer existed.

He was *it* for me.

As impossible as it sounded, he was my one.

"You look so serious." He slowly unwrapped his arms from my body. "Is this because I promised you dinner and didn't feed you?"

It would have been easier to agree, make a joke and laugh it off. I mean, we had been doing serious with Scully and the baby and life, this was supposed to be the fun part.

Why couldn't I just lie?

"No, it's because part of me is waiting for all of this to fall apart."

He rolled onto his side facing me. "Why would it fall apart? And if this is about the press, I told you, they'll get bored. Ignore them."

"It's not about the press." I swallowed, wishing my only concern was whether or not they thought I was hot enough for him. "But because, we weren't really meant to happen."

I had danced around it since the first day on his doorstep, giving him just enough so I wasn't a total fraud, but not the full truth. Not entirely. I had no idea if he would be flattered, or if he would think I'd somehow tricked him. That I had orchestrated our reconnection, seducing him with smoke and mirrors.

"That story you read, was never meant to see the light of day. It wasn't written for you, it was about you."

God, it sounded bad.

So.

Fucking.

Bad.

But I had already started so there was no point stopping now.

He listened intently, raising an eyebrow as I took a breath. "I had writer's block and I just couldn't do what I needed to do. Everything I wrote sucked. And then one day, I started writing about you. Not to sell, but to let the thoughts I had in my head play out on the page to see if there was any hope at all."

"Nick and Blaire?" He laughed. "Come on, Claire. I'm not an idiot."

"So you knew what it was? What *I* was?"

His finger traced my jaw, lifting my head to look him in the eyes. "Here's what I knew. That a beautiful woman, I'd met years ago, wrote a funny and compelling story that very conveniently had me as the main character. Which ironically, is exactly what I know now."

"But I'm—"

"Really fucking adorable." He chuckled. "And for some strange reason you're into me. *Really* into me. Like you couldn't be any more into me if you tried." The smugness radiated off him like he was the sun, the situation itself seeming to please him to no end.

I rolled my eyes, too far gone to be embarrassed. "You're really enjoying this."

"Oh," his eyes lit up like a Christmas tree, "like you wouldn't believe."

"Well, so there's more."

Did I really have to say it? Things were going so well.

Yes, it's now or never and he deserved to know.

Did he really? He seemed cool with it up that point, let's just assume he was fine with everything else.

No. We are doing this.

"The night you were drunk, I was going to break into your house to steal my story back." The words came out in a rush, needing to say it before I chickened out and hoping it would silence the mental tug-of-war I had going on in my head.

He threw his head back and laughed, like I had delivered the best punch line in the world. God, I hoped that punch line hadn't been me.

"You were going to break into my house? Wow, you really are a psycho, that's kind of hot."

"Stop laughing." I elbowed him in the ribs. "This is what you've signed up for. I was a crazy person with bad intentions, who contemplated breaking into your home."

"Claire, look at me." He stopped laughing. "I don't give a fuck what you think your intentions were. You didn't break into my house; I let you in. And then what did you do with all your crazy, bad intentions? Nothing. Jack. Shit. You're a good person. When I was lying there and you could have done something crazy, bad or both, you didn't. You know why?"

Honestly, I didn't know how he had an answer when I had no clue. "Why?"

A smile spread across his lips. "Because, despite what you've told yourself, we *were* meant to happen."

Stop.

My heart.

"Nick, you are going to kill me with all this sweetness."

I wasn't even kidding, my heart felt like it was primed to explode and he would be the reason.

He shrugged, seeming to be unconcerned at my possible demise. "Just remember how sweet I am when I forget to lower the toilet seat."

CHAPTER 21

"OH SCULLY, HE is so precious," my mother cooed while holding Sebastian. "You must be so proud."

One thing I loved about my parents—well I loved a lot of things, but the most important thing—was they were good people. While other moms might have judged Scully's decision to bring a baby into the world with no father figure and no real plan, my folks didn't bat an eye. They respected her for her decision, right or wrong, exactly like they would have if it'd been me.

They may not agree with everything I'd done, but they loved me. Which was why I had avoided telling them when I hadn't been doing so well. Because deep down I felt guilty for the blind love and support I'd been given.

"Thanks, Carly." She looked at her son in the arms of my mother. "He's pretty darn cute."

"Speaking of *cute*." My mother's lips quipped into a smile. If she was trying to be coy, she really sucked at it. "How's Nick? And when am I going to get to meet him?"

I rolled my eyes. I knew she'd waited patiently so she could slide it into conversation and pretend it was a coincidence, but she'd been dying to ask since she walked in the door. "Tonight.

You get to meet him tonight, but don't like . . . bring up anything embarrassing."

"What could I possibly say?" She scoffed, looking at me like I was being preposterous. "That my daughter had a mild obsession with him and used him for inspiration for fan art."

"Fan fic," Scully corrected, the two of them obviously coconspirators in the effort to make me squirm.

"I already told him, so your blackmail material will do you no good," I warned, glad for once my mouth had actually gotten me out of trouble rather than in it.

Scully huffed. "Well, there goes our fun."

"You were planning on having fun without me? I swear, I need better friends." Luke walked in, surprising us by coming home in the middle of the day.

"Luke, so lovely to see you." My mom's eyes lit up, kissing Luke on the cheek while she rocked Seb. "I thought you were at work today?"

"Great to see you too, Carly. And I'm in between meetings. I wanted to come by and check on my main guy." He leant down and kissed Sebastian's head.

Like the rest of us, Luke was smitten. Totally wrapped around the finger of a tiny human who would play us all like violins the minute he worked it out. But even so, it was surprising to see him randomly come home and say hello.

"Well, make sure you don't need to work late tonight, we're having a family dinner so Mom can meet Nick. And Scully and Mom have been plotting all day so I'm going to need someone on my side." I stood and gave him a hug.

"Oh, so you don't want me to mention the storage tub in your room of bonus material?" Luke grinned, shooting me a wink. "Done." His hand ran along his mouth like he was zipping it.

"Maybe it's *me* who needs better friends." I nudged him. "You want to grab some lunch? We have leftover sandwiches in the fridge."

I wasn't entirely sure what was going on, but the food was a good distraction. I also figured that if I could get him alone, then maybe I could find out why he'd decided to stop by in the middle of the day.

He nodded, giving me a smile. "Trying to bribe me with food. I'll take it because I'm hungry, but that bullshit about a way to a man's heart is through his stomach is a lie. I'll still talk if given enough motivation."

I grabbed his arm and tugged him into the kitchen making sure we were out of earshot. "What's going on? And don't tell me it was only to see Sebastian."

His eyes glanced to the direction of the living room, Scully and Mom's voices floating through the open plan. "Your room." He tipped his head to the hall.

I hadn't snuck around in my own house since I was sixteen, but I didn't question him, following Luke into my room and closing the door.

My mind was swimming with possibilities and all of them were bad.

"Whatever it is, you need to tell me now because I'm about to freak the hell out." My hands wrapped around his arms trying to keep my voice low. "Is Nick cheating on me?"

I'm not sure why I said it, but it was honestly my first thought. Things had been going unusually well for us and he was so perfect. Maybe a little *too* perfect, which was why I secretly wondered when something was going to come and mess it all up.

"You think Nick's cheating on you?" Luke asked, a genuine look of surprise on his face.

"No, I don't think so. Or at least I didn't. Please, just tell me." I couldn't even think straight let alone talk, my heartbeat thundering in my chest as I waited for whatever bad news I knew was coming.

"I have no idea if he's cheating on you, and if you suspect it, then maybe you two need to have a talk. But that's not what this is about."

Luke had chosen his words carefully which meant it was definitely about Nick. Until now, Luke had been one of the biggest supporters of our relationship, only trumped by Scully.

"But it is about him, so spill."

He shoved his hands in his pockets. "I had a meeting today about a new contract, working on *The Blue Line.*"

"Oh my God, you'll be working on Nick's series? That's great." I threw my arms around him feeling myself sag in relief. It was wonderful. With both Nick and Luke on set maybe I wouldn't feel so weird when I visited.

Except.

He wasn't smiling, the joy I felt one-sided as I pulled away from him. "Why do I feel like this isn't a good thing even though it sounds like it's a good thing?"

"It is a good thing . . . for me. They have a big budget and I'll be staying for the entire season, maybe even longer if it works out. But when I was there, Audrey Rydell was there too. She had some meeting with the director or something. And while I was waiting, we got to chatting."

"She's married," I fired back, knowing that while I'd had stupid suspicions about her before, I'd done my due diligence and investigated. Besides, Nick had hardly mentioned her, so if he was even remotely interested in her, then he was CIA level at hiding it.

"I know she's married." He rolled his eyes. "Stop hypothesizing and listen. So, she has this meeting and I could tell she was nervous. Anyway, we got talking about jobs and she mentions that she is unsure about staying on. You know, they are probably going to let her write some episodes, let her get her feet wet but she was approached by someone else to be a main writer on something new."

Luke had a talent for making people talk. Scully and I had often joked his smile was laced with sodium pentothal or that his eyes were capable of hypnosis. Five minutes with his charm and you were spilling all of your secrets whether you wanted to or not.

"So you guys besties now?" I laughed, wondering if this was his subtle way of telling me I'd been replaced. "Because she might be more successful than me but she will not con her way into Salvatore Ferragamo to get you those loafers that were apparently sold."

"The story she was asked to adapt, the one where she'll be the main writer, is yours, Claire." His words shot out. "A director has given her *your* story and asked her if she'd be interested."

No, that was impossible.

"Well that's crazy, Jeremy hasn't even optioned it yet. It hasn't been sold to anyone." I tried to laugh, but not able to manage it.

"You're smarter than that, Claire," he warned, looking pissed off, and I wasn't sure if it was at me or the situation. "You think a network is just going to hand over money without getting a second opinion? You're a script reader at the moment, it is literally your job to read something and give your report before anyone puts any cash on the table."

Well, sure, I guess that made sense. But wouldn't I have been told or something, a little heads up?

"What are you saying, that there's a possibility that someone is going to buy it but they want *her* to adapt it?" I hadn't even considered the possibility, the words sticking in my throat as I said them.

"Yeah, it means you need to call your agent and find out what the fuck is going on. Someone is trying to sandbag you, and I have no idea if Nick is in on it, but he's definitely who they have in mind for the lead."

I felt my body lower as I sat down on the bed, feeling dizzy as

I tried to work out exactly what he was saying. He joined me on the bed, holding my hand as he told me the whole story.

Audrey was rumored to be getting her chance to write an episode or two, but it was a long shot that she'd replace anyone fulltime. Not unless one of the regular writers left or was embroiled in some sort of drama. So, if she wanted her chance to move up from the kiddie table, she was going to have to look elsewhere. Or stay, and push someone down the stairs.

Luke—his good looks, sympathetic ear and hypnotic charm— had managed to tease out of her what project she was considering. Not because he'd suspected it had anything to do with me, but because he was a nosey bastard like the rest of us and liked to be in the know. He was a good friend to have around who knew more about people in our industry than even I had assumed. Probably how he was able to get me the job as a script reader in the first place, something I hadn't questioned at the start because I didn't want to know the answer.

"Are you sure it's mine, maybe it's something that sounds like mine. I mean, it's not like there's anything original in Hollywood anymore." I was grasping at straws, hoping against hope he was mistaken.

"It's the same. She even mentioned Nick, saying that it would be good to work with a leading man she was already familiar with. Apparently they've been looking for a project together for some time."

I knew that, Nick had told me earlier, and it had been something I'd hoped *we*—as in me and him, not Audrey—would have together as well.

But I'd told both Nick and Jeremy I wanted to be the one to adapt my story. Worried that someone else would screw it up, take my words and make it look stupid. If it had been something else . . . maybe it wouldn't feel so personal, but this was *Nick and me.* I had to be the one.

It was *supposed* to be me.

I felt like I was going to be sick.

My head fell into my hands as I prayed for the room to stop spinning, the questions overwhelming me as I tried to make some sense of it.

Did he know? Take me to his agent, get me to agree so he could have a custom made role and then cut me out? He wouldn't do that. He just wouldn't.

"Claire, call Jeremy find out what's happening and then call Tyler."

My head snapped up in a panic. "Your friend the lawyer?"

He rubbed my back in an effort to try to comfort me. "Just make sure you know where you stand okay? Jeremy is going to look out for Jeremy. He's an agent, not your friend."

It wasn't true.

I couldn't let myself believe that a man who I'd fallen in love with would do that to me. Use a weakness in me and exploit it. It made no sense. I'd told him, he *knew* what I wanted. There was no reason for him to do this.

Nick was already successful, he'd won awards, was in magazines, had the critical acclaim—he didn't need me or my stupid story. Why?

"He isn't involved. He just isn't." I shook my head refusing to believe he knew. "He's not some nobody looking for his big break, he can literally pick and choose his projects, scripts are tossed at him like confetti."

"Yeah, like he's working on something now?" Luke's eyebrow rose with suspicion.

"He's on a break, maybe he decided to take the summer off."

It was true that the last couple of years Nick would do side projects during *The Blue Line's* hiatus. Nothing huge because his filming schedule started back in the fall, which didn't allow much time, but he always seemed to do something. I assumed after his drunken night and then later confession about the pressure he'd been under, he'd decided to take a break. I was even hopeful that maybe I had been a reason, his lack of projects giving us time to be together.

Luke put his arm around me, pulling me close to his chest. "Maybe he is, maybe he isn't. I don't know, Claire. But you owe it to yourself to find out what's going on."

He was right, and I refused to be a dumb love-struck moron who thought it was better to bury their head in the sand than know the truth.

"Thanks." I hugged him back, knowing that no matter what happened, he and Scully would be my safe place to land.

"I have to get back to work, but I'll be home in time for dinner." He kissed the top of my head. "You know I love you, Claire. And the last thing I want is to see you get hurt."

"I love you too. But please don't say anything to Nick until we know for sure."

Who knew how long it would take before I got some answers, but I couldn't confront him until I knew where I stood. After all, if he was manipulating me, I didn't want to give him the opportunity to figure a way out.

"I'll let you take the lead." He gave me a warm smile. "I'll see you when I get back."

Luke left without the lunch that I'd promised while I sat in my room wondering if my world was falling apart. Other than knowing that Audrey Rydell was considering my story, I literally knew nothing else. And I hated not knowing.

Putting on my big girl pants I picked up my phone and dialed Jeremy's number. My hand shook and my pulse raced, the seconds it took before someone answered feeling like an eternity.

"Levin Murphy, this is Jessica."

Damn it.

In my effort to extract the truth, I'd completely forgotten that Jeremy's personal assistant was also Dave Larsson's girlfriend.

Great.

"Hey, it's Claire Becker. I was hoping to talk with Jeremy."

"Oh, hey Claire, how are you?" Jessica responded, sounding warm and professional like she always did.

"Doing great," I lied. "How are you?" I figured I needed to at least pretend I was polite even though the last thing I wanted was to make small talk.

"Good to hear, I'm good too, thanks for asking. Jeremy is with a client right now, is there something I can help you with?"

Yeah, sure, can you tell me if your boss is trying to cut me out of my own story and my boyfriend is an accomplice? Thanks, that would be great.

"I'd actually prefer to speak to Jeremy if that's okay."

I hated that I was asking permission, that I didn't demand she put him on the phone right now and tell me straight out what was happening. But I couldn't rush it, especially when all I had at the moment was hearsay. Sure, my source was reliable—Luke had never given me misinformation before—but it wasn't like I could admit my best friend and roommate had beguiled Audrey into talking.

There was a pause, and I was almost positive she was going to tell me that Jeremy had a full schedule and would call me back later when he had time. That was industry speak for *fuck off* and I'd heard it more times than I would have liked.

"He has an opening at four-thirty, do you want to come in?"

What?

I didn't know if she was throwing me a bone or it had been divine intervention. Either way I was taking it before she had a chance to change her mind.

"Yes, that would be great. Thank you."

"No problem, Claire. We'll see you then."

The call ended with no clue as to whether Jessica was an ally or enemy, but the opportunity wasn't something I was going to squander.

"Hey is everything okay?" Scully poked her head in my doorway. "We saw Luke leave and when you didn't come back, I was wondering where you went."

"Yeah, I had needed to make a call, nothing important."

I hated lying to her, but if I told her the truth, the minute Nick walked in the door—guilty or not—she'd have him up against the wall threatening him with the baseball bat we kept in the closet.

"Well, okay." She didn't seem convinced but didn't press. "We're going to put Sebastian down for a nap and binge watch your boyfriend on cable. I think it's important your mom appreciates how fine a man he is." She smirked, bringing her hand up to her mouth in mock surprise. "Oh, is it weird if we objectify him while you're in the room?"

I laughed even though I didn't feel it. Not because I cared that she and mom were going to see Nick's naked butt on television, even though it might be slightly awkward. But because I had so much else going on in my mind.

"Would you guys mind if I went out for a while?"

"You're seeing him in a few hours, Claire." She laughed. "But fine, if you want to go have sexy time with your boyfriend, I'm not going to stop you."

Ha! If only.

"Thanks Scully, you're the best." I got to my feet and pulled her into a hug.

I purposely didn't correct her, knowing it was easier for her to think I was with Nick.

"Yeah, yeah. I know, I'm awesome." She rolled her eyes, moving back to the doorway. "Just make sure the two of you are back in time for dinner. Luke is cooking so you know it's going to be good."

"I promise I'll be back." I crossed my heart even though sitting through dinner was the last thing I wanted to do.

Scully tossed a "have fun" and a smile over her shoulder and left. Meanwhile I had a few hours to fill, hoping in that time my mind wasn't overrun with every worst-case scenario.

I picked up my phone and scrolled down my contacts until I got to Tyler. He'd been amazing when we went through my contract with Jeremy, and from everything I'd heard, he was a damn good lawyer. Plus, he was a good friend to Luke, which meant he was someone I could trust.

"Tyler Woods." He answered his cell immediately.

I took a breath, steading myself. "Hey Tyler, it's Claire Becker. Have you got a minute?"

"Claire." There was a smile in his voice. "Good to hear from you. You're in luck, I'm in between meetings."

I walked over to my closet and pulled out a skirt and jacket. "Thanks, I wanted to ask some advice."

"Give me a second." There was a pause and then the sound of a door closing. "Okay, tell me what we're looking at."

A slow breath eased past my lips.

If something was too good to be true, it usually was.

CHAPTER #22

TALKING TO TYLER put a lot of things in perspective. Jeremy could pitch my story to whomever he wanted. He could wheel and deal and make all kinds of promises, but until I signed the final contract, releasing my rights as the author, he didn't have shit.

Granted, that also meant that *I* didn't have shit—the chances of someone else picking it up and pitching it again not great—but I wasn't as powerless as I'd felt. Which was why I'd put on my nicest skirt and jacket, a killer pair of black heels and held my head up high when I'd walked into Jeremy's office.

Jeremy leaned back in his seat, his hands tented in front of him. "Claire, what a nice surprise."

Is it, asshole? I was tempted to ask but managed to bite my tongue and smile.

"I wanted to check on the status of my story, see if you had any bites?" I eased in, giving him a chance to tell his version of events.

"A couple." He nodded, giving nothing away. "But these things take time and it could be months before anything is settled and a deal is made."

I tipped my head to the side wondering if he was generally prickly or if it was just for new clients he hadn't made money off yet. "Funny, word on the street is that it was given to Audrey Rydell for consideration. Sounds like some kind of *deal* has already happened."

Honestly, it was hard to remain calm. I even tried all that breathe-in-breathe-out bullshit Pru had taught us from the ill-fated baby class in an attempt to not grab him by his expensive business shirt and demand answers.

"Where did you hear that?" he asked cautiously, his smile not faltering.

Not a denial, which meant I wasn't wrong. "Oh, I have my sources. When were you going to tell me?"

I was calling his bluff, hoping that if he thought I already knew that he would fess up. It was a calculated risk but one I felt confident making. It was either that or I leapt over his desk like I had wanted to when I'd walked in.

"Okay." He shook his head. "Nothing is set in stone, but one of the premium cable channels wants it. We have a handshake deal, but it hinges on Audrey coming onto the project. And of course, Nick will be the lead."

I felt the air rush out of my lungs, hearing it confirmed so much worse than I thought. "But it's my story, shouldn't I be the one to write the screenplay? We discussed this, I told you it had to be me."

It was difficult not to sound like a child throwing a tantrum but I didn't understand. I was a screenwriter; I was more than capable of turning a good story—mine—into a workable script.

"Claire, as I said when I read it, I liked it. It's funny, good story—all that other stuff I mentioned—but no one knows you. And I *never* promised anything." He leaned forward in his desk to illustrate the point.

I tried to remember the conversation, thinking back to what his words had been.

He'd never agreed.

He'd never said that it would be me.

Even when I told him point blank that I wanted it to be me, he'd never said that it would be.

And when I signed the contract for representation, it was just that—*representation*. There wasn't a clause to spell it out, and I had mistakenly believed that it would have been taken care of if or when we sold it.

I'd fallen for the oldest trick in the book.

"Your resume isn't one I can pitch to a network or a producer. They like the *story*, but they need someone with a proven track record before they pony up the cash. It's not personal, just the way it works."

It was hard not to take it personal when it was the person—me—they didn't want. *Thanks for the great idea, we'll take it from here.* It felt like a giant fuck you.

"But if you gave me a chance to write it and present them with it, they will see I have the talent to do it. I may not have Audrey's resume, but I am a damn good writer."

It wasn't about ego. Okay, so it wasn't *just* about ego. I knew that I had the talent and most of all the determination to make it shine. The screenplay I'd recently finished was by far my strongest work yet. I had learned so much in the past weeks, not only about myself but about the craft, courtesy of the script reading from Marconi.

Jeremy shook his head, my impassioned plea falling on deaf ears. "And in time, you'll get your seat at the table. But right now, I'm offering you a foot in the door. Your name will be on the backend credits, and you get to see your concept make it onto the screen. You know how many screenwriters out there would kill for that?"

"What about creative input? Do I get a say, get to collaborate at least?" I offered, hoping there was some way I could still be a part of my own project.

"Sorry Claire, Audrey is the debutante. The studio wants to use this as a chance to show everyone else what they've missed out on. She's the only one who will be working on it."

Funny, he didn't sound *sorry* at all.

"So that's it, I'm supposed to hand it over and sit down and be grateful?"

Do not cry.

Do not yell.

It was a mantra, going on in my head in a loop, as I sat there wanting to cry *and* yell.

"Yes, and count the money you made by selling it."

Money, it always came back to money. I felt like I'd been kicked in the gut and asked to be grateful, and I couldn't have been more hurt.

I swallowed, knowing that my beat down wasn't even close to being over. "What about Nick?"

"What about him?" Jeremy's eyebrow rose, waiting for me to continue.

The control I had on my emotions frayed as I demanded. "Come on Jeremy, you're not a lawyer or a priest. Has he agreed to play the lead?"

"Well look at that, didn't think he had it in him to keep his mouth shut but he surprised me." The bastard actually had the nerve to smile. "Yes, he has agreed. Not only does Audrey get her day in the sun, but your boyfriend gets to carry a series on his own name. Being part of an ensemble is good for him, but if he wants the big dollars he needs to step out without a security blanket."

He knew.

The whole time I had tried to convince myself that it had been all Jeremy's doing, but it wasn't. How long had he kept it a secret, how many times had he seen me, slept with me and not said a word? Everything I thought I knew about him was wrong.

My mouth opened and then closed, not able to find any words I wanted to say. There was *nothing* left to say.

"Look, for the record, this was not how I wanted to tell you. I wanted to be sure there was a deal and then present you with it. But it is what it is."

To his credit, he'd stopped looking smug. Not sure if he found some humanity or he just thought if he tried to be more sympathetic I would leave without making a scene.

"What if I don't sign?"

"Then the deal is dead."

"Will you try and get me something else?"

He shook his head. "Claire, I'm not trying to be an asshole here, but I'm your agent, not your life coach. I have gotten you the best possible outcome. Your words turned into a series. Now it might not be exactly how you saw it in your head, but that's life. And ultimately it is your choice. You say no, it's no. But I can't promise that it won't be the same exact outcome every single time."

"What you're saying is that no one will buy anything of mine until they know my name. But how can anyone know my name if I don't get a chance?"

"Easy, the same way everyone else did. Eat humble pie and wait your turn. It will come around, and it sucks, but it's the only way. There are no overnight success stories in this town, Claire, only a bunch of people who have been working their asses off until they finally got noticed."

It was a bitter pill to swallow, made even harder because he wasn't being an out and out prick. Don't get me wrong; I wanted to hate him. Pissed off that he had cut me out of something I had created and was giving it to someone else. And I didn't have it in me to be grateful. But I knew it wasn't entirely his fault.

"Well, thanks for your time." I stood up, feeling numb, like I was part of some weird dream.

He stood too, watching me as I walked to the door. "So will you sign the deal?"

"Send me the contract." I kept my eyes forward, hesitating at the door and took a breath. And without looking back, I walked out.

I SHOULD HAVE gone home, but I didn't, too consumed by emotions that instead I got in my car and drove. I didn't even know where I was heading, figuring it was easier to be alone than pretend that everything was okay. Oh, and I still had to sit through dinner with Nick, because *that* was what I wanted to do.

My phone had been shut off since before I'd gone into my meeting with Jeremy and I hadn't bothered to turn it back on. So when I eventually walked through my front door an hour later than our dinner was supposed to start, it wasn't pretty.

"Jesus Christ." Luke had his phone at his ear and a worried look on his face. "I've called everyone I can think of, no one has heard or seen you for hours."

"I'm fine, I just needed to drive." I didn't bother to explain, walking past him and into the living room.

Scully immediately grabbed me, balancing Sebastian in her arms as she hugged me tight. "You had us worried sick, thank God you're okay."

My mom also hugged me, her face full of concern. "Is everything all right, baby?"

Unable to answer, I nodded, even though everything was far from all right.

And there he was, the liar himself. "Claire, where have you been?"

"Sorry, I missed the memo where I had to check in with you," I bit back, anger and hurt taking turns as to which emotion I felt the most.

Luke cleared his throat. "Ladies, why don't we give her a minute." He tipped his head to Scully and my mom who were obviously confused.

How could they know? I was positive Nick didn't walk in, meet my mother for the first time and announce, *"Hi, I'm your daughter's boyfriend. I'm also an opportunist and have a problem with honesty. But I've told her I love her and I'm great in bed, so that should make up for it."* Probably too much of a mouthful, especially with all those lies taking up so much space.

"Sure, we'll be in . . ." My mom searched for something to say.

"My room," Scully finished. "Seb probably needs a change anyway."

They both walked down the hall to Scully's room and closed the door, leaving me, Nick and Luke.

"You want me to stay?" Luke glanced at me before looking at Nick.

I shook my head, "No, I'm fine," even though I wasn't.

He eyed Nick hard as he walked away. "I won't be far."

The air around us crackled as our eyes connected, Nick proving he wasn't an idiot by not moving any closer. "Jeremy called me."

"Really, you guys have a nice chat?" I asked, trying to keep my voice calm. *Wouldn't want anyone to think I was taking it personally.*

"Claire—"

"How could you?" I didn't want to give him a chance to give me excuses. "You knew, you *knew* that he was going to give it to Audrey. Was that always the plan? When I went in there for my meeting with him and he told me how much he *loved* it? Was it just so you could steal my story, give it to someone else to write and then get your solo shot?"

No matter how many times I thought it, hearing it out loud was exponentially worse. It made me feel like a loser and a fool, which I probably *was* for believing my life could turn on a dime and I could have everything I'd ever dreamt of.

His muscles were tightly coiled, his hands, fists at his sides. "It wasn't the plan, at least it wasn't *my* plan. I brought Jeremy your story because I thought it was awesome. And yes, I thought it was a perfect opportunity for me to lead, but I wanted you to write the screenplay."

"Do you want me to thank you? Bow down at your feet because you thought I had talent? You should have told me, the minute you knew that I was being cut out of my own story, you should have told me."

Out of everything, that was what hurt the most. Sure, I was embarrassed and feeling sorry for myself—no one liked to be rejected. But I would have survived, I *had* survived, and maybe I would have even agreed with them. Okay, that was probably a lie, I would never agree someone else could have written my screenplay better than I could have, but I would have been reasonable.

"I couldn't tell you, Claire." He took a step toward me and I raised my hands to stop. "I signed an NDA. If I did say something and the network found out, it would have been my ass. Not to mention the deal would have been dead in the water. Besides, as far as I know there is no contract yet."

"It was an NDA, not the launch codes for nuclear weapons. You could have found a way to tell me something, or even give me a hint that it was a consideration. Instead you let me believe—"

"I let you believe that you would sell your manuscript. That something you wrote would get made into a series. I thought you would be grateful."

"Get. Out." It tore out of my throat so fast and so loud I was sure everyone on the block had heard me. And I didn't care, not willing to be told that I should be thankful for being treated like a child.

He reached for me, moving forward even as I backed away.

"Claire, look, that came out wrong."

"No, I think that it came out *exactly* how you meant it. So do us both a favor and get out of my house." I pointed to the door, praying he didn't touch me so I wouldn't be forced to rip off his arm.

"You need to leave." Luke's voice came from behind me, giving me a reassuring hug as he came to stand beside me.

Nick shook his head, his jaw tense. "No, not until I explain."

"Nope, she wants you gone, you get out. And don't think for a second that I won't drop you, I don't give a fuck what your last name is and how many magazines you've been on."

Luke wasn't as big as Nick but he wasn't far behind, and I didn't doubt for a second he'd be able to hold his own if he needed to.

"Just go. There is nothing left to say."

And wasn't that the truth. Looking at him just hurt, reminding me of all the things I thought I had, when really I didn't. All of it was an illusion, a fake reality that would eventually be exposed. I wasn't even sure he'd really loved me at all. Maybe it had been gratitude, feeling like he owed me.

I could tell he wanted to stay, his feet hesitating as he stood his ground. He didn't care that Luke was shooting him looks that could kill, ignoring him entirely as his gaze locked on me.

"Claire."

It was too late.

My head shook as I fought back tears, not allowing him to get that from me. Instead I stared back defiantly, letting the over-whelming hurt bubble up inside of me but keeping it locked down.

Nothing.

After I had opened myself up and shared so much of myself, he wouldn't get one thing more.

Why the hell wouldn't he just leave?

"Go." The one word all I could manage through my gritted teeth, praying to God that I could wait until he walked out the door before I fell apart.

His hands fisted at his side and he took a breath, the "okay," more of an exhale as he finally moved.

I watched every step he took to the door, stood there and looked as the man I thought I was in love with opened it, turned around one last time and left.

Finally.

My body sagged the minute the door closed, the effort to keep it standing exhausted, as my knees gave way.

"I've got you." Luke's arms came around me, keeping me close to his body and not allowing me to fall. And finally, I let myself cry.

He didn't ask me to explain or wait for me to tell him what I needed, instinctively knowing as he picked up and carried me to my room and laid me on the bed. Scully and my mom appeared at my doorway, the look on their faces telling they'd heard the whole thing. It wasn't exactly like they could have missed it, and in a way I was relieved I didn't have to repeat anything and explain.

My mom sat on the edge of my bed, her hand stroking my hair like she was comforting a child. "I am so proud of you," she said, without explaining why.

As if sensing my pain, Sebastian cried from the other room.

"I'll be right back." Scully excused herself as she went to go get him, returning a few minutes later with her beautiful son in her arms and his tears all but stopped.

At that moment, I envied him. That all it took was a hug to make everything better. I wanted that so desperately, to not feel like I'd been torn in two.

Scully hopped on the bed, laying Sebastian between us and then put her arms around me. We didn't speak, just laid there facing each other, like her hands were all that was holding my two halves together.

Maybe they were, maybe I'd become that fragile.

Luke joined the party on my bed too, taking a seat on what little room there was left and rested his hand on my back. He was the first one to speak.

"I know it doesn't feel like it now, but you are going to be okay. We are all here and we love you."

And that just made me want to cry more.

I rubbed my eyes, wiping away the tears as I felt every single one of the emotions within me.

Hurt.

Anger.

Betrayal.

Fear.

Not dismissing any of it and giving myself permission to feel each of them both singularly and as a collective.

Luke was right.

It wouldn't be tonight, but at some point I would be okay.

Hours passed—or maybe it only felt like that—before my mom kissed my forehead, told me she loved me and left me on the bed. Next it was Luke who performed the ritual, leaving the room so it was just Scully, Sebastian and I. Seb had fallen asleep, cocooned between us, his little snores a reminder that time hadn't stood still.

"You want to talk about it?" Scully said, her arms had to be hurting, and yet she kept them right where they were, locked around me.

I sighed, the tears all cried out, my head throbbed, and reality had set in. "Part of me even understands why he did what he did, but it doesn't make it easier."

"What do you mean?" she asked cautiously. "Because if you're about to tell me that you're partly to blame for this mess I'm going to have to beat you. I won't enjoy it, and would prefer my son didn't see his mom go *Lemonade Beyoncé* on your ass, but I'll do it."

I laughed, unable to help the soft chuckle from escaping my

throat with the visual of Scully, a baby tucked under one arm, swinging a bat with the other.

"No, I'm not saying it's *my* fault. Hell, I even tried to tell him all the crazy he was signing up for in the interest of full disclosure." I didn't want there to be secrets between us, for there to be something that would eventually be revealed that could be seen as dishonesty. Turns out, it wasn't me that had to be worried.

"I meant that I get why they chose Audrey over me. It still stings like hell, and I hate how *good* she is," *And I wanted to hate her, even though she was not responsible for any of it,* "but I know why they did it."

Ego aside, I understood I was a small fish in a very large pond. Maybe not even a fish, possibly even smaller like a sea monkey. And no, I wasn't fishing for compliments; I knew I was talented. It was about knowing that no one was going to gamble millions of dollars on an unknown. Those Cinderella moments only happened in front of the camera, not behind it, so I got it.

Loud and clear.

And, if I could put my bruised self-pride aside for a second, I'd be glad that my words were going to be molded by a strong and talented woman who I knew would do my story justice. Man, I hated being reasonable.

So, as I explained to Scully all the reasons why, yes, I understood, and yes, it still sucked, it wasn't being "shut out" that hurt the most.

"He didn't tell me. And here I am wondering if it was because he didn't trust me enough not to behave like a spoilt brat, or he figured I would be so fucking thankful that I'd be too distracted to care, or because his motives weren't honorable from the start." All of them blew hardcore, and none of them said good things about me or him.

"All he had to do was tell me; look me in the eyes and say, *this is what they want to do, I love you, and it's shitty, but I wanted you to hear it from me."*

"Yeah, well. It's not like he didn't have time." She shook her head, cursing under her breath. "So what are you going to do?"

And wasn't that the million dollar question.

"I told Jeremy to send me the contract. If the price is right and the conditions are fair, I'm not going to withhold my work out of spite. Besides, it would probably be career suicide, and I really don't want to read scripts for the rest of my life."

Scully stared at me, a smile edging at her lips. "When the hell did we become grownups? Egging Baby Daddy's house was a lot more fun than being rational."

"Yeah, well. I'm positive I still have some irrationality in me so don't get too excited." I laughed. "As for Nick, well . . . maybe some things are best left as a fantasy. I just don't know if he was one of them."

She nodded, not trying to persuade me one way or the other, which was a good thing because no one wanted a sermon when they were hurting.

Time would tell if he should have remained just my muse, or if our meeting was needed to put me on a different course and change my destiny. But whichever he turned out to be, it would not break me.

CHAPTER #23

HAVING MY MOM around was a godsend. She not only helped with the baby, but brought me ice cream in bed like she used to when I was younger and broken hearted. Choc chip didn't heal the hurt, but it did make it slightly more tolerable.

Dad called a bunch too, threatening to jump on a plane and "straighten that boy out." He wasn't a violent man by any means, but I didn't doubt he'd give Nick a stern talking to. My little brother, Cody, told me he thought Nick was a hack, casually mentioning his acting sucked and I could do better. I didn't know if he genuinely meant it, but it was nice he'd say so if only to try to cheer me up. And Courtney—my little sister who dearly believed love conquered all—cried along with me.

It was hard being away from them, knowing that even miles away they were rallying for me. But I felt their love and knew that at a second's notice they'd be on a plane if I asked. And when I said goodbye to Mom, her time with us coming to an end, I promised I'd call more.

I wished we all lived closer, but the distance didn't diminish our connection. I was indeed lucky when it came to my family and friends; maybe it was too greedy to believe that I would be lucky in love too.

Nick's calls, texts and messages were all avoided and ignored. I'm sure he probably thought I was being an unreasonable bitch— care factor non-existent—but I needed space and time to think. That space and time was used productively watching cult 80's movies, where despite the guy screwing up, he found a way to make it up to the woman he loved with a grand gesture. Cheesy and predictable, I cried during every one. Who didn't love a grand gesture? They sure didn't write them like that anymore.

I'd convinced myself the heavy immersion into retro cinema was research, looking at the evolution of screenplays over the years. But realistically it was the only way I could avoid seeing Nick or one of his family members on television, in a movie or in a magazine. Not great when you were trying to forget one of them.

It also helped avoid seeing any speculation about me, and mine and Nick's relationship. Scully had not so discreetly slammed her laptop shut when I'd recently walked into the kitchen. I didn't know if it was another article wondering if he'd finally gotten sick of "slumming it," or if it was something new and he'd been seen with someone else. Neither possibility made me feel good, but one would definitely hurt more than the other.

Ugh, I needed to get a better handle on my feelings, they weren't doing me any favors.

Besides, I had a contract to negotiate, and I wasn't going to make business decisions emotional even if it sort of made sense in this instance.

"I want my name on opening credits. I don't care if it's small and tossed in with someone else, but I won't be buried on the backend behind the caterer."

Tyler and I had gone through the contract with a fine-tooth comb. It was reasonable but there was room for improvement, and I wasn't going to be called a diva for fighting for what I believed was what I deserved.

Jeremy scribbled in the margin, thankfully not fighting me or Tyler as he made notes. "I don't see it being a problem if you will give up full creative control."

"That's fine," I agreed, the concession made easier given the distance of a few days.

Tyler added a few other changes—extra protection legally—but other than that, I just wanted it over. I felt like the loop had been completed, something that had started because of it, would end because of it, and I could move on.

"I'll hopefully get back to you in an hour or two with an answer from the studio. They want to move on this so we should have a new contract drawn within a few days for you to sign." Jeremy shuffled the papers on his desk as he rose from his chair to shake my hand. "Let me know if there is anything else."

Would there be anything else? Who knew?

I wanted to ask about Nick—because as much as I pretended I didn't give a shit, I did—but I didn't ask. I had promised myself to be unemotional and I couldn't do that if I brought him into it. There would be no getting around that, and no human would have been capable. Certainly none with a heart, and I very much had one of those.

We said our goodbyes, exchanged bullshit pleasantries and Jeremy walked us out. It had been so bittersweet, and not how I imagined the sale of my first work would be. It just went to show, dreams don't always turn out the way you saw them in your head.

"Why don't you let me buy you dinner?" Tyler hesitated at my car door. "Seems like a fair trade since you did most of the negotiating in there."

I shook my head, glad that I'd had him by my side as backup. "I thought lawyers were supposed to be greedy, with no soul. You sure you aren't going to get kicked out of the fraternity for being kind and considerate?"

"I won't tell anyone if you won't." He nudged my shoulder. "Come on, I won't even make small talk, you can just tell me if Luke is dating anyone and then forget it even happened. Client attorney privilege prevents me from mentioning it unless you do."

I'd had my suspicions that Tyler's relationship with my room-mate wasn't as friend-like as Luke believed. Tyler's willingness to help me, take my calls whenever, and a more than generous fee reduction, didn't speak to that of just a "friend." I *might* have been wrong, but I didn't think so, especially with Tyler's admission all but confirming he was interested in more.

Pity I was still firmly in the camp of love sucked.

"You know I'll be terrible company. I'm still pretending that Nick Larsson didn't break my heart; it's taking up more mental space than I'd really like to admit. And I was trying so hard to be unemotional in the meeting with Jeremy that I'm sure I'm due for a cry soon too." It felt good to be honest with my feelings. Even if it was to a man I was paying to have my back and keep his mouth shut. Considering the last one I'd trusted on instinct, I was happy for the insurance the retainer gave me.

He thought a moment, stroking his chin like he was consid-ering it. "Yeah, even with the crying, I'm still pretty sure that your emotional breakdown will be more fun than dinner by myself."

Wow, sounded like his life was even more depressing than mine. "Well then, I guess we should get going. We've got a busy evening of dinner and tears, and we're wasting good crying time by standing around on the sidewalk."

So, with our evening plans agreed upon, we hopped into our cars and I followed him to a place of his choosing. Since he was insistent on paying, it should be his choice as to where our food consumption/emotional breakdown would take place. Who knows, maybe it wouldn't be so bad.

Tyler had excellent taste, choosing a small bistro rather than a large popular restaurant not far from Jeremy's office.

It was renowned for being closed off from the press, the frosted windows not allowing outside eyes to peer at who was dining inside. Convenient when crying was on the agenda. And not that I had mentioned it, but I hated the idea of some random photographer catching me in my vulnerability. I'm sure they had more than enough for their stories about our break up; I wasn't going to give them the tearful confirmation they craved.

We had a drink at the bar, both our phones receiving a message from Jeremy that the studio had accepted our demands. And as we sat down at our table and looked at our menus, I was actually looking forward to dinner.

"Luke know you're interested?" I asked, taking a sip of wine as we waited for our food. "I have to be honest, if he knows, he hasn't said anything." And considering what we'd been through lately, I'd have hoped he would have mentioned it.

Tyler swirled the wineglass between his fingers as he tried to hide his grin. "Nah, he dated my college roommate so I don't even think I'm on his radar. You know, can't date your friend's ex and all that."

God he was adorable, a perfect gentleman who dressed well and had a good job and seemed to have a good heart. Exactly the kind of man I'd want for my best friend if I weren't too busy being miserable. "No, you got it wrong." I laughed, the first genuine one all night. "If Luke dated *your* ex or you date *his*, that's when you have to invoke brocode. Dating friends of friends is allowed, unless there was shady behavior involved by either parties, and then no."

"Sorry?" he asked, obviously missing my very clear explanation of dating etiquette.

I tried again, hoping to be more successful the second time around. "Did either Luke or your college roommate cheat, lie, steal or kill anyone during the course of their relationship?" Kill was a little extreme, but we needed to cover all our bases.

"No, Tom accepted a job offer in New York, and neither wanted to do the long-distance thing."

"Well then you are in the clear. It's not high school where you swore some allegiance or something. Everyone is an adult, so no boundaries crossed. You should let Luke know though, I think you two would really hit it off."

"You think?" He sat up a little straighter. "Thanks, Claire. I might give him a call tomorrow and ask him out."

"Just be yourself, and whatever you do, don't lie to him," I warned. It was a sad sorry state of affairs when *I* was the one handing out dating advice, but if I'd learned anything, it was how much it hurt when it went wrong.

The rest of the dinner was great, and I even managed a few laughs here and there. It might not have changed anything, but I felt good to be able to forget for a little while.

The problem with forgetting was, when that inevitable memory returned, it wasn't any less painful.

I was contemplating dessert—it was a coin toss between the crème caramel and the chocolate gateau—when Nick Larsson strolled into the bistro. The eatery I'd been so impressed by up till a minute ago, had now been sullied beyond repair. And I also definitely needed the chocolate gateau, because caramel wasn't capable of curing a heartache.

He wasn't alone either, flanked by Jeremy, Dave and another guy who was blond and bore a family resemblance—obviously related. What did you call a pack of Larssons? A crew? A mob? A pride? Yes, pride sounded about right, let's go with that.

The pride of Larssons—and Jeremy—moved to their seats with seductive efficiency. The three of them together bent the laws of physics with their ridiculous beauty, I had to almost turn away so I wasn't blinded by their good looks. Thankfully I was able to focus on Jeremy, who wasn't a Larsson and therefore not genetically blessed, saving my eyes from the all-out slaughter that would have befallen them should I have gazed upon the pride.

It was also conceivable that I wasn't as sober as I thought, but I was too busy with inner commentary to worry about that.

"Shit," I muttered under my breath, wondering if I should hide behind a menu and hope he didn't see me, or keep staring at him like a loser . . . and hope he didn't see me. Either way it was clear I didn't want to be seen.

"You want to leave?" Tyler asked, following my line of sight and spotting the pride. "I can drive you home and then Luke can come back and get your car."

That had been the plan when I'd decided to finish the bottle of wine all on my own. Tyler would drive me home, then pick up Luke to collect my car, thus giving them an excuse to be to-gether in a confined space to talk *and* give me the opportunity to celebrate—or forget—a little. Everyone got something out of it, and the good mood that had started with dinner would hopefully continue so I didn't feel so empty when I went to bed that night.

But life—that cruel, cruel bastard—decided that my plans weren't worth shit, throwing a pride of Larssons at me like I was a wounded hyena.

"No, no, it's fine." *Oh, it was not anywhere close to fine.* "They probably won't even notice us. Let's just ignore them and order dessert like we'd planned." That would also give me the opportunity to investigate, find out if their congregating was for the purposes of good or evil.

So. Should. Not. Have. Drank. That. Wine.

I could see from his face that Tyler didn't agree, short of throwing me over his shoulder and carrying me out, there wasn't a lot he could do to convince me otherwise.

Tyler glanced over at the table, the four men sitting down and looking at their menus. "Huh, that's Roman Pierce. An amazing attorney but has a tendency to be a massive dick."

"Oh, so *that's* Roman." I narrowed my eyes having difficulty trying to focus. "Well that would make sense, it's a family trait."

Being big dicks.

Having big dicks.

No, that wasn't what I meant. It was definitely *being*. They were big, huge, massive dicks. Of which I wanted no part.

None.

"Roman is related?"

I wasn't sure how well Tyler knew Roman—or why he had a different last name—but he was definitely one of them. If not for the obvious *good-looking Larsson pride* features, there was the matter of the big dick. Of which we'd already established . . . shit, I'd lost my train of thought. What was I say—

"Claire, I think we've been spotted."

"Shit."

My head snapped up to four pairs of eyes looking directly at me. Jeremy, Roman, Dave and Nick, all with their menus down and their gazes locked on our table.

"Why did it have to be tonight?" I cursed under my breath. I was having fun, trying to forget him, and the minute I'd lowered my defenses—bam, there he was. Now I had lowered defenses, no chocolate gateau and a future full of trouble.

Tyler stood, reaching for his wallet and pulling out some cash. "Come on, Claire, let's go."

You know what? He was right; it *was* time to go.

It took most of my effort but I managed to stand without looking like a ragdoll. My feet worked just fine, keeping me steady as Tyler walked around and offered me his arm. *Such a nice guy.* He and Luke were going to be so happy together when I eventually got home so they could hurry up and fall in love. But that would have to wait a minute, my feet taking steps toward the table instead of toward the door.

"Claire. This is not a good idea." Tyler followed me, continuing to be a gentleman and putting his arm around my waist. It sure made the walking easier, so kudos to him for that.

His advice was probably solid and should have been heeded, so it was a pity that it was ignored. Instead, I strode forward, my smile widening as I reached the edge of the Larsson pride—and Jeremy—at their table. "Hello gentlemen, how nice to see you." Each word was delivered so clean and precise that I was seriously impressed.

"You must be Roman." I continued my excellent run, turning to the blond good-looking one I hadn't met before and held out my hand. "I've heard a lot about you but haven't had the pleasure to meet you."

Roman's eyes dropped to my hand, a smug grin spreading across his lips as he glanced at Nick and then stood. "And you must be Claire. Trust me when I tell you, the pleasure is *all* mine." His words delivered with a throaty chuckle.

"Fuck," I heard Dave mutter under his breath, shaking his head and trying to suppress the grin as he stood. "Hey, Claire."

I said hello to Dave while continuing to ignore Nick. His focus hadn't moved for a second, his gaze on me so intense that I could feel the heat of his stare burning my skin like a laser.

"Let me get some more chairs." Roman flagged a waiter, still wearing his smug Larsson grin. He reached down to where his brother was sitting, smacking him playfully at the back of the head. "Nick, where are your manners? Say hello to Claire."

Nick stood, his eyes following the lines of my body and the male arm around it. "Claire."

"Nick."

Our names tossed at each other like grenades as our gazes locked. Maybe it was petty, walking up to him when I hadn't returned his calls, but I was too mad, still hurt and too wine'd to stop. Besides, no man—famous or not—was going to make me feel like I had to hide in a corner like that redhead in "Sixteen Candles." She had a problem with paperwork falling into the wrong hands too if I remembered correctly. In any case, I wasn't backing down, the tension so thick you could have parted the air like a curtain.

Tyler—the sweetheart, man I hoped he and Luke got married—tucked me closer to his body, as he waved Roman off. "We don't need chairs, we were about to leave."

"I won't hear of it." Roman grinned, holding out his hand. "Tyler Woods, right? You worked the DeNezza case, I've heard good things."

Showing he had incredible dexterity—Luke was going to be a lucky man—Tyler shook Roman's hand while keeping the other wrapped around me. "Yeah, thanks Roman. Similarly heard good things about you."

I didn't care what they were talking about, too busy staring down Nick and making sure I wasn't the first person to blink. I hoped he did soon though, because my left eye was starting to twitch, and I didn't want him to wrongly believe I was flirting with him. Because I wasn't. The dick.

Jeremy, who'd remained silent up to that point, decided he needed some skin in the game, rose to his feet as he patted his client—well one of them—on the shoulder. "Why don't we all take a seat? Wow, did it get chilly in here." He laughed. "Nick, Tyler is Claire's attorney." In what I'm sure was an effort to get him to stand down.

Ha, good luck, buddy!

"Nice suit." Nick's jaw tensed, tipping his chin to Tyler. "I'm Nick."

"I'm Tyler." He returned the chin tip and then turned to me. "You want to stay?"

That was his way of subtly telling me it was time to leave without telling me what I had to do. Because Tyler—unlike Nick—communicated. But as happy as I was to take Tyler's suggestion under advisement, we would not be leaving. I felt empowered, strengthened by the resolve to hold my head up high—possibly with the benefit of alcohol—and told him what a jerk I thought he was.

"I think we'll stay." I smiled, accepting the seat the waiter had brought over. "Thank you so much for the invitation, Roman."

"Anytime, Claire," his smile beaming.

Tyler sat beside me, squeezing my waist as he settled. He might not be happy about our change in plans, but he wasn't leaving a fallen soldier behind.

Jeremy clapped his hands together in an effort to call us to attention. "So, what's everyone drinking? I'll buy the next round."

"Nothing for us thanks. We just finished dinner—"

"Actually," I cut Tyler off before he was able to finish. "We should order champagne to celebrate. To acknowledge and honor mine and Nick's shared success."

Nick's body tensed, his eyes hadn't left me since I'd walked up to the table and while I had no idea what was going on in his mind, I was pretty sure I was taking up some sizeable room in his headspace.

Good.

"Well let's not get ahead of ourselves, contract hasn't been finalized yet." Jeremy laughed nervously. "But, yeah, let's get some champagne." He flagged a waiter and ordered something I hoped was expensive.

"So Roman, did Nick tell you about his *amazing* new upcoming role?" I ignored Nick and his staring competition. "It's fantastic, going to be such a *good* career move for him." *I mean, I should know considering I wrote the damn thing.*

Roman tilted his head, giving me his full attention. "Well, yes I think he mentioned something about it. But I'd love for you to tell me more."

"Roman, don't," Nick bit out, murderous sight daggers thrown at his brother.

"Claire, it's been a while," Dave added, no doubt trying to play mediator. "How's Scully and the baby?"

Oh, nice try at deflection.

Not today, Dave.

Not.

Today.

My cheeks hurt as my smile widened, positive I was in danger of pulling a muscle in my face, but I didn't care. "Scully and Sebastian are doing great, thank you so much for asking. You should come and visit, maybe then she can give you something else of mine to read. I know how fond you guys are of my work."

"Claire, let's go talk." Nick shot out of his seat and was beside me in an instant. It was impressive—his fancy feet moving so quickly—not sure I could have managed the chair-to-Claire maneuver so seamlessly.

I waved him off, not having anything to do with his attempt to silence me. *Was he embarrassed?* Good, he should be. "Oh Nick, but we haven't even gotten to the champagne yet. And I'm happy, sitting down and chatting with your brothers. Not so much you, Jeremy, because well, I'm not your biggest fan. No offense." I turned and smiled at Jeremy.

He held up his hands and laughed. "None taken."

Nick's body was dangerously close to mine, his sexy scent lingering in the air like an evil seductive elixir. "Claire." His hand moved inches from my arm.

"Don't even think of touching me," I breathed into his face

as I jumped to my feet. "Do. Not."

I wasn't quiet about it, diners turning around to see what the commotion was about, but I didn't care. I wasn't going to allow him to put his hands anywhere near me. And not only because I was angry, but because I was also confused and didn't need lines blurred where I might kiss him. Because I was mad. And I wanted to kiss him. So he could not touch me.

His hand dropped, but he didn't move away, refusing to give my body and my mind a reprieve from his sexiness. I hated that I still thought he was sexy, probably why I'd been avoiding him.

"Okay, but please let me talk to you. Please." His eyes softened, and if I didn't know what such a skilled actor he was, I might have bought the sentiment. Begging was a nice touch. But, no, I was smarter than that.

"Claire, I need to tell—"

"I don't care what you need to tell me." I sneered at him, inadvertently putting my face closer.

So close.

I pulled back, taking my lips away from the temptation of kissing him as I tried to look away. "I want to celebrate. I sold my first script." I chuckled, rolling my eyes. "I know it's not *really* a script, but I'm going to be grateful."

"I'm not doing it." The words shot out of his mouth like bullets, stunning me to silence. "The fucking series. I'm passing on it."

"What?" I asked confused. It was only a few hours ago I'd been in Jeremy's office discussing the series that he was now saying he was *passing on*.

"I said I'm going to pass. I wanted to talk to you, to tell you how sorry I was about this whole fucking thing." He ran his hand through his hair. "Look, I didn't use you, but I screwed up and I should have told you the truth the minute I knew, regardless of the NDA."

"Nick, take a seat." Jeremy laughed nervously, standing up and patting Nick on the shoulder. "Everyone is a little emotional now, so let's not make any hasty decisions."

The softness in Nick's eyes was gone as he looked at Jeremy. "No, fuck that. I said I was out and I'm out. Your intervention with Dave and Roman isn't going to work, you know why? Because I'm a man and I own up to my mistakes. And this was one of them." He turned back to me. "I love you, Claire. I'm sorry, and I will keep saying it even if you don't want to hear it. And I'm *not* going to do something that will remind me for the rest of my life how I lost the girl of my dreams."

Well . . . fuck.

I couldn't breathe, my lungs froze as everyone's eyes landed on me. He'd said exactly the words I'd wanted to hear, and yet I couldn't answer him. I loved him, wanted to wrap my arms around him and kiss him like the end of all those cheesy 80's movies. I mean, as far as grand gestures went, this one was pretty big. But I couldn't, not wanting to be the girl who made up with a guy just because he said sorry.

"Goddamn you, Nick." Lust, love, anger, hurt, confusion and passion swirled through my head as I tried to decide if it was the most epic romantic thing anyone had ever done for me or it was simply plain dumb. "Couldn't you have just stood on my lawn with a boom box?"

"What?" It was his turn to be confused as he shook his head.

Man, I was pissed. So annoyed at him, and me, and the world. "I don't want you to give up the role. It's *you*. Who else is going to play it? I don't want some asshole who can't do you properly, to play *you* and mess it up. That's just going to make me look bad. And another thing." I held up my hand. "You aren't doing me any favors by turning it down. It will get tossed in the trash and forgotten about, and I won't get to see you play the *you* I wrote, even if someone else changes the you a little."

There was silence. If the entire bistro hadn't been looking at us before, they sure as hell were now. No one moved, not even the wait staff, as they watched a real-life episode of "Nick and *Claire*" right in front of them.

"You *want* me to do it?" His voice dropped to almost a whisper, almost as if I was the only one he'd intended to hear it.

I nodded, hating that I couldn't just hug and kiss him and tell him it was all going to be forgotten. I couldn't do that. *He'd hurt me.* I couldn't take him back right now even if he was adorable and loveable and it almost hurt more not to hold him. "Yes, I want you to do it."

"Claire." His hand reached out, hovering near my face, seeking permission.

I just couldn't give it.

As desperately as I wanted to, I couldn't have him touch me right now.

"Bye, Nick." I hated the words, knowing it was both the right and wrong thing to do.

"Tyler, I'd like to go home."

CHAPTER #24

NICK HAD TRIED to stop me from leaving, begging me to just talk to him. But the closing credits were running on the current Nick and Claire episode, and the script for the next one hadn't been written yet.

So as hard as it was, I turned my back and walked out of the bistro with Tyler, wondering if "goodbye" was the last word we would ever speak.

"For the record, the way you handled yourself in there was pretty badass." Tyler reached across and gave my arm a squeeze. "You sure you don't want to consider a career in law? I could use someone like you in the courtroom."

I laughed, staring out the windshield as we drove. "Funny, I don't feel badass."

We arrived at home and I walked silently up to my front door. Tyler had already texted Luke to let him know his driving services were required so I handed over my keys, wanting only to go inside.

"Tell him how you feel, okay," I warned, grabbing Tyler's arm before opening the door. "Don't assume he knows or wouldn't want to know. Give him the information and respect him to make the choice for himself."

Tyler nodded, leaning over and giving me a hug. "You are an amazing woman, Claire Becker. I'm looking forward to all the contracts we're going to negotiate together in the future."

I wanted to tell him not to get his hopes up, but I didn't want to ruin the mood. Instead I smiled, opening the door so that maybe he could get started on his happily ever after. Maybe I was just better at writing someone's story, rather than my own.

Scully and Sebastian were sleeping so at least I was spared having to relive it all, well at least until the morning. Instead I went into my room and took off my clothes, shuffling under my covers even though I knew I probably wouldn't sleep.

My phone beeped.

Claire, I know you probably won't read this, but on the slim chance you do, I'm sorry. x

Ugh, God I wish I could go back to ignoring him. I pulled the phone into bed with me, hiding under the covers as I typed.

Just do the part, Nick. Audrey is going to do an amazing job.

This isn't about the part.

No, it's not. Which is why you need to do it. I want this for us, even if the "us" isn't together. Besides, think of the money. Jeremy is probably having a heart attack by now anyway.

I don't give a shit about Jeremy.

I laughed, sending my response.

Yeah, well, I don't either.

The little dots that jumped while he was typing had stopped, and for a minute I thought it was over. I held my breath as I watched the screen, not really wanting it to be.

You looked beautiful tonight. Tyler's a lucky guy.

Even though I didn't owe him any explanations, I didn't want there to be any confusion.

It wasn't a date. He's my lawyer.

Still lucky, he got to have dinner with you.

I rolled my eyes trying to stop the smile. God, he was charming.

Aren't you being rude by being on your phone? Go spend time with your brothers. I really like Roman by the way, tell him I said hi ;-)

Firstly, no one likes Roman, so you might be the only one. And secondly, I'm crushed I didn't get the winkey face. :-(

You have to earn that.

Tell me how.

I shook my head, pressing the phone to my chest as I shut my eyes. *Tell me how,* God I wish I knew. I wanted to trust him again, to know that he would trust me. To know while we weren't at the same level outside, when we closed the door, we were. And even if he said exactly that right now, I wasn't sure I would believe it. Because I didn't only need to hear it, I needed to *know.*

My finger hesitated on my screen, thinking of what I wanted to say.

Remember how you did it the first time. Goodnight.

It seemed like forever ago, the night at his house when he could barely stand. And I had no idea if he'd even know who I was.

Or that I would end up loving him like I did.

EVERY TIME I closed my eyes I had the same reoccurring dream—Nick on the red carpet of his new series, looking amazing in a black suit. I was a few steps behind, wearing a stunning full-length gown, watching as the crowd screamed to him from the sidelines. They adored him, holding out their hands to touch him as he made his way up the carpet, posing for pictures as reporters asked him questions. I called out his name, wanting to see his smiling face and tell him how much I loved him. And right when he was about to turn—his hand about to touch me—I'd wake up, and Nick, his beautiful suit and smiling face were gone and I was alone.

I hated dreams.

Groaning, I pulled myself from my bed and got showered and ready for the day. I had been reading scripts for Marconi for a couple of months and things were going really well. He liked my notes and suggestions, and while it wasn't the job I had dreamed about as a kid, it was actually pretty cool. I got plenty of time to get my own writing done, having finished the screenplay I'd started the first night at Nick's and had already started another. And I got to read some pretty good pieces of work from my peers. Some not so great, but I was always honest.

The back and forth of paperwork was usually done either by email or courier, but today he'd requested a meeting. I had no idea why he'd asked me to come to his office, hoping it wasn't to tell me my services were no longer required.

I tried to remain positive, reminding myself that I had done good work and there was no reason for him to fire me. But in case I was wrong, I dressed in my best power suit and made sure I wore waterproof mascara.

"Sit down, Claire." He was waiting for me, watching me as I took a seat in front of his desk. "How are you?"

I adjusted my skirt as I tried to smile. "Good, really good, and you?"

Small talk was never good in a business situation. It was stalling, filler, and someone like Carl Marconi, had no time for it. So why he was trying to inquire about my wellbeing was both worrying and confusing.

"I'm doing fine." The corner of his mouth curved up in what was a poor attempt at a smile. "Can I get you anything to drink?"

I was getting fired.

All the talk of how I was feeling and whether I wanted a beverage, only useful to cushion the blow. So I didn't tell everyone he was a heartless bastard when he handed me my walking papers. Goddamn it. Did I have to lose literally everything? It was bad enough I didn't have the dream job *or* the dream guy, but now I had to give up whatever other happiness I had too?

"Mr. Marconi, with all due respect, sir, you didn't invite me to your office to offer me a drink. If there is something you wish to say to me, then I would prefer if you simply said it."

I mean, if I was getting fired anyway then why bother trying to draw it out? Might as well get it over with so I could go look at putting in my application at Starbuck's.

"There's no bullshit with you." He laughed, leaning back in his seat. "That's why I like you; you read, give me your unfiltered opinion and then move on. You don't try to sell me anything."

"It's not my job to sell you anything, sir. If the script doesn't sell itself, then there is nothing I can do for it."

He nodded, agreeing with me as his fingers drummed on the top of his desk.

So I assumed by his admission that he "liked me" that I probably wasn't getting fired, but I was no more enlightened either.

"I heard a rumor about you." He leaned in closer, waiting for my reaction. "You and Nick Larsson."

Fucking. Nick. Larsson.

"Sir, it wasn't a rumor, we were dating for a while. But it

doesn't have any bearing on my work, and of course any material you gave me was kept confidential and—"

He held his hand up, stopping me midsentence with a single lift of his palm. "Heard you developed the idea for a new series starring Nick. Heard that the executives over at ShowPlace are creaming their pants, and the contract will probably be finalized later today. You want to tell me about that?"

"Yes, it was my idea, and I'm expecting a contract in the next few days." I took a breath trying not to sigh and show my disappointment. "But Audrey Rydell will be writing the screenplay. I'm sure she's going to do an amazing job and of course Nick will be a fantastic lead."

He shrugged. "That piss you off?"

"Yes."

I figured I hadn't bullshitted him in the past, and I wasn't going to start now. Besides, it felt good to say I was pissed off, and I was allowed to be disappointed.

"Good, so give me something else."

I wasn't sure what exactly he was asking for.

"Something *else*?"

"Another screenplay, Claire," he clarified, his hand slamming down on the desk. "Let them have that series. Take their money and enjoy it. I'm not interested in television and neither are you. Give me your other idea, the better one, and let's see if you have what it takes to be on the big screen."

My heart pounded in my chest, barely allowing myself to breathe as I asked, "How do you know the *other one* is better?"

His grin widened. "Because you would have never have sold your best work and let someone else write it."

"I have something." I couldn't say it fast enough, wishing I had a banner and a parade for emphasis.

"I know you do, so let me read it. Because if it's as good as I suspect, the money you are going make on your network deal will be pocket change. And unlike those idiots, I won't let the person who thought up the idea walk out my door."

"Won't the fact I'm unknown make it difficult to sell?"

Don't get me wrong, the idea that he wanted to read my work was outstanding. When I'd started I hadn't even hoped for it, not daring to ask if I could even submit something. But I'd been encouraged before, only to have it ripped from my hands and given to someone else. That scar was still fresh, and I wasn't looking for a matching one so soon.

He threw his head back and laughed. "Is that what they told you? You were too big of a gamble?" He shook his head in disgust. "*Television*, I don't think you could find a pair of balls in those hallways if you tried. Send me the screenplay, Claire."

It wasn't an offer, and there was no promise of anything other than him reading it, but as I left his office, I felt like I had wings. Years of trying to get my work in front of people and in the space of a few short months I had one being adapted into a television series and a big producer wanting to read the other.

And I still had a job!

Oh my God, I was practically swimming in good fortune, my Toyota not going fast enough as I drove home.

"Scully!" I screamed, throwing open the door and thankful there was someone home to tell.

She ran into the living room looking terrified. "What, what's wrong?" Her groggy voice and glassy eyes hinted that I'd woken her from a nap.

"Shit, you were sleeping?" I looked around, forgetting that loud announcements weren't a good idea anymore. "I hope I didn't wake Sebastian."

"He's fine, I have the mobile with the music going in his room." She waved her hands, trying to hurry me. "Now stop stalling and tell me before I pee my pants. And I'm not talking fake pee either."

"Marconi is going to read one of my screenplays," I squealed, trying to keep my voice down as I did a happy dance.

She joined me, happy dancing away as she grabbed my hands and squeezed. "Yay, I'm so excited! That's huge news, and to think you thought you were going to get fired."

"I know, for a minute there I was worried." I fanned myself. "What time does my little boyfriend wake up, we should go find Luke and celebrate."

Scully looked at her watch, her face pulling into a frown. "He just went down twenty minutes ago, I was hoping he'd sleep for a couple of hours. We can do dinner though," she offered helpfully. "We can go out, anywhere you want."

"Yeah, yeah, we can do that." I tried to not be disappointed. She had a baby for God's sake, she couldn't drop everything to be with me. "Dinner, we'll do dinner."

"Why don't you call Luke and see if he's free? Maybe he can sneak out and you guys can go for midday martinis."

Guilt rocked me, feeling silly that I couldn't wait a few lousy hours. "It's fine, we can celebrate tonight. I'll just stay home with you."

"Claire, go, I am going back to bed in the hopes of having a nap. And trust me when I tell you, that right now, that is waaaaaaay more exciting than a martini." She hugged me, spun me and then pushed me toward to door. "Go find, Luke. Tell him to make reservations for tonight, he has an in everywhere." Well, she was right about that.

My arms circled her for a quick hug back and then I was back out my front door and into my car. I swear, when I eventually got paid, I was buying something decent. Nothing flashy, but nicer than my boring old Toyota, I think I'd more than earned it. I dialed Luke and then pulled away from our house, hoping to get him on the phone and meet him somewhere.

"Hey gorgeous, what's happening?" He answered after only the second ring.

"The mission, if you chose to accept it, is to meet me at a bar of your choosing for a midday martini. Marconi is going to read one of my screenplays," I screamed into the phone, the danger of waking babies no longer an issue.

"That's awesome, Claire. Shit." I heard him shuffle the phone. "I've got a packed schedule and can't get out of here until five. You want to do dinner? Tell me where you want to go and I'll organize it."

My heart sunk, again, selfishly disappointed that I was celebrating alone. It was stupid. I had friends, *good* friends, and it wasn't their fault they had busy lives right now. "Yeah, dinner is a good plan. I would really like that. And I don't care where we go but make sure they are kid friendly. I don't want Scully feeling unwelcome."

"You're a good person, Claire." There was a smile in his voice. "We love you and are proud of you."

"Yeah, yeah, I'm so wonderful." I rolled my eyes. "Now let me get off the phone so I can find a bar and have a drink on my own. See you tonight."

It wasn't ideal, but I wasn't going to not celebrate. Besides, who knew if the lack of company was going to be my new normal. Scully was a new mom and Luke worked a lot. And if he and Tyler did eventually go out, he would probably have less time to deal with his pain in the ass friend. Besides, being by myself wouldn't be so bad, and if I couldn't stand my own company, what were the chances anyone else would.

Trying to remain upbeat, I parked near a restaurant I knew served cocktails and made my way to the bar. I would have my midday martini, toast my success and not have to share my French fries with anyone. See, there were benefits to drinking alone, you just had to find the silver lining.

The draw back? You had no one to stop you from doing something stupid. Before I could stop myself, I'd pulled out my phone. And because I was curious, I decided to pull up Nick's social media. I mean, there was no harm in only looking, was there?

My finger flicked over to *Instagram* figuring it would be safest. I wasn't strong enough to see if he'd changed his relationship status on *Facebook*, and I didn't have the stomach for all the hashtags of *Twitter*.

Oh my God.

There were at least a dozen new pics, all taken in the last few hours. *All of them* with Nick topless, eating an ice cream, similar to the first photo I'd accidently "liked." Man, he looked good. I swirled my drink, taking a sip as I contemplated my next move. My thumb swiped the screen and opened my text messages, our last exchange staring me in the face.

This was a bad idea.

Know if Roman is busy? I need a drinking partner. If I could have his number, that would be great.

Sent.

My phone beeped with an incoming message not even a minute later.

If you are asking for Roman then you are already drunk and you should probably stop drinking. I make a very good coffee partner though, help sober you up?

I smiled stupidly at his response. It changed nothing, but . . . there was no harm talking to him. Maybe we could be friends? Or maybe the drink was stronger than I thought and should take his advice.

Boo, where is the fun in coffee? Guess I'm drinking alone.

I snapped a selfie of me holding my glass and sent it with the accompanying text.

Looks delicious.

It's okay, I've had better. I took another sip.

I wasn't talking about the drink.

I sprayed whatever drink was left in my mouth all over the bar. Okay, so drinking and texting wasn't a good idea. I grabbed some napkins, cleaning myself up and wiping the top of the bar, thankful it was early and the place was still empty.

As I balled up the dirty napkins and put my drink aside—I think it had done enough damage—my phone rung, I picked it without even looking at who it was.

"Delete my number." Nick's voice curled in my ear, stopping my heart.

My hand squeezed the phone at my ear, remembering he'd asked me that once before. "What number? I already deleted it." My heart thumped in my throat as I waited for his response.

"Good, then you won't be able to call and tell me not to come. I'll be at your place in half an hour. Sitting on your doorstep. And in case you're wondering, I *will* be sober."

"Wait—" It was too late, the phone going dead before I had a chance to tell him not to go. "Shit," I cursed, leaving what was left of my drink and fries and tossing some money on the bar. If he said he was going to my house, then he was going there for sure. Which meant I needed to get home before Scully killed him.

"Shit."

CHAPTER #25

I DROVE MY Toyota like I'd stolen it, pushing the speed limit to the edge of negotiation and running any light that wasn't a hard red. I was probably risking a ticket, but I figured the fine was going to be less of a hassle than the jail time Scully was going to get when she murdered Nick Larsson.

My brakes screeched to a stop as I pulled up to the front on my house, and already parked there was a silver Mercedes coupe. No prizes for guessing who it belonged to. I seriously needed a better car.

I jogged to my front door finding Nick sitting on my stoop as promised. He not only appeared sober but he looked good, dressed down in denim and a T-shirt that did good things for his chest. "Did you fly here?"

He glanced over my shoulder at my worn-out Toyota. "You know my car is faster."

"Yes, yes. It's faster." I looked around anxiously, ready for the front door to open at any second and my baseball bat wielding roommate to be on the other side. "Why don't you show me how fast it is and drive us out of here."

His brow rose, probably not expecting me to suggest a field

trip. "Okay then, let's go." He laced his fingers in mine without asking, leading toward his car and opening the passenger side door.

Shit.

I really hadn't thought this through.

Oh well, it might not be ideal, but getting out of the vicinity of my house was still the main objective. Without another thought, I slid into the car and waited for him to get inside, my eyes locked on my house the entire time, waiting for signs of movement.

He hopped in the driver's seat and started the ignition, putting the car into drive and peeling away from the curb. "I'm glad you called." His voice pulled me from my view, my house disappearing as we drove. *Phew, that was close.*

"I didn't call. You did." I reminded him, putting it on public record in case that was important later. I still wasn't sure how it was all going to turn out.

He turned his head and grinned. "Well I'm glad you texted then."

"Didn't you read it? I was looking for your *brother*." I rolled my eyes, pretending to be annoyed as I folded my arms across my chest.

He laughed, reaching out and touching my knee ever so gently. "Claire, I love you, but his *wife* barely tolerates him. I think it's time we got you professional help."

Between avoiding Scully, getting in the car and pretending to be the president of Roman's fan club, I had barely noticed how much Nick was touching me. My fingers when he led me to the car, my knee when he was talking, and now his thumb was rubbing the back of my hand. I could have pulled it away, but I didn't. Instead I pretended I hadn't noticed it and let him keep touching me. It wouldn't be the first time I pled ignorance when it came to him.

"Sooooo." I tried to think of something to say that was safe in friend territory. "I hear we're getting our contracts today, that's exciting."

He glanced over, his hand steady as his smile hooked a little at the side. "You worried I'm not going to sign, screw you out of your deal?"

"No," I scoffed. "And if anyone got screwed out of not signing, it would be *you*. How you going to maintain your decadent lifestyle eating ice cream shirtless if you don't get the millions they are probably promising you?"

He threw his head back and laughed. "You know I still have a job on *The Blue Line*, right? I think I'll manage. And speaking of ice cream." His head tipped to the windshield, a small ice cream shop coming into view.

It was tiny; the single fronted shop barely visible at all except for the faded yellow and white awning. He parked the car on the curb and killed the ignition, bringing our linked hands to his lips. "I need consent." His mouth twitched, hovering above my knuckles.

I rolled my eyes, trying not to smile. "My hand and nothing else."

His eyes stayed on mine as his lips touched my skin—gently, teasingly—stroking my hand as he kissed it.

The confined space of the car made it difficult to breathe, especially when he was looking at me like he was and being so sweet. "I know what you're doing," I whispered.

"What? Taking you out for ice cream?" His brow rose, the mix of faux innocence and surprise he was trying to convey only hampered by his wicked grin. "I thought you *liked* ice cream, or was it *me* eating it?"

I swallowed—hard—as I slowly extracted my fingers, trying to maintain my smile as I opened the door and stepped outside.

It was either that or leap into his lap and make out with him in the car. Oh, I still hadn't forgiven him, far from it, but that didn't mean the man couldn't turn me on with a glance of his sexy brown eyes. And sex didn't have to be emotional, maybe just fucking him would work out some of the aggression and clear my head so I could think clearly.

No.

I couldn't sleep with him.

Ice cream, we were going to get ice cream and then I'd go back to being mad at him. Or hurt by him. Or whatever I had been feeling that wasn't turned on.

"You know," I shuffled indignantly onto the curb, "I wasn't mad because they gave it to Audrey."

He got out of his car, leaning against the side as he nodded. "I know."

"You *know* what?" I asked, wondering if he was only saying it to appease me. You know, just nod, agree and let it blow over. But that wouldn't work.

"I know it's because of me, because I lied to you."

Okay, so maybe he knew.

Weren't we supposed to be getting ice cream or something? The conversation felt way too serious to be had on the sidewalk.

"So you gonna take your shirt off too, or is that just for Instagram?" I tipped my head to the store behind us, hoping to break the moment.

He laughed, sauntering to where I was standing and whispered. "Someone's been stalking my page."

"A cursory glance, barely even noticed." I smirked, pushing the door open and strolling into the store.

Inside was empty, the rundown theme of the place carried through in its worn out tables and chairs, whose color had probably bled out right around the time Ronald Reagan was president.

There wasn't much "color" in the woman behind the counter either. She was polite enough, but barely cracked a smile, serving us our cones and completing the transaction like we'd been at an ice cream ATM.

"I swear, nothing I do impresses her." Nick laughed as we walked outside to the single table in front of the store. "Eric and I came in here once and left a five hundred dollar tip, she nodded her head shoved the money in the cash drawer and wiped down the counter like we'd handed her a fiver. If you ever need someone to keep your ego in check, she's the woman to do it."

"That why we're here, you need your ego checked?" I asked, licking my cone and taking a seat on one of the plastic outdoor chairs.

He took the other chair, paying more attention to my ice cream than his own. "No, we're here because I wanted to talk to you and didn't want to take you to my house. I needed somewhere we wouldn't be bothered." He looked around to the mainly deserted street. "The ice cream is just the bonus."

I ignored his comment about the ice cream and the way his nostrils flared every time I took a lick. It may have given me more pleasure than it should, but to be fair, the ice cream was really that good. "You *didn't* want to take me to your house?"

When we got in the car, trying to put distance between us and Slugger Scully, I'd assumed his house was going to be our destination. I hadn't really thought much about it, other than getting away from my house. So I was surprised when that was where we didn't end up.

"I'm trying to be respectful, but I'm not a fucking saint." He blew out a curse. "If I got you into my house, alone, I'm not sure I would have been able to stop myself from pushing you up against a wall and kissing you."

My tongue stopped mid-lick, my body heating at his suggestion. "Well . . ." I paused, making another pass along the base of the cone as I looked up at him. "I guess my tongue is getting action either way."

The cone in his hand disintegrated, crushed as his fist tightened around it, the ice cream dropping to the ground. Fire burned in his eyes, his tongue swiping across the bottom of his lip as he swallowed hard. "I'm going to say what I'm going to say and you're going to listen." His voice a rumble. "After that you can choose, we can get in my car and I'll take you anywhere you want, and you can go back to hating me. Or we get in my car and I take you back to my house. And Claire, it won't be only to kiss you, so make your choice carefully."

It was my turn to swallow, feeling my body ignite like he'd stripped me bare and spoken those words directly into my core. "Okay." I nodded, losing interest in the ice cream and tossing it into a trashcan beside us.

"Jeremy called me the morning after Scully went to the hospital. I was home waiting to hear from you and checking the clock every ten minutes gauging how long I should wait before getting in the car and coming back."

I nodded, letting him know I was listening and urging him to continue.

"During the course of the conversation he told me that Show-Place read it, fell in love with it and wanted it. But they wanted Audrey and me—the package deal."

"And you just agreed?" I shot back defensively.

"No, I didn't just agree." He ran his hand through his hair in frustration. "I told him how shady it was and that I didn't like that they would bring on another writer. But I'm not Eric, Claire. I'm a main character on an *ensemble*, and I haven't sold anything on my own name. He told me to be smart, take the part, and while it wasn't ideal, that you would still get credit. It was a step forward."

I rolled my eyes, the whole idea I should be thankful for the scraps that were tossed my way was infuriating.

"Claire, listen to me." He grabbed my hands. "One of your best friends was in the hospital, and no one had any idea if Sebastian was going to be okay. I made an executive decision. I signed the stupid NDA, Jeremy went into negotiations, and *we* worried about getting Scully through the next couple of weeks. I couldn't risk you getting upset and something happening to any of you."

"What do you mean?" I narrowed my eyes, trying to understand.

He blew out a breath, the weight of it obvious as his shoulders sagged. "I am not justifying what I did, Claire. I'm not trying to manipulate you after the fact."

"About what?" I shook my head still not getting what he meant.

"I didn't want Scully to lose the baby, okay," he cursed out, his eyes flooded with torment. "I didn't want you to be upset, tell Scully, and it put her further at risk. I like your friends, Claire. They've been good to me and they love you. And given the choice of dealing with it—no matter how badly—and giving you a break, I was going to take it. You weren't sleeping, hardly remembering to eat and going out of your mind with worry. Be pissed at me, hate me, if that's what you need, but I did what I thought would hurt you and your friends the least."

Timing, they say, was everything.

It felt like a bomb had gone off, the pieces of what I knew and what I *thought* I knew scattered as I tried to hold them together.

I had no idea of the timing, no idea that when I had been sitting by Scully's bedside, hoping, praying and doing whatever else I could think of, that had been when Jeremy told Nick. And yeah, things were tough, especially those couple of days until her contractions stopped. I felt like I couldn't breathe until Sebastian was born, safe and healthy and out of danger.

Words didn't come. Anything I could think of saying felt inadequate.

"Claire, I'm sorry. The last thing I wanted out of any of this was to hurt you."

I couldn't hear anymore, I pushed away from the table and stood. "Please, don't say anything else." I held my hands up, wanting him to stop talking.

He still should have told me. And yes, things had been intense during that time, but I would have been okay. But his reasons for wanting to protect me and Scully were so freaking sincere, it was difficult to be angry.

Nick rose from his seat, grabbed his keys from his pocket and started walking toward the car. "Pretty much all I had to say anyway, so let me know where you want me to drive you and we'll go."

He was already standing beside his car, hitting the lock, holding the passenger side door open, and waiting for me to get inside. I followed him, stopping when he was in front of me and looked into his eyes. "Goddamn it, Nick." I pulled him toward me and kissed him like I'd wanted to do since I saw him sitting on my steps.

Our mouths met in a heated rush, his eyes widened in surprise but it only took him a second before he took what I was giving him and grabbed it with both hands.

He grabbed me too.

My body was pushed against the side of the car, his fingers holding my face as our kiss intensified. I was burning, so in need of getting close to him that I literally couldn't get enough. I leaned into him, desperate to touch him as a low growl traveled up his throat.

"Get in the car, Claire," he groaned at my lips. "I need you alone."

My kisses lingered, the idea of tearing myself away offensive, as I held onto his body. Every part of me ached, the wanting so intense, I thought I would split apart.

"Car. Now." He pulled himself away, his eyes so fevered I was surprised he was able to stand.

I didn't argue, folding myself into the car and slamming the door as he jogged to the other side. He threw himself into the driver's seat, starting the car and putting it in drive before I'd even had a chance to fasten my seatbelt.

"Nick." My hand grabbed his thigh, traveling up toward the front of his jeans. "I want you inside of me."

"Jesus Christ." His knuckles turned white, grinding his teeth as he tore down the road, weaving through traffic to get to his house.

Not able to stop, my fingers palmed the hard ridge in his pants, rubbing him through his jeans. My own body responded, fierce tension unfurling in between my legs as I rubbed my thighs together.

Nick looked down at my hand, biting his lip as his chest rose and fell with heavy breaths. "When we walk in that door, I'm going to fuck you. I wanted this to be sweet and gentle, but I don't think I am capable of that now."

"Yes," I moaned, my nipples straining against the front of my blouse, just wishing he would do it already. Between my legs, I felt myself get wet, the building tension making me slick and hot and desperate for release. "I thought you told me this car was fast, drive faster."

He didn't disappoint, speeding toward his house like we were in pursuit. And in case he needed any extra encouragement, I stroked him through his jeans, feeling him harden under my palm as he cursed under his breath. Slamming on the brakes, we skidded into his driveway and came to a stop. We didn't speak, getting out of the car like it was on fire and running to his front door.

"Fuck." He grabbed me, kissing me hard against his door while his hands fumbled with the keys. "God, I want you." The metal click of the key engaging, popping open the lock as the door gave way from behind me.

I felt myself tumble, Nick's hands steadying me as he pulled me against his body as he kicked closed the door and started what he finished outside.

Arms and legs tangled as I tried to pull off my jacket and he undid his pants. He dug in his wallet for a condom, slipping it on before even sliding down his boxers, his cock in his hand as hard as a rod.

"Inside of me," I begged, pulling up my skirt and pulling down my underwear.

Undressing was taking too long and if he didn't fill me in the next second, I felt like I might explode. He didn't miss a beat, yanking down his jeans around his hips and pushed me against the back of his couch. His fingers gripped me tight as he rubbed his hard length along my opening. "You ready for me?" he asked, my body flooding with desire as the head of his cock circled my slickness.

"Fuck. Me."

The two words were all he needed to hear, driving into me in a fast thrust that filled me root to tip. My body seized, the invasion amplifying the deep desperate throb between my legs as I closed my eyes to feel him. Every part of me was awake, my pulse racing as he drew out and slammed back in, the shiver felt in my body and my soul.

I wanted it.

I wanted it hard and fast and without apology, making me feel that he was there, in me, wanting me as desperately as I wanted him.

We didn't speak, kissing and moaning as our hips rocked, the dam inside of me feeling like it was going to burst.

"Claire." My name tore out of his throat as I felt my muscles tense, and with one more swing of his hips I was shouting his name over and over again as my body trembled.

Every part of me felt like it had been lit on fire, pulsing, as the wave consumed me whole. He held on, chasing it until he came with a raw guttural growl.

"You okay?" His lips found mine as he tried to catch his breath. His body was slick with sweat, his hair a mess, and his face so full of concern it made my heart ache.

I nodded, unable to answer as the freight train in my chest tried to get back on the rails. If that had been just sex, I was sorely mistaken. It might have been fast and hard, but there was nothing about what we did that wasn't deep and emotional as well.

He pulled me toward him, holding me close as his heart thumped loudly beneath his chest. I loved the sound, the strong, steady beat reminding me what we'd just done.

"Does this mean you forgive me or was that just angry sex?" I felt his grin as he leaned down and kissed the top of my head. "Either way I'm not complaining. Just need to know if I have to get you angry again later."

I pushed against his chest, shaking my head. "That was frustrated, built up tension, I missed you, sex." I laughed. "And all you need to do later is be hard." My core squeezed his cock still inside me.

"That is not a problem." He lifted my chin and kissed me. "Probably achievable sooner than you think."

His mouth languished over mine, slower, taking his time over every inch of my lips as I felt him pull out. My body shivered at the loss, seeking the warmth of his touch even though we'd just had sex. It was like I'd been starved, needing to binge on him in order to make it feel real.

"You want to take this to my bedroom?" His thumb traced my jaw leaving a trail of tingles in their wake. "I really want to get you out of these clothes and love you properly this time."

I looked down at our half-dressed state, items pushed up, down or aside in haste, and laughed. "I think you did pretty good the first time, but getting out of my clothes sounds amazing."

He kicked off his shoes, stripping out of his clothes before scooping me up in his arms. I nestled close to his chest, kissing it as he strode to the bedroom like I weighed nothing.

My back hit the mattress as he lowered me onto the bed, kissing my neck before whispering, "I'll be right back."

His perfect body turned giving me an amazing view of his ass as he walked into his adjoining bathroom. Man, I could get used to that view. Not just his ass—although, hello, it was pretty spectacular—but him, telling me he would be right back.

I rolled to a sit, using the time I had to unbutton my blouse and slip it off. Next was my skirt, my fingers twisting to the side trying to find the zipper and finally getting it down. And by the time he'd returned, I was laying leisurely on the bed—naked—trying to look seductive.

He stood at the doorway between the bathroom and his bedroom, leaning on the jamb as he looked at me. "I thought I was going to get to do that." He pointed to the pile of clothes on the floor. "I was looking forward to peeling them off you slowly and showing you my appreciation with my mouth."

Man, he was *such* a giver.

Almost made me want to put them back on if only so we could take them off, my body shivering at the thought of his hot mouth all over me.

"So." He strolled to the edge of the bed, leant over and captured my chin. "You never answered my question."

"Yes." I smirked looking down at his naked body and not imagining I'd be saying anything else to any request he had. Maybe even *hell yes*, and even more likely, a string of breathy *yeses*.

"You have no idea what I'm talking about, do you?" He knelt on the bed, stalking closer to me and kissing my neck. "Having trouble with your attention span, beautiful?"

Well when he kissed me like that there wasn't a lot of anything I could keep track of. "Of course I know what you're talking about. You wanted to know if I wanted to crawl under the covers so you can." *Kiss, kiss*—his mouth was unrelenting. "Screw what was left of my brains out."

He lifted his head away from my skin, his finger tracing the bridge of my nose. "Trust me when I tell you, I'll get to *that*. But first you need to tell me, are we good here? Because I'm not letting you out of this bed until this is a permanent thing."

My pulse raced, finding the proposition both endearing and sexy as hell. I mean, if I had to be kept somewhere *permanently*, Nick Larsson's bed sounded like a good place to be. "You going to tie me to the bed and hold me hostage?"

"If that's what it takes," he smirked. "I'll try not to enjoy it."

That smile of his was dangerous.

Always had been and always would be.

"I love you." It was the only answer I could have given him, the only one that made sense when he talked about being together. "I'm here, and you don't have to hold me hostage."

He pulled me into a hug, his body engulfing me whole. "I love you too."

I didn't want to be angry anymore. And in my heart of hearts, I knew he did what he did because he cared. There was no way that behind those beautiful brown eyes that held so much tenderness, there could ever be malice.

I saw that now.

And sure, maybe we needed to work on things, but there was always room for improvement.

But there was no way I could let him go.

CHAPTER #26

"YOU KNOW THIS isn't going to be easy, right? You hurt me, so they hate you." I looked over at Nick, his hand relaxed on the steering wheel.

He laughed, unconcerned about the litany of expletives that was awaiting him the minute we got back to my house. If Scully didn't curse him out—her swear ban in place because of the baby—then Luke would more than make up for it with a few choice words for him for sure—both of them furious for the heartbreak I'd suffered.

"I like to live dangerously. Besides, what's the alternative? Sneak around behind their backs and pretend we're *not* in a relationship? I don't like your chances of me doing anything that doesn't involve us being together."

Man, I hoped Scully had gotten a decent nap. Anger, sleep deprivation and her baseball bat were a deadly mix.

Still, it did sort of thrill me that he was willing to go to my house even though he knew he'd probably be unwelcome. That he felt the need to make it right, even at the expense of being cussed out and probably asked to leave.

Doing *that*—putting me ahead of his own personal

preservation—was probably the most romantic thing ever; beat the *hell* out of standing on my lawn with a boom box.

"Okay, but don't say I didn't warn you." I shrugged, knowing that trying to convince him otherwise was a lost cause. "Also, have I told you that I love you?"

His grin widened, bringing our interlocked fingers to his lips. "Yes, but I never get sick of hearing it. I love you too, beautiful."

As we approached my house, my guts twisted in a knot. I was excited and nervous all at the same time. My friends were important, and while there wasn't a chance I'd give him up, their opinion mattered so much to me. I didn't *need* them to be okay with it, but I really wanted them to.

Nick parked his Mercedes in the same place it had been before, cutting the engine and turning to look at me. "I love you, Claire. Not Scully, Luke or anyone else is going to convince me that being with you isn't a good idea. I don't care what amount of shit I need to crawl through to make it work, it is worth it to me."

Jesus.

My Heart.

The overwhelming feeling to grab him and hug him so strong I had to clutch my chest. He was my forever, no matter how hard our road was going to be, he was it for me. Scully would see that and be happy for us.

Reaching across I gave him a quick kiss, pulling back intentionally because I knew anything more and I probably wouldn't be able to stop. That would not be a good way for either of my best friends to find out we'd rekindled our relationship, seeing us making out in the car in the street.

Taking a deep breath, I stepped out of the car, Nick joining me on the sidewalk. He grabbed my hand, clutching it tightly as we walked up to the door and watching me with a smile while I opened it.

"Claire? Is that you?" Scully called from the kitchen. "Luke said he made reservations tonight at—"

She stopped, having walked around to the living room and seeing Nick Larsson with his arm around me. "How long was I asleep?" She looked at me, searching for an answer.

"Hey, Scully." Nick tipped his head in her direction, playing it cool.

Her eyes hardened, thinning her lips into a tight line that could only mean bad things. "Don't *hey* me. We're still mad at you." She turned to look at me. "We're still mad, right?"

"Well . . ." My hand rested on his chest as I tilted my head to look into his eyes. "No, we're not still mad."

Scully's arms flopped to her sides dramatically. "But he hurt you, Claire."

Loaded with the words of his defense, I'd opened my mouth when Nick stopped me. "I did, and I'm sorry. And I promise I'll never do it again."

No excuses, no explanations—zip.

It would have been easier if he told her the truth. That we had been ear deep in crisis when he found out about the deal, and he thought he was doing the right thing. And that even though his motives were sound, he still wished he'd done it differently. He could have told her all the things he'd told me, knowing that once she'd heard them she would have probably thawed. How could she not, especially when he'd been so concerned about her and her son. But he didn't, willing to carry it all, even if it meant things were difficult for him.

She glared at him, swinging her eyes back to me and noticing my smile before shaking her head. "I love Claire like a sister, and if you ever—"

"I won't." He cut her off, the smugness in his smile dropping. "I won't. And if I do, you won't need to take me out, I'll do it myself."

Scully sighed, tossing her eyes to the ceiling. "Why does he have to be so damn charming?"

"I know," I agreed, laughing as the tension in the air eased. "He really is hard to be mad at."

Her face softened, the hard lines of anger easing as she walked over to me. "Well if you're happy, babe, then I'm happy."

Nick chuckled. "I'm right here, Scully."

She held her hand up, pretending to ignore him. "Uh-uh, you might be charming, Larsson, but I'll push that to the side if my Claire isn't bursting at the seems with contentment."

I nodded, reaching out and hugging her. "I am, really and truly bursting."

"Fine." She rolled her eyes. "Then we're all happy." She tossed her arms around Nick and pulled us into a group hug.

Our feel-good moment only lasted a minute before we were interrupted by the sound of crying.

"Duty calls." Scully loosened her hold, giving us a smile. "That vibrating chair thing that all the blogs swear by is bullshit. He'll only sit in it for thirty minutes before he hates it."

Scully walked to the direction of the crying, leaving us in the living room by ourselves. "One down, one to go," I whispered.

"Don't worry about, Luke." Nick kissed the top of my head.

I pulled back, curious as to why I *didn't* need to worry about the man who until recently wanted to put his head on a spike. Dramatic I know, but Luke had just wrapped up working on a period drama and had sourced many a spike and found them to be most efficient as well as decorative.

"Luke came to see me this morning."

"What?" I don't know if I could have sounded more surprised if I'd tried, unable to add *"the fuck"* after it.

His hand rubbed against my arms, his brow furrowing in concern. "Look, don't get mad, it wasn't about you. And even though

I tried everything I could to get him to talk about how you were, he wouldn't budge saying that he wasn't telling me shit."

"So *why?*"

He bit his lip, cautiously choosing his words. "Because I'd let him know there was an opening in the wardrobe department for next season."

"Scully?"

"I swear, Claire, I wasn't trying to use it as an opportunity to get to you." The sincerity shone in his eyes. "But Rita quit, and I knew that Scully had given up her job the night she went into labor."

I remembered that night. How considerate he'd been, inviting her out to try to cheer her up, and how concerned he was for her when it all went bad. She'd given up her job, with no plans for the future, something we hadn't even talked about since Sebastian's birth even though I knew she was worried.

"She's got experience and it would mean she'll get the rest of the summer to be with Sebastian. Then in the fall, come to work with us. It's a solid seven-month contract, and I'm on good terms with the producer so he took my recommendation. Plus, we're a family show, she can probably bring her son on set." He grinned. "And then I can hang out with my little buddy between takes."

I shook my head, not understanding his reasoning if it wasn't an attempt to win me back. "But why would you do that?"

"Because Claire, like I said to you back at my house. I like your friends, and I had the power to fix something. Maybe part of me hoped that with both Luke and Scully working with me I'd win them over and convince them to tell you what an amazing guy I was." His smile hooked at the side making him look adorable.

I laughed, wondering if he was crazy, willing to wait until filming started again in order to try to win me back. "That was one hell of a long game."

He shrugged. "It was the only one I had."

"Are you and Luke BFFs now?" I pushed lightly at his chest, pretending I was concerned at being replaced.

He scrunched up his nose, shaking his head. "Not quite, but I told him I was going to do everything I could to get you back. We shook hands, deciding that you would make your own decisions and he wouldn't stand in my way if that was what you wanted."

"Oh, really?" I planted my hands on my hips, admiring that the two of them had worked out their differences. It couldn't have been easy, Luke was fiercely loyal, but he also knew I wasn't someone that could be told what to do. I guess he figured if I ended up back with Nick, then he—like Scully was—would be happy for me.

"Jesus, Larsson." Luke slammed the door behind us, shoving his keys in his pocket. "You work fast. Thought you would give it a day or two."

He walked over to me, studying my expression as he gave me a hug. "You okay, sweetheart?"

I nodded, giving his arms a squeeze. "I'm good," looking up at Nick, "Really good."

"Scully seen him yet?" He looked down the hall where Scully's bedroom was. "You know she still has that bat."

"She's seen him and she's happy for me too." I moved my arms to Nick. "And she hasn't even heard about the job offer yet."

A sheepish grin crossed Nick's lips. "I figured I had to win her back on my own merit. Then, if I fell short, I'd toss it in as a sweetener."

On cue, Scully walked in with Sebastian cradled close to her chest. The little guy looked content in his mother's arms while Scully looked like a natural. Fuck Pru and her classes, my best friend was rocking motherhood.

"We're not mad anymore." Scully tipped her head in Nick's direction, leaning over to give Luke a kiss on the cheek.

Luke nodded. "I see, what a surprise." His face showed

anything but surprise. "Well, I guess I better call and add an extra to the reservation."

"You guys had plans?" Nick's eyes moved from Scully to me. I'd been so caught up in our reunion, there hadn't been time to tell him my good news.

When Marconi had told me about wanting to read and possibly work with me, I hadn't imagined being able to share that with Nick. The gratitude that I could, flooded me as I grabbed his hands. "I might have a project on the horizon, Marconi wants to read my work."

"We're celebrating," Scully added.

"Claire, that's amazing." He yanked me close to his body. "He's tough to impress."

"Yeah, well let's not get too excited. Nothing has happened yet." I was trying to be cautious and not get too ahead of myself. It was hard though, feeling so happy there wasn't a lot that could sour my mood. Even if he hated it, told me that what I'd written wasn't for him—I'd still *be* happy. Because despite what Marconi or anyone else thought, I *knew* I was a good writer. There wasn't anything in the world I'd rather be doing, and even if it was going to take a while before I got my success, I was willing to wait.

Besides, how could I go wrong when I had my muse as my boyfriend? The opportunity for inspiration would be endless, and I wasn't above capitalizing on what I had.

"Looks like we've got a lot to celebrate tonight." Nick smiled. "The new series, Marconi reading Claire's work and Scully's new job." He glanced at her waiting for her reaction.

"What new job?" She frowned, bouncing Sebastian in her arms. "I know I should be looking but I am struggling with just getting a shower in the morning, let alone job hunting. I figured so much is on summer break right now anyway, what was the point."

"Well there's a job with us if you want it." Nick glanced at me, waiting for me to nod before continuing. "You still have to interview, but they know who you are and the work you've done."

"With *The Blue Line*?" Her eyes widened, misting at the edges. "You got me a job?"

He shook his head. "I only mentioned your name, Scully. The rest will be all you. But it's a great crew, regular work and I know you'd be an awesome addition to the team."

Luke leaned in, adding to the argument. "And I'll be there, we all know that is going to be a huge selling point. We haven't worked together since . . ." He took a minute trying to work out when was the last time they worked together.

"Since *Crash*," I answered, reminding them that the last time they had worked together, I had been there with them. And ironically, so had Nick, his minor role of the sexy bartender starting this train of craziness.

"Wow!" Scully's eyes got huge. "How freaky is that? All those years ago, barely even knowing each other and now we're all together."

Nick put his arms around me and kissed my forehead gently. "Nah, it was meant to be. Some of us needed to get our shit together first. Fate just made sure we came back to what was meant for us."

My.

Heart.

Anymore and it was liable to burst, and I didn't care, willing to have it explode in my chest as I loved this amazing man.

"Stop it Nick," Scully warned. "I'm still hormonal and if you make me cry, I will beat you."

"Don't stop." I grabbed his shirt, holding it tight in my fingers as I looked into his beautiful brown eyes. "Don't *ever* stop."

There was no way of knowing what would have happened if *Crash* hadn't been canceled. If, five years ago, I'd have worked up the nerve to ask him out or if he would have. Maybe we'd have dated, ultimately growing apart because we had so much more to do with our lives. He had to become a super star, and I had to do some developing of my own. What I did know, was that show getting canceled had seemed like the worst thing in the world.

And now I knew better.

It had been the best.

"TELL ME, NICK," Roman leaned across, his grin bursting at the seams, "does it bother you your fiancée has won an Academy Award before you?"

It had been less than twenty-four hours since I'd walked off that stage, a gold statue in my hands, and I felt like my feet hadn't touched the ground. It was beyond my wildest dreams, the award coming as a shock when I'd heard my name called, with Nick by my side clapping the loudest.

Nick shook his head, smiling at his brother. "You do realize I've won two Emmys, a Golden Globe and a Screen Actors Guild award."

Roman chuckled, looking less than impressed. "Always the bridesmaid, never the bride."

"Don't listen to him, he's an idiot." Lauren—Roman's beautiful and extremely talented wife—sat down and rubbed her swollen belly. "And congratulations, Claire. We're so happy for you."

"I never said I wasn't happy." Roman wrapped his arms around his wife. "I'm fucking ecstatic."

She rolled her eyes. "Like you're *ecstatic* about Alex's new job offer?" Her lips twitched into a grin. "Straight out of college and he gets headhunted by Young, McMillian and Walker. Quite an accomplishment. Tell us, Roman, where did you start again?"

"Please, I coached him the whole way through," he scoffed, the smugness in his smile dropping. "If I'd had *me* as a guiding force through law school, I'd have had more than just *one* fancy offer."

Alex—the youngest Larsson, and the man in question—walked over, dropping a kiss on his sister-in-law's cheek. "Roman talking shit again? You sure you want to expand that DNA?"

He'd graduated magna cum laude from Berkeley Law School, and as Lauren had gleefully pointed out, received an incredibly prestigious offer from one of the biggest law firms in L.A. But rather than take the offer the minute he was able, he instead took a few months off and traveled. And that *fancy* firm had been only too happy to wait. It figured that all the Larsson men were fiercely competitive, even the two who weren't in show business.

Alex turned to me, the famous smile that all his brothers seemed to have widening on his face. "Hey Claire, congrats on the award. Maybe one day Nick will win one too."

"You're not going to bait me, Alex." Nick's smile not faltering as he put his arm around me. "I don't care, and I'm incredibly happy for Claire."

That was not a lie, he had absolute zero animosity that I had won the coveted accolade before he had, something none of us expected.

While Nick had continued to earn critical acclaim on *The Blue Line* for multiple seasons, he'd also expanded his small screen dominance with *Nick and Blaire*—the show I'd created. As expected, Audrey Rydell had done an amazing job with the adaptation, earning herself a Golden Globe for the writing. Not going to lie, that had actually stung. But the blow had been softened by my very own screenplay achievement, a small motion picture with moderate success at the box office.

Marconi had put his money where his mouth was, and not only produced the first screenplay I'd given him, but he also bought the second. And *that* next one, well, that had been the game changer.

Not only had it been my best writing to date, it smashed all earning predictions, and put me on the map. Directors and production houses who had previously given me a hard pass were falling over themselves to read my work, it was incredibly vindicating. And when award season came, it was *my* name being read in nominations.

"Hey! We made it," Jessica Larsson, Dave's wife came running in minus her husband. "Dave's parking the car, the traffic was terrible. Hi Claire, congrats on last night."

"Thanks." I smiled and nodded for the millionth time in the past few hours, my cheeks heating every single time.

It was so weird to be the center of attention, and not something I had gotten used to. Especially considering the company I was keeping. Also strange was to be called an overnight success despite years of rejections and working hard behind the scenes. Even weirder were the questions Nick got on the red carpet, about how it felt to be one half of Hollywood's newest power couple. The famous actor and the acclaimed screenwriter, we were a force to be reckoned with.

It was a massive contrast to what they had said about me before. Not going to lie, I smiled smugly at their cameras, my success a special "fuck you" to all of them who had called me plain and ordinary. Funny how they'd forgotten all of that.

Our upcoming wedding had also attracted quite a bit of attention, with reporters desperately trying to guess when exactly we were going to be tying the knot and who was going to be there. The invites more sought after than tickets to the MET Gala. But our wedding *wasn't* tonight, that was for damn sure.

"Christ," Roman cursed, the door swung open revealing what looked to be thirty colorful balloons.

Dave poked through the mess of streamers and helium as he

strolled into the room, "Hi everyone, did I miss it? Oh, hey Claire. Good win last night. Let's get our people to talk to each other. I'm anxious to work with you."

"We're getting married soon, your *people* are going to have to wait." Nick shot a look of warning toward his brother. "And you need to get in line like everyone else."

"She's going to be my sister-in-law, surely that means I get to jump the line." He smirked, turning back to me. "You know there's still time to say no and back out. We'll still all love you and you won't have the hardship of being married to him."

Nick flipped him off, shaking his head. "You are such a dick."

Jessica stood, grabbing the balloons from Dave's hand. "Sit down, baby, we're still waiting. And play nice, this isn't a bar."

Waiting had been the theme of the night. Nick and I hadn't been far, being the first to arrive after Nick's mom, Kate, called us. She was positively buzzing with the impending birth of her new grandchild, and while she wasn't in the birthing suite, she was right outside the door, not bothering to sit in the waiting room with us. The rest of the group had been summoned as well and had slowly filtered in. And while it was only seven P.M., the lack of sleep from the previous night meant I felt like a zombie.

I needed coffee. Or wine. Or maybe both, not sure which one would get me through what potentially could be a very long night.

"You need anything?" Nick dipped his head, his lips brushing against my ear. "You look exhausted."

"I'm fine." I leaned my head against his shoulder. "And I'm tired, but there is nowhere else I'd rather be."

Last night hadn't only been a huge night for me, but Eric had also walked away with a statue. Only problem was, he hadn't been there to collect it. Tia was two weeks overdue with their second child, and none of the gods—including the Viking ones—were going to be able to convince her to go anywhere there wasn't a birthing center. Eric wouldn't go without her, which meant the director collected it on his behalf. Not that Eric was concerned, he was too busy being blissfully happy with his three-year-old son, Ethan, and his pregnant wife, who currently was in labor with their daughter.

Which was why there was a *pride of Larssons* in the waiting room of Roland Regan UCLA Medical Center.

My phone buzzed discreetly in my pocket and I tried to ignore it. It had been going most of the day, with the calls either being people to congratulate me or people wanting something from me. Amazing how many friends come out of the woodwork when your name was read out on television. Thankfully my family had been really cool about it. Ignoring the media attention that they had inevitably received, with my mom and dad circling the wagons and making sure no one talked to the press. They were the best kind of family, all of them excited beyond measure to be adding Nick to it. Not because he was famous, but because with him in my life I was happier than I'd ever been.

My phone buzzed again.

Whoever was trying to reach me was being persistent, the repeated attempts to silence the damn thing met with more buzzing.

"I'm going to step out for a second." I pulled out my phone from my pocket holding it up to show Nick. "Come get me if there's any news."

He nodded, giving me a kiss as I got up and walked out the door and into the hall, the calmness of the birthing oasis left behind as the bustling of the hospital surrounded me.

"Hey."

When I'd held up my screen to show Nick, the caller had also been revealed. Scully wasn't the kind of woman to be silenced, which was why she was hitting the redial like it was going out of style.

"Oh my God," Scully squealed into the phone. "Where have

you been?"

Not much had changed in all the years I'd known Scully, and her excited phone calls demanding to know where I was, usually meant trouble. "I'm at the hospital, Tia's in labor. What's going on?"

"Tyler proposed to Luke," she screamed down the phone. "They're getting married."

I laughed, knowing that Tyler had been planning to propose to Luke for months. I'd been with him when he'd chosen the ring, sworn to secrecy until he finally worked up the nerve. Guess the day would be one a lot of us didn't forget, even if it was for different reasons.

"That's great, I'm so happy for them."

Warmth spread through my body, both incredibly happy and relieved I no longer had to keep the secret. Plus, with Luke getting married, Scully could finally help to plan the extravaganza she didn't get from me. Nick and I were going to have an elegant—and simple—wedding. Luke, well Luke liked things a little more flashy.

"You don't sound surprised. *Why* are you not surprised?"

I bit my lip, trying not to smile. "Because I knew."

She gasped, sucking in a gulp of air. "You knew, and *didn't* tell me, you're supposed to be my best friend. You're Sebastian's godmother, for God's sake."

"I know." I shrugged, not feeling any of the guilt she was trying to put on me. "But it was their news so wasn't mine to share. Besides, I wanted you to be surprised when Tyler asked you to help plan the wedding."

"Tyler is going to ask *me* to help plan the wedding?" she screamed into the phone, people around me turning around having heard her voice barreling down the line.

Well.

Shit.

"Scully, do not say anything, I thought you already knew."

I tried to cover, hoping like hell Luke or Tyler wouldn't be mad.

When Tyler told me he was going to propose to Luke, he was worried that with his caseload he didn't have time to help with the details. Hell, he'd have been happy to fly over to Vegas and make it legal, but he knew Luke wanted something grander. So after I helped him choose a ring, he asked me whether involving Scully would be a good idea. I knew that next to him proposing to Luke it was the best idea he'd had.

"To the grave, I miss you and I won't tell a soul," she whisper-yelled into the phone. "Finally, we get to have the wedding I've always dreamed of. You let me down in that regard."

I laughed, not the first time I'd been told of her disappointment. "You know, you could just get married yourself. Most people get their dream wedding when it's *them* walking down the aisle."

"Pleeeeeease," she scoffed, "I'm happy being a single mom and dating whoever I want. I only want the party."

"Claire." Nick had come out into the hall, his face positively beaming. "It's time, she's about to deliver."

"Gotta go, Scully, Bye." I pulled the phone from my ear without waiting for her to respond.

Then without wasting another minute, I walked up to Nick and kissed him. A full, on the mouth, desperately in love kiss and I didn't care who was watching.

"Not that I'm complaining, but what was that for?" He grinned, nibbling on my lips.

My hand moved to his chest, feeling the steady rhythm of his heart beneath my fingers as I looked at him and smiled. "Because every now and again I like to remind myself how lucky I am."

He laughed, his eyes filling with mischief as he dropped another soft kiss on my lips. "You want to find an empty room so I can show you how much *luckier* you can get?"

It was my turn to laugh, the idea more tempting that was

probably appropriate considering we were waiting for our niece to be born.

"Nick," I pretended to be scandalized. "You know I just won an Oscar and that kind of behavior is not something that would impress the Academy. You don't want to ruin your chance for the future, do you?"

His lips spread into his trademark mischievous grin, "Fuck the Academy, I won you."

THE END

ACKNOWLEDGEMENTS

AS ALWAYS, MY first and most enthusiastic thanks goes to my family. Gep, Jenna, Liam and Woodley. I love you guys so very much.

Thank you to rest of my crazy crew, those who share blood ties and those who are here by choice. I adore you all and thank you for your unwavering support, constant understanding and immeasurable love. Back at you x 2!

Thanks a million to the team at Brower Literary and Management—Kimberly, Aimee and Caroline!! Come visit me, I have Tim Tams!

To my amazing editor, Nichole Strauss, from Insight Editing, you gave me permission to take a breath when I needed it. There is not a doubt in my mind if I had handed this in when it was supposed to be done, it would have been complete and utter shite. You waited, giving me the time to find my voice again. Thank GOD it is back. #LetTheInsanityContinue.

MK, lord, no words for you. Love your insight, thank you for all the work you do for me.

Thank you to Christine Borgford from Type A Formatting. It is always a pleasure working with you. Not only are my pages prettier but your ability to get it "right" every time has me in awe.

HANG LE! Lady, look how far we've come. I've lost count how many times we've worked together, but it is a privilege and a pleasure to continue the tradition. You are generous of heart and have an amazing mind. Oh, and you make me look good ;-)

Thank you to my amazing proofreaders MK, Lisa B, Jackie R

and Rosa! Your sharp eyes make things so much better.

To all my author peeps, LORD, I LOVE YOU!!! Thank you to each one of you for your continued awesomeness. Not only do I devour your words—I will always be a reader—but some of you have become very dear friends. I expect you to be excellent character witnesses should the need arise. Please and thank you in advance. P.S. Thanks for all the laughs and your shoulder through the tears. P.P.S. I wished we saw each other more.

A HUGE and ROWDY thanks needs to be extended to the bloggers, reviewers and promoters. Whether you are part of a big page, small operator, new or OG—I appreciate you. Those pimps, reviews, shares, and noise you make are invaluable to me and my books. Thank you for everything and your continued support.

Thanks to KP, Jessica and Team InkSlingger! It's been a pleasure working with you guys. Thank you for helping me with PR and promo "stuff"—it has been awesome having you in my corner.

To Liz, MJ and Jillian at 1001 Dark Nights. Thank you so much for making me feel like I'm part of your incredible family. I still feel like fraud, not sure what I'm doing there, but you have all been so gracious and kind. I'm so glad Liz found me and the insanity of the #1 series or I might never have gotten to know how awesome you all are.

THANK YOU to the T Gephart Review Crew and Entourage. Whether you belong to one or both, I absolutely adore you and am so thankful for the love you show my book babies. Review Crew—those shares and reviews mean everything!! Thanks to Michelle Clay who mobilized when I needed her and got the show on the road and to every member of the team. Entourage—thanks for the silliness and making it such an awesome, drama-free and fun group. Sorry I'm not in there as much as I should. I'll work on that.

And of course, a MASSIVE thank you goes to my readers. I don't care if this is the first book or you've read every single one,

I am grateful you found me. Thank you for your support, kind words and encouraging messages. Being able to do what I do is amazing but I wouldn't be able to keep doing it if there weren't people buying, reading, sharing and reviewing my books. Every single one of you is important, don't let anyone tell you different.

Lastly, thank you to the "Larsson" who was partly responsible for me starting this wild ride. Who thought the crazy insanity would have lasted five books? Certainly, not I. Hope our paths cross again, but if they don't, I'm eternally grateful for the inspiration.

Thank you.

Thank you.

Thank you.

ABOUT THE AUTHOR

T GEPHART IS a USA Today and International bestselling author from Melbourne, Australia.

With an approach to life that is somewhat unconventional, she prefers to fly by the seat of her pants rather than adhere to some rigid roadmap. Her lack of "plan" has resulted in a rather interesting and eclectic resume, which reads more like the fiction she writes than an actual employment history. She'd tell you all about it, but the statute of limitations hasn't expired yet. But all those crazy twists and turns have led her to a career she loves—writing romantic comedy.

When she isn't filling pages with sassy and sexy characters with attitude, she's living her own reality show in the 'burbs of Melbourne with her American husband, two teenage children, and her fur child—Woodley.

She loves adventure, to laugh, travel, and strives to live her life to the fullest.

CONNECT WITH T

www.tgephart.com
Facebook
Goodreads
Twitter

BOOKS BY
THIS AUTHOR

The Lexi Series

Lexi

A Twist of Fate

Twisted Views: Fate's Companion

A Leap of Faith

A Time for Hope

The Power Station Series

High Strung

Crash Ride

Back Stage

The Black Addiction Series

Slide

Sticks

Stand

#1 Series

#1 Crush

#1 Player

#1 Rival

#1 Lie

#1 Muse

#1 Love (coming 2019)

Collision Series

Train Wreck

Car Crash (coming soon)

Standalones

The Fall